No Time for Daddy's Girl

Dorothy Collins

Dorothy Collins

AUTHOR TO TODAY THE WAITING

ISBN: 978-1-9991691-0-7 (sc)
ISBN: 978-1-9991691-1-4 (e)

In Memory of my late daughter Bonnie
She inspired me to publish the novels I wrote.
Thank you to my son Barry and his wife
Jeannie for their support.
and
Thank you to Terry Unger in appreciation of
her encouragement.

Chapter One

Ted had risen that morning with every intention of it being just another normal day. But normal wasn't to be. Ted's morning ritual of shower and shave was interrupted by a scream. Why would he hear a scream way out here? "Nah, it can't be." He went back to his shaving. He still had half an ear trained to outside sounds.

This time he couldn't ignore it. That was definitely a scream from somewhere nearby. He had to find out the source. He was only half-dressed, but he ran to the door anyway. Old jeans that hugged his hips like glue were covering his male anatomy. His feet hit the boots and planted themselves inside on the run out the door.

Another scream pierced the air.

Ted ran in the direction of the scream which emanated from nearby, coming from a car in the region of the waterfall which flowed over the cliff on the next property behind his place to the left. He was not able to see inside the car because it was tilting precariously on the edge of the bank over the cliff-side, and the weight of the waterfall hitting the auto was making it seesaw.

Ted knew it was only a matter of time before the car went over. The water was hitting the hood, then continuing its journey, cascading into the valley below. He knew this could be a death scene all too soon. He did not relish the scenario before him.

Ted sped over the ground like a sprinter in a dead heat. He literally ate up the distance, barely hitting the dirt on each boot's descent. He was no sprinter, but his legs churned with fear. He knew he had to get there by covering as much ground as possible without delay. As he ran towards the car, he could detect movement inside. The vehicle was tipping more than the effect of the waterfall.

A girl's face was plastered to the side window as he viewed the car up close. It was tipped sideways in his direction because the undercarriage was wedged on a rock on the far side, stopping it from going over.

The cascading water normally looked especially picturesque in sunlight, causing dancing lights and colorful rainbows. That was not the case today. It was a surging threatening body of water about to cause annihilation if it succeeded in sending the car over the edge.

Why was the car here? No one should be driving in this area. The road stopped just past his driveway with just enough room to turn. Ted, a loner, was living far away from everyone, leading a quiet lifestyle. He depended on his job as a stevedore to give him his excitement in life.

Who is this girl? Surely, she couldn't have panicked pressing the gas instead of the brake. Ted thought the first thing he had to do was calm the girl before she aided the car in its downward plunge. He knew this was going to be no easy feat. The natural instinct is to escape.

Finally, he made it to the car as the auto dipped once more towards completing its downward passage. No time to think this out, he had to act fast, pulling at the door. The car's angle held by the rock dissuaded the door from budging.

Next, he yelled at the girl through the partially open window to be still. The girl was too terrified to stop screaming. She was moving about as though in a jumping jack motion. Every upward movement was restrained by the seatbelt, casting her down again.

Ted put his hand against the window where her face pressed against the glass. He did it with a stroking motion talking soothingly. Gradually she stopped pitching and screaming, just blinked her eyes. Those blue azure eyes were now silently pleading for help.

Even in her distress, she was eye-catching. She was a girl that could camp in his dreams anytime. Blond curls framed her face covering the window pane.

Ted was happy to see she was lying immobile at last. He yelled, "I will get you out if you stay, motionless." Yeah right! Like I'm a hero?

He had no idea what to do. He knew this would need deliberation as the car was in too precarious a position. The pulsation of the water from the gushing waterfall was still rocking the car none too gently. Just then, it slipped forward on its rock wedge to confirm his fears.

"Can you open the window more?"

"No, I tried, but I guess my weight on it won't let it open."

Ted ran around the car to see if he could get the other door open, but both doors were jammed. There was a hanging branch from a tree beside the car. He wedged it under the handle, hoping that would help brace the vehicle from going over for a while longer. He ran back around the car, noting it was a Camry. Camry's are solidly built cars, so there were no possibilities of prying open the windows.

Windows!

Ted quickly looked around for a rock to smash the rear window. He figured he would have to ease himself in that way, mainly to keep the car from slipping over the cliff.

He found a rock and smashed it with force, but not too much power as he didn't want the glass particles to shower the girl. The first whack, the window just cracked in every direction like a spider web in the sunlight. Again, his arm came down with more force, and the window appeared to buckle but bounced back. No choice, Ted's next blow was so forceful that glass exploded in a whoosh into the interior of the car, forcing more movement to the already precarious auto.

But there was nothing he could do about that he just had to get in as fast as possible. He used the rock to bang out most of the glass so he could safely get in and out of the car with the girl.

Please, God, help me to do this right.

Not that Ted was a religious man, but right now, he figured he needed all the help he could get. With the glass particle removal, as best he could in his hurry, he climbed onto the trunk of the car. His weight stopped the rocking motion as he was a big man six foot four and 205 lbs. of brawn from his stevedore work.

He also knew his muscular build was going to be a problem, getting through the window and inside the car. It just may be the final factor in sending the car on its dismal journey into the valley.

Ted eased forward. The car started to rock. The girl was shifting around, trying to see him. "Please stay still," he pleaded, sweat forming on his brow. "I know it is hard under the circumstances, but you must. It is imperative."

The girl froze in place. Ted's head was inside the car. He was waiting until the vehicle stopped shifting around, grating on the rock threateningly.

"You must not move unless I tell you all right?"

The girl whispered in fear. "Yes."

"Can you move in slow motion and release the seatbelt after you turn off the car that is?"

The girl reached forward and turned off the car. Easing her hand back and reached for the seatbelt. When she released it, it flew back in the direction of the door as the belt quickly retracted into its holster like an attacking hissing snake. The car rocked again. The girl squealed.

"I'm sorry, I didn't warn you to hold on to the seatbelt, so that wouldn't happen. Now keep perfectly still. I am going to try to ease inside a bit more and see what I can do to help you." Ted eased forward. "Are you hurt?"

"Yes, my foot was caught in between the pedals somehow. I wrenched it when I hit the rock. It is quite painful to move. My hand went through the steering wheel, and I hurt my wrist."

"Can you move your foot? Slowly," he warned, "ever so slowly being careful not to rock things."

The girl gasped in pain, but she said gamely in a small voice, "I think it will be all right enough to get me out of the car. It is not trapped."

"Good." Ted was inching forward as he talked so she wouldn't panic if the car started moving again. The upper part of his body was in the car. He felt the car start to rock more.

"Don't move," he yelled.

"I won't," she whispered.

"I can't come in any further, so now it is up to you." Ted eased back a bit, knowing his weight was what he had to concentrate on if this rescue was to be successful.

"What is your name?"

"Emma."

He could tell her teeth were chattering in fear by the way she said her name.

"Hello Emma, I am Ted. Emma, I want you to turn ever so gently until you are kneeling on the seat. You are going to have to do it in slow motion. If the car starts to rock in any way, stop that is important, very important." Ted stressed. "Can you do that?"

"I'll try." Emma's voice was still wobbly but a bit stronger. He took that as reassuring.

"Emma, are you a teacher?"

"No."

"Are you a librarian?"

"No."

Ted was trying to get her mind past the fear that was surrounding her. Keeping her calm was necessary.

"Are you a nurse?"

"No."

"Are you a trapeze artist?"

"No." Then she giggled.

"What are you?"

"Daddy's girl," she replied with feeling. That was why she was in this predicament.

Ted was surprised but kept his voice nonchalant.

"What does Daddy's girl do?"

"Daddy's girl does the books for his business, but Daddy doesn't want me to call myself a bookkeeper. He insists I call myself Daddy's girl."

"Okaaay??" Ted's voice was far from reassuring after that comment.

This girl must be at least twenty-three if he was any judge of age now that he could see her better. Somehow Daddy's girl didn't work for him, but then he didn't have any children. Maybe her father had a reason, but Ted couldn't quite understand it.

Now that she had calmed down. He had to get her out as fast as possible as the pounding water was slowly inching the car forward even though his weight was holding the car more stable.

"Emma, now you can start to move. Slowly, slowly is the key here."

She tried to ease herself around, but the car only swayed.

"Stop! Don't move anymore," Ted yelled but not too loudly as he didn't want to frighten her.

"Can you push yourself up with your feet? Lift your bottom until you are almost standing and at the same time, put your arms back over the seat and see if you can reach my hands. Slowly is the key here."

Emma started to raise her derriere, but the steering wheel was trapping her legs.

"I can't do it." Emma's voice was scared and defeated.

"Emma, do you know the workings of the car? Does it have a tilt steering wheel?"

"Yes."

"Good. Now ease your hand forward and make the steering wheel tilt out of your way. Gently!"

"That's it. Now ease yourself up as I said before." Emma's body was rising. "That's it. Keep coming slowly, now reach up."

Emma was whimpering in pain from her ankle, but she knew she had to do this, needing rescuing.

"Emma, I can't reach you yet. I daren't move in closer, so you are going to have to reach back much further. When our hands meet, I will grab hold of you. You will have to push with your feet to project yourself backward. I know this is difficult from your awkward position. But we have no choice in the matter." Ted tensed his muscles to receive her weight on hand contact.

"Just a little bit more Emma, we are just about touching. I can hear it is hurting your foot by your moans. Try to ignore the pain. I know that is easier said than done, but it is the only way I can get you out." Ted was trying to reach in further without his moving forward into the car.

"Stand up on your toes if you can, that might be enough to make the difference."

Emma moved up on her toes with some difficulty and groans. Ted touched her hands. Success! But before he could grasp fully, she plunked down with a squeal of pain.

The car rocked drunkenly and with a grinding noise inched over the edge more. Ted shimmied backward, trying to stabilize the auto.

Emma was crying now. She knew it was hopeless. Any effort she made might send the car cascading into the deep gully.

"Emma, don't cry, please. You have to concentrate on trying again. I almost had you in my grasp. I am strong enough to pull you out if you only give me a chance." He let that sink in before he said, "now wait till I tell you to move. This time give one big push with your feet. I know it hurts, but we need that extra effort to propel you upward so I can grab your hands. I will do the rest once we make contact. Okay?"

Emma knew it was pointless. She continued to cry, trying to curl up in a ball of grief. "Go away. I want to die."

"What do you mean you want to die?" enquired Ted with an appalled voice.

"That is why I am in this location. I tried to drive over the cliff, but the car got stuck on the rock." Her voice pathetically thin barely above a whisper. "Then, I started screaming. Not because I was scared, but because I hadn't accomplished my mission to plunge over the edge."

Ted strained his ears to hear her confession, then reaction set in.

"Emma, are YOU crazy? YOU don't want to die! YOU are too young!" Ted was yelling at her in horror. He was inching forward.

"Yes, I do."

"Why for heaven sakes?" he asked in disbelief.

"Daddy's books don't balance because someone is ripping off the company by altering the data. I think my brother Jimmy is involved. If I kill myself, then Daddy will think it was me hopefully, then Jimmy will stop." Emma whimpered.

"That is silly. What kind of notion is that? They will still find out about Jimmy because as soon as you die, they will audit your books and find the same thing you did. They will know it wasn't you. Especially when they realize this is no accident."

"No, they won't. The documents have a similar signature to mine as my twin brother, and I write almost the same."

"Emma, this wasn't very brilliant of you, you know." Ted had eased back into the car again more fully as he now knew this was going to depend on him reaching her when she made the next effort. He felt this time; it would have to happen or else...

"Emma, we are going to try once again. Do you hear me?"

"NO! I want to die." Emma's voice was quite positive about this. Her purpose in coming here was to die. The waterfall's power would eventually take care of the balancing action of the teetering car. She sank deeper into the seat, recoiling lower away from him as she said, "go away. Let me die."

"Emma, if you won't help me, I will have to crawl in there. Then we will both die. Is that what you want?" Ted asked, trying to compress his frustration.

"No."

"Emma, I will not leave you to die. The only way out is for you to try again."

"NO! I came to die. I want to die!" Emma's voice had gained conviction much to Ted's horror.

"Emma, I cannot stop myself from rescuing you, so either you help me out here, or we both die. I am twenty-eight. I am certainly not ready to die. I have a whole life ahead of me. Things I need to do and see, and so do you."

"No, I don't. I want to die. You can leave me here and walk away."

"Emma, I am not going to walk away. I am coming in. Then we will both die, got that," he declared vehemently.

"NO, don't come in," Emma yelled back.

"Let's try once more, and if we don't succeed, I promise to leave you, okay?" Ted had no intention of leaving, but he was willing to promise her anything if only she would try again.

"Ted, I don't want you to die, but I have to die. It will be all right. Just leave that's all, and nature will take care of things." Emma's voice was getting adamant.

Ted shook his head. Then he tried a new tack. "All right, but I am going to phone Jimmy and tell him what you are doing. Do you think Jimmy will care enough for his twin to confess his wrongdoing to his Dad knowing an audit is imminent? Of course, he would. Then your death would be for nothing. Jimmy would go to jail. Your father will be devastated over your needless death."

Ted paused, giving Emma a moment to digest this concept. At that moment, the car shifted forward again. The car's nose lowered a few more degrees, increasing its exposure over the cliff's edge. The pounding water on the hood was working in Emma's favor.

Chapter Two

Emma, Emma," Ted yelled. No answer. She sat crying.

"All right," Ted made sounds like he was scooting backward. "I will phone Jimmy and let him know the sacrifice you made for him."

"NO," said Emma pushing herself up agitated. Ted grabbed her hair that had swung out from her head over the seat.

"I have you now, Emma. Put your arms up, or I will pull every hair out of your head if necessary." His hold on her hair was stopping her from dropping back into the seat. He knew it was hurting her by her piercing shrieks. He would not give in. This was the only possible way for him to convince her.

"Emma put your arms up, or I will pull your hair out by the roots." Ted was sweating now and hating himself for putting her through so much pain. Her tautly stretched hair held in his firm grip. He jerked it more.

Emma squealed loudly. It was hurting so much she had stopped crying. Her feet were pushing up to release the sting in her scalp. Her screams of pain shot through him.

"Arms up, Emma," Ted commanded.

"Okay, okay, release my hair," she screeched loudly.

"No, Emma, not until your arms are up so I can reach them. Come on, or I am going to tug some more. You will lose your hair." He yanked once more threateningly.

"Ouch! You are a bastard. Do you know that?" Emma screeched

out. With her hair pulled tautly, her facial skin drawn back so much. It was difficult to talk properly. "Ted, let me go."

"No Emma arms up. NOW!" Ted gave another pull on her hair. He hated himself inflicting pain, but he would hate himself more if he didn't succeed in saving this girl. The next fifteen minutes were crucial in convincing her, or they both would likely die. There was no doubt in his mind that he would have to keep pulling her hair until she gave in. Some strands had already separated from her scalp. He could feel them curling around his hand after his last yank.

Ted was a gentle person by nature. He hated pain of any kind. Here he was imposing pain on this poor girl with his cruelty.

Emma was a petite small-boned pretty girl except for her face distortion caused by his taunt hold on her hair. A few more hairs gave way, springing up to curl around his hand. The feel of them was starting to make him panicky. How long could she stand the pain? What if she kept refusing? In desperation at the thought, he yelled.

"Emma arms up. GET THEM UP NOW!" Ted was getting fearful of her stubbornness.

The hair pulling, and the yelling at her fueled her pigheadedness. She ignored Ted.

He tried a gentler voice in the hopes she would listen. His commands were ignored, as though she was infuriated. "Please, Emma, I beg you. This is hurting me more than you." He gave another yank. He couldn't believe how strong-willed this girl was to die, how she withstood the need to put her hands up, to release her hair from his painful clutches.

"Ouch! Let go, you bastard. I know what I want. You can't stop me." Emma spat out.

"Emma, you are coming out of there even if I have to pull you out by your hair," Ted yelled. Forget the need to be kind. He started pulling on her hair now as the car shifted again under his struggle to get her out. He knew definitely that the car was going to respond to the combination of the pounding water and his movements.

Emma's arms flew up to stop him from pulling her hair. He grabbed her hands and pulled at the same time. The car slid forward. Ted kept pulling, sliding backward at the same time. His facial expression was distorting with the effort of pulling her weight and moving backward.

Ted's feet hit the ground as her head came through the window. There was a loud grinding noise as the car finally dislodged itself from the restraining rock. The car shot forward. Ted felt Emma going away from him. He braced his legs. He held on for dear life. She came back towards him again. Her foot caught on the window ledge. The force of the car dipping forward into the yawning space pulled Ted towards the cliff edge.

"Emma, pull your foot free," Ted screeched. He wasn't going to lose her now.

"Lift your leg, so your foot comes free." Ted was desperate as he was losing traction.

Were they both going over in spite of all his efforts? No way!

Ted gave a final jerk and threw his body backward with all his might. Emma's foot came free. The car plunged over the cliff. Emma landed on her back on top of Ted. His breath whooshed out of his body.

Emma recovered faster than Ted, who was still breathless and traumatized by fear. They had almost gone over with the car. The sound of the car crashing into the gully and breaking up was still echoing in his ears.

Ted also became aware that his back had landed on something very sharp. It had sunk deep with Emma's dead weight falling on top of him. Lying there, he became aware that his bare torso had shattered glass particles embedded in his upper body from the uncleared broken window. If only he had taken the time to grab a shirt, that would have helped protect him. But there was no point in having regrets now. He was thankful they were both alive.

Emma was squirming around on top of his body. She rolled over and started pummeling and screaming at Ted. He was shocked at her frenzied rage. Why wasn't she happy to be alive?

The pain was excruciating like a hot poker was delving into his back. He had to calm her, to save himself from further injury, or he would be no help to her.

"You maniac, you saved me. You tore my hair out. You took away my right to die. I hate you. You atrocious man, why didn't you let me die?"

Ted was having trouble restraining her. Sharp rock ripping his skin as it pierced his back. She viciously pounded his chest and cavorted on top of him. The rock was thrusting deeper and deeper. She gouged his eye with her flailing hands. Black and blue tomorrow no doubt.

He grabbed Emma's hands, trying to stop them from doing any more damage to his already battered body. With her arms restrained, Emma fell forward, burrowing her head into his neck. She started to cry. All her fight dissipated.

Emma's weight as she fell against him caused a sharper pain to penetrate his body. But Ted ignored it as best he could in his concern for Emma. He was too kind-hearted. He hated to see anyone cry, particularly the deep sobs racking her body. He tightened his grip, the hot poker thrust ever deeper. He was sure the blood was running down onto the ground.

Ted didn't know what to say to comfort this tormented girl. She seemed to be shriveling in his arms in grief. "Emma, please stop crying. We have to get back to the house before you go into shock." In her rage, she had not reacted to the traumatic events of the past half-hour. Could it have been only that long, he wondered? He wrestled them to a sitting position. "Emma, we need to get up now. It is important to get back to the house."

He had no choice but to push her over onto the ground, easing her down as gently as he could. Ted doubted she was even aware of what he was saying or doing, deeply buried in her grief. He hated to let go of her, but he knew he had to get up.

Ted sprang to his feet, wincing and staggering in pain from his back. Emma was his priority as he relaxed his shoulders to lessen the pain so he could bend over to pick her up. The pain was excruciating, but somehow, he managed. He held her close against his body, turning to head for the house. A great roar came from the gully. He looked back to see the leaping flames and black smoke shooting up from the ravine, curling towards the sky. The car had exploded.

Ted sighed in relief at the close call they had. If her foot hadn't broken free, it would have dragged them over too. He would never have let go. He just couldn't. Those flames would have consumed them both. No time now for disturbing thoughts.

He again turned to the house as Emma had collapsed against him. Grief, shock, and viewing the explosion had finally taken its toll. His back was still feeling like a hot poker was twisting in it, but that didn't stop Ted's booted feet from covering the ground quickly in half running gait. He gritted his teeth and kept going.

Reaching the open door, Ted strode inside, knowing his bleeding back was causing weakness in his extremities.

He didn't stop in the kitchen but headed to the front of the house. To the bedroom with his unmade bed that he had so recently vacated. Had it only been half an hour or so? It seemed like forever. He placed her on the bed, rolling the blanket around her to warm her body.

Then he went into the living room to the liquor cabinet to obtain some brandy and a glass. He hurried back to the bedroom to see if Emma had moved at all. She was lying with her eyes fully open, staring into space as though in a trance. It was frightening to see.

He opened the bottle of brandy, pouring some into the glass. Holding the bottle to his lips, he took a big gulp, then another. It seemed to fortify him a bit. He took another big swallow before he placed the bottle on the bedside table.

Ted lifted her as he sat down, pain shot through him. He ignored it, pulling her blanketed body across his lap. Her head fell sideways. She was limp as a Raggedy Ann doll.

He braced her head with his left hand. Then he managed to reach the glass from the night table, hampered by her passive body. He brought the glass to her lips. Her mouth was slightly open. Would she be able to swallow? The brandy trickled into her mouth, but she didn't respond, because it was trickling out.

He eased her head back, forcing her mouth gently open, in the hope he could pour the brandy down her throat. He was worried she might choke, but he had to take the chance.

He poured more brandy into her mouth. This time the liquid must have gone down because she automatically swallowed. He waited for a second, pouring more. He carefully observed her reaction. She swallowed, giving a big shudder, like her body's tension was released by the brandy.

Emma's body went into shivers. Her teeth started chattering. He realized he had to get more blankets and hot tea for her. He laid her down only to notice all the blood on the bed. How could she be bleeding? Then he realized, he must be bleeding profusely. No wonder he was feeling light-headed. He grabbed the cotton sheet from under her, folding and wrapped it tightly around him, grabbing a shirt to keep it firmly in place. Emma was more critical now, or he could lose her. After saving her, he wouldn't let go of her life, despite her wishes.

Some of the excess sheeting was hanging down, ballooning around him as he walked towards the kitchen with blood drops in his path. He had no time to let them concern him. At the stove, he grabbed the kettle, moving to the sink for water. The water sprayed before he maneuvered the kettle under the tap correctly. 'Oh damn!' Dually placing it on the stove, maximizing the heat.

On his next trip to the bedroom, he grabbed some blankets from the hall closet. Thank goodness his mother kept him supplied each Christmas because he kept the place too cool.

Although she seemed still in a trance, her body was shaking. He could hear her teeth chattering as soon as he cleared the door. Ted placed the blanket around her blanketed body then added another for good measure. Surely three blankets should be enough.

Plodding to the kitchen, he felt the sheet was slipping. He grabbed the excess, and with the aid of a knife, ripped a wide strip folded it over and over and wound it around himself after removing the bulky sheet and shirt. There was a rope hanging on a hook behind the door, using it to tie the makeshift bandage tightly. He felt sharp stabs of pain as he must have forced glass chips deeper, into his skin.

He pulled his shirt back on but did not do it up. He thought, perhaps he should call for help. What if the blood continued to flow, would he pass out? He went to the phone to call his brother Tommy.

Tommy was leaving late for work because Sally's excessive morning sickness had delayed him. He was always most sympathetic staying until the worst was over. He was heading out the door when the phone rang. He was already late, should he answer it? Yes, he had better, or Sally would try to get up. He had just convinced her to go back to bed for a while.

"Hello."

"Thank heavens. You are still there. Can you come over right away, I need help? I am injured, and I am losing blood. I am afraid of passing out. I have a girl who is in shock. I am trying to revive her."

"What happened?"

"Haven't got time for details. Just come." Ted hung up the phone.

Tommy decided to call the ambulance and gave them directions to his brother's place on Old Canyon Road. He didn't like the weak sound in his brother's voice. Then he raced out of the house and got in his silver truck, heading out with a squeal of tires.

* * *

Ted rummaged in the cupboard for a teapot and cup. He kept for his mother's visits. Ted looked for the teabags hiding in the back. Dumping the last teabag into the teapot, reaching the kettle poured the water over the teabag. Ted reached for the sugar to lace the tea liberally, to offset the shock. Ted had read that somewhere. He headed for the bedroom. He noticed he was moving sluggishly. The loss of blood was taking its toll.

Ted managed to get to the bedroom, although he had bounced off the walls a few times on his staggering journey there. Fortunately, he hadn't spilled any of the tea much to his surprise. Her teeth were still like castanets.

He sat down gingerly on the side of the bed half-turning, wincing in the process. He tried to ignore it, as he lifted her into his arms. Taking the teacup off the nightstand, he took a sip to make sure it wasn't too hot. Conveying the cup to her lips, Ted helped Emma to drink some of the tea.

She was still staring vacantly, but she did blink a few times after a few sips of tea, which was encouraging. He tilted the cup up a bit more, but the liquid seemed to run down her chin. "Emma, try to drink the tea."

This time when he tilted the cup, it went into her mouth and stayed there. "Swallow, Emma," Ted ordered. "That's a good baby," he said when she complied.

"You are going to be all right. Please let yourself be thankful I saved you." Ted looked down into her azure unseeing eyes. The blank look was disturbing.

"Emma, you need to drink some more. Please help me here."

Ted continued to tip the tea into Emma's mouth. She swallowed, letting the liquid trickle down her throat. "More baby," he kept coaxing as he tilted the cup further. "That's it, Emma."

He could tell the hot tea was doing some good because the chattering had ceased. She was trying to move her arms that the blankets held restricted.

He gazed down into her lovely face. At that moment, Ted fell in love. How could this have happened? He did not believe in love at first sight, but now he knew it was possible.

He continued to rock her. This girl who had tried so hard to fight the escape he offered to her. To sacrifice her life for her twin so Daddy would be unaware of Jimmy's deception. Why didn't she realize her death wouldn't make him behave? Jimmy would only continue in his corrupt ways until he was caught red-handed. Then her good intention, at the cost of her life would be for nothing.

Emma was now trying harder to get her arms free, but Ted didn't want to release her yet. He just wanted to hold her like this gazing at her lovely face. He put the cup to her lips once again. Emma drank freely this time.

"That's good, Emma. You will be okay now. I feel it."

The relief that ran through Ted felt so good.

His eyes drooped down as a bout of weakness hit him, draining him like it was draining his soul. Now that Emma was going to be all right, his own body was responding to the excessive blood loss.

Ted vaguely heard a noise outside in the direction of the front of the house as he fell sideways against the headboard, slipping into unconsciousness.

Tommy burst into the bedroom just as Emma cleared her one arm from the nest of blankets. She started yelling and hitting Ted even though it was a weak effort, but her voice was clear. "I hate you. I hate you. I will never forgive you. I wanted to die. I needed to die." Then Emma fell over Ted's limp body in a faint.

Chapter Three

Wondering what in the world had happened, Tommy was alarmed by the scene before him. He was thankful that he had called the ambulance before leaving home. He heard a screech of brakes outside. His heart calmed. Good, now he is rescued. Running to the front door, he saw the ambulance. They were removing a stretcher. Leaping out the front door, Tommy was yelling.

"Hurry! Hurry! There are two of them. But I have no idea what happened or how badly they are hurt. I see blood around the house and on the bed where both of them are unconscious." Tommy ran on excitedly. "The girl seems to be angry with my brother because he saved her from dying, then she passed out," Tommy said in wonderment.

As the paramedics proceeded into the house, Tommy said, "one of the victims is Ted Maxwell, my brother. A girl who is a stranger is the other victim. I think it is my brother that is bleeding but not where."

He led the two paramedics into the bedroom, leaving the stretcher in the hallway. They found the couple passed out together as if, in an embracing sleep. The paramedic quickly loosened the blankets around the girl and threw them to the other side of the bed. One slipped to the floor.

He eased the girl down, laying her flat, trying to determine the extent of her injuries by running his hands over her gently. Her ankle appeared swollen. He couldn't find any other physical injuries, only pieces of glass particles in her skin and hair. The ambulance driver strode over to the other side of the bed, avoiding the bunched fallen blanket, to reach Ted. His partner was taking the girl's vital signs, while the driver tried to ease Ted down on the bed. Hesitating because of the excessive blood.

The blond man said, "this girl's vital signs are almost normal, so I think she is okay but probably passed out in shock. Throw me the blankets." The driver reached down to pick up the blankets and covered her again with his partner's help. Then the driver, Hank, came around the bed and said, "I think it would be best if we put the man directly on the stretcher."

Tommy was easing the bulky stretcher into the room as the blond guy Bill reached for the stretcher to pull it into position. Hank had no precise knowledge as to the extent of the male victim's injury. "I think it will be difficult to lift this unconscious man without causing more damage to him."

"We have no choice if we want to get him out of here," Bill said. "Tommy, you hold the stretcher firmly while we try to grab your brother. Then you ease it around while we get him off the bed. We know he is bleeding, but we are not able to determine where. It could be his side or back from the distribution of the blood."

"Ted, can you hear me?" Bill was saying over and over. Ted did not respond. Hank had managed to take Ted's upper body against his own and eased an arm under him as Bill lifted his legs. They lifted Ted off the bed, moving toward the stretcher. Tommy was trying to maneuver it as close as possible. They finally got him on the stretcher. Bill took his vital signs, which were showing they were beyond normal but not life-threatening.

"Tommy, you and Hank take the stretcher. I will bring the girl. I think that is the fastest way to get out of here."

They made slow progress into the narrow hall with the stretcher while Bill reached down for the girl, and was soon following.

"What could have happened?" inquired Tommy mystified.

Hank said, "there is no clear evidence of rough play here, only blood, so it would seem whatever happened must have occurred someplace else."

After they reached the front door, they had further difficulties with the stretcher manipulating the stairs as Tommy unused to maneuvering the bulky stretcher around like the experienced paramedics.

Bill moved past them on the wide steps to put the girl on the ground. He came back to take over from Tommy.

"Tommy, you go ahead, open the ambulance door. Hank, and I will get the stretcher in place. I want to start an IV first."

Bill was rummaging inside for the case, holding the IV paraphernalia and other life supports.

"I am worried about the amount of blood loss." Bill was pressing the IV needle into Ted's hand. "It is more important to get to Emergency. I'll attend to things back here once we are on the road."

Bill and Hank worked skillfully in getting the two victims into the ambulance. The girl was reclining on a sloped chair. Tommy entered the ambulance with Bill, while Hank proceeded to get in the cab for the journey to the hospital.

Bill was now taking Ted's vital signs and giving the information to Hank, who was in contact with the hospital, giving them their ETA.

The girl was stirring. Tommy said, "the girl has come around. Do you think we should question her?" He was anxious to find out what was going on between her and his brother.

"You can try," said Bill, "but don't press her if she reacts negatively. She still looks too dazed."

Tommy looked down at the girl. She seemed to be breathing okay. Bill could tell her condition wasn't critical by the sound of her breathing.

"What happened to you?" The girl stared back at Tommy but didn't say anything. "What happened to you and my brother?" Tommy requested again but not too harshly.

She whispered, "I hate him. I hate him." Then she clamped her mouth closed and said no more. Tommy decided due to her hate-filled answer, not to press her further until she had proper medical attention.

Tommy asked Bill. "How is my brother?"

"I think he needs a blood transfusion. I wish we could have determined where he is bleeding, but we felt it was best to get him to the hospital as quickly as possible. The makeshift bandage seems tight enough to suffice until we get there."

Tommy's voice held shock when he said, "I wonder why she hates him so. That is twice, she responded to him in that way." Her eyes were closed again. Bill looked over, but he felt she had closed her eyes to avoid any more questions rather than being unconscious.

The ambulance arrived at the hospital in San Luc. It was the town nearest to where Ted lived.

After the screeching halt of the ambulance, the hospital emergency doors burst open as a bevy of white exploded from within. There were two nurses and two doctors. One nurse pushing a wheelchair.

The stretcher with Ted was the first out. They wheeled it through the doors and into a cubicle at the far end. Bill assisted the blanketed girl into the wheelchair that he had taken from the nurse. They stopped halfway down the room, easing her into a small cubicle. Bill helped her onto the gurney, being careful of her swollen foot. "How are you feeling?"

The sullen-faced girl made no answer.

The doctor attending Ted was removing the blood-soaked bandage from his body with surgical scissors. He didn't know what to expect. He appeared to have lost a great deal of blood. The doctor had ordered a transfusion as soon as he got the vital signs.

The two doctors shifted the big muscular man over on to his stomach as there appeared to be no significant injury in his chest area other than embedded glass fragments. They were horrified to see the ugly gaping hole in his back. The wound was torn and jagged and very deep. There were particles of rock or some such substance projecting from the injury. "It must have been excruciating for him to lay on," the doctor stated.

"No wonder he passed out from profuse loss of blood and pain," said the second doctor.

The first doctor nodded his head. "We will have to get an x-ray immediately," yelling to the nurse. She responded to the doctor's clipped order by leaping to the phone to order the x-ray. "An incoming patient requires imaging of a back wound." Turning, she noted the stretcher was already out the door to x-ray. The patient had not regained consciousness.

The x-ray department handled the unconscious patient with care. They were moving him as little as possible to get the image taken. The young female technician was proficient, but she was so small she needed help from the male orderly that had delivered the inert victim. After the x-rays, the stretcher headed for the operating room, where a team of doctors and nurses were suiting up awaiting Ted's arrival.

Again, the wound was exclaimed upon in the OR. "It looks like he has fallen on something sharp. Something that forced his body to tear, ripping his skin in a very injurious jagged way."

The x-rays had arrived along with the patient. The two doctors were viewing the damage on the x-rays on the bright screen. The wound was quite deep, but no severe damage to any internal organs seemed to be evident. The x-rays showed several shards of substance in the cavity of the gaping wound. The doctors were discussing the trickiness of removing all of the fragments. The wound was bleeding again, due to the manipulation during the x-rays. They started carefully removing the particles that indeed were rock chards and glass. The tearing destruction of the skin required an extensive skin graft.

Tommy was pacing the waiting room. Ted had been in the operating room for three hours.

Finally, Ted was lying in the recovery room. The black was starting to recede. How was Emma? Where is she? Did they manage to keep her from getting away? All he remembered, was her yelling and hitting him, spewing out words of hate. He had fallen in love with her. How weird could that be?

Ted wanted someone to tell him how Emma was, but he couldn't move enough to locate a nurse. Magically a nurse did appear to check on him. Ted was lying on his stomach, so it was difficult to see her from his prone position. The nurse was checking his vital signs. He tried to use his voice, but it came out as a croak.

"Where'ss... the... girlll?"

The nurse bent over, observing his face. "Do you want something?"

"Howw'ss the girll?

The patient was trying to push himself up.

"Please don't move like that. You have lost a lot of blood. The operation on your back is serious, and you aren't supposed to move physically yet. There are needles and tubes. If you lie still, I will see if anyone knows about a girl with you, okay?" She quickly went to the phone to call emergency.

"My patient, a man with a back injury, is asking about a girl? Did a girl come in with him?"

"Yes, there was a girl with him. She was in shock and had shards of glass removed from her body along with bandaging a swollen ankle, and she seems depressed. A car accident, I would think. That is all I know."

The nurse from the recovery room replied, "there was the oddest thing I noticed about the patient I have here. He arrived with long blonde hair wrapped around his hand. I have never seen anything like that before."

The emergency nurse said, "yes, the girl has long blonde hair, but I don't know the explanation for such an odd occurrence."

"I wonder what transpired between them."

"Neither patient has been coherent enough to tell us. But I understand that the brother of the man is here, and he doesn't seem to know either." The emergency nurse continued. "We will just have to wait to see what happens when either patient recovers enough to talk."

Ted was continually fading in and out of consciousness due to the powerful painkillers they were feeding him intravenously. He was trying to fight the fog of fuzziness until the nurse came back with the answer about Emma.

He saw a white-clad body in his peripheral vision. "Mr. Maxwell, the young lady that came in with you, they say is okay. Just some glass fragment wounds and a swollen ankle. We are admitting her because she was treated for the shock but is still in a trancelike condition."

Ted was not able to fight the drugs any longer. He was just relieved that Emma was detained for observation. He knew why she was depressed then he slipped into a shroud of darkness.

* * *

The next time Ted awoke, he could see his brother sitting in the chair beside his bed. As soon as Tommy was aware that he was awake, he leaned down and said, "how goes it, buddy?"

Ted tried to respond, but he felt his throat had closed up. He tried to speak. "Wat? Wat?"

"Wat, oh, you mean water?" Tommy reached for the cup with a straw sticking out of it. He held it to his brother's lips.

Ted drank slowly. It was so difficult to swallow. He didn't know if it was the position he was forced to lie in or the drugs. He tried sipping some more to ease his throat somewhat.

"Not too fast; take your time. You will be okay, or at least that is what the doctors are saying," Tommy said quickly to reassure his brother. Their roles had reversed. Ted was three years older than Tommy. Ted had always been the one to do the reassuring. It was strange to see him so incapacitated and vulnerable.

"Try some more water, then we will see if you can speak more clearly," Tommy suggested. Ted sipped. It went down a little easier.

Tommy sent an inquiring look at Ted. "Can you talk now? The police were here. When you were in surgery for so long, they left. They went out to your place to look around first. I still don't know what occurred exactly other than the rock fragments along with the glass in your body meant something drastic happened. The girl isn't talking, although she is conscious. The nurse in the recovery room mentioned that she had removed quite a few long blonde hairs from around your hand. What was that all about?"

Before Ted could reply, the door opened. A stern-looking police officer appeared. "Is he awake yet?" he asked gruffly.

"Yes," Tommy said, "but he hasn't been able to talk yet. Did you find out what happened at his place?"

"Yes. We found a car in the gully near the waterfalls. It had exploded and burned to a crisp. We are assuming your brother Ted managed to pull the young lady out first." Another cop appeared at the door. Tommy glanced his way as he answered the first officer.

"That may explain the blonde hairs wrapped around my brother's hand. Did you find anything else?"

"Some scrape marks on a boulder like it had been wedged there. Also, a sharp rock, with plenty of blood and some skin on it. That rock must have been what injured your brother. It was near where the car appeared to go over. We have a crew going down to see if there is anything left of the car to identify the girl. She isn't talking so far, according to the nurses." The officer had introduced himself as McNally and his partner Officer Anderson. McNally removed a book from his pocket. He flipped through the pages until he found what he was looking for.

"I was in to see the girl first. She isn't feeling like talking other than to ask how you are," Officer McNally said.

McNally looked at his notes again then peered over at Ted. "It looked like it was a blue model car by the structure, but that is all we can determine at this time. The mystery is, why would the vehicle go over at that point? It isn't realistic considering the distance from the road. Even an erratic driver couldn't have gone that far off the road."

Ted was lying still taking this in. He knew Emma had tried to kill herself and why. But he was not about to tell the police, nor Tommy. He hated that he couldn't be honest with his kid brother. They had never had secrets from each other, not even when they were younger.

Tommy turned to Ted. "Can you talk now, big brother?"

Ted had closed his eyes, pretending to be unconscious as he wanted the officers to leave.

Tommy leaned down to study Ted. "I think he has passed out again, or the drugs have put him back to sleep. He seems to fade in and out like that."

"Okay, but if he awakens call us. We will be right down the hall at the nursing station." McNally motioned the other officer to follow him.

Tommy settled back in the chair to wait for Ted to recover when he noticed Ted's eyes were opening. "You were playing possum, weren't you?"

Ted croaked out. "Yes." His throat was still dry.

Tommy reached for the water cup again. Ted started sipping thirstily as a nurse appeared in the room.

"Is he awake yet?" The nurse asked as she advanced to the bed.

Tommy replied, "yes."

"How do you feel, Mr. Maxwell?"

Ted replied with a stronger voice. "Like a Mack truck ran over me."

"Well, it seems you have had quite a time of it. Could you possibly have been in a car accident?" She had heard there was a car involved from the police officers. While she had been talking to Ted, she had been taking his blood pressure and temperature, writing the information on the chart.

Ted was silent, but Tommy asked. "How is the girl now?"

"She is conscious, but that is all I know as she is on another floor."

"Mr. Maxwell, you must try to drink as much water as you can. Your diet will be mostly liquid as long as you are on your stomach. I have put pillows along your body to stop you from rolling over in your sleep. You will be on intravenous until you can start eating normally."

She puffed the pillows up against his body. "Another nurse will be in soon to give you a sponge bath." She headed for the door as it opened, admitting the doctor.

"Nurse, how is our patient doing, awake yet?"

"Yes, doctor." Turning towards the bed to be of assistance to the doctor during examining Ted. "I am Dr. Murray. I came to see my handy work. Mr. Maxwell, I want to look at your back." He was removing the padded bandage as he spoke. Tommy was horrified at the hugeness of the laceration on his brother's back. He could see the damage must have been extensive. Ted winced and groaned as the doctor probed the skin near the wound.

"Nice work, even if I say so myself. We have to hope we were successful in removing all the particles of rock before we sealed you up. I would recommend you stay on your stomach for another three days to give that skin graft a chance to heal." Ted emitted a groaning sound.

"I know it is difficult, but it is in your best interest, believe me." The doctor changed the bandage. "The chest cuts aren't deep, and the back will be fine with the skin graft. In just a few days, you will be able to get up for a bit." The doctor left the room. He didn't seem to expect Ted to talk, which was good because he was compressing his teeth against the pain of the doctor's probing. The nurse left after replacing the covers and pillows around him.

Tommy sat, waiting. He observed Ted's compressed lips, which spoke of great pain. Ted physically forced his body to relax enough to speak.

"Tommy, can you go and speak to the girl for me. Her name is Emma. Tell her I am okay. Play down my injuries and tell her I love her. I think she needs something to bolster her right now," Ted said a little above a whisper.

Tommy's mouth dropped open at his brother's declaration of love. Ted wasn't the type to fall in love without sharing that this girl was part of his life. Who was she?

"Tommy, please give me some more water before you go. Then after you talk to her, come back and tell me what she said." Ted's hand administered an extra shot of painkiller.

Tommy reached for the water and held it to his brother's lips. Ted took a few sips.

The painkillers were taking their toll from the added surge, taking him under into drugged sleep. Tommy left the room and headed for the nursing station. "Do you know where the girl that came in with my brother is? Her name is Emma."

"Yes, I heard she is on the third floor. So, her name is Emma. So far, she has refused to give us her name. I don't know if they will let you see her unless you are a relative. But you can try considering the strange circumstances that they both came in under." The nurse explained.

Tommy went the elevator scanning the indicator for the level it was on presently. When it finally came, he pressed three. His dilemma was, how do you ask for a girl if she hasn't supplied her name? Arriving on the third floor, he was about to find out. Approaching the nursing station, he looked at the young nurse with expectation. She was busy entering something in a binder.

Tommy had his smile ready for when she looked up. "There was a young girl just admitted. Do you know in which room I can find her?"

The nurse reacted to his smile with one of her own. "Yes, she is in 308. Are you a relative?" Knowing full well, he wasn't by the vague way he had asked for the patient.

"No, she came in with my brother, who is a patient on the fifth floor."

"I will have to call the doctor to enquire," she said with a smile that matched his.

"Please tell him, my brother is anxious about her condition. He has asked me to see her in his place. My brother's name is Ted Maxwell." Tommy supplied the information, hoping that was going to make the difference. The nurse spoke into the telephone for a while then hung up. The overhead speaker started paging a doctor requesting he call 3244. The phone rang.

She spoke into the phone. "Can Mr. Maxwell's brother visit the patient in Room 308? He says his brother is concerned about her. Apparently, they came in together from the same accident."

"The doctor said you could go in to see her provided she doesn't get upset, or you will have to leave immediately."

Answering with a polite yes, Tommy headed down the corridor looking for room 308. He was wondering about Ted's strange message. Ted had always been a loner, a regular guy that had dated. His social compatibility of late was nonexistent, making Ted's message bizarre. How long had he known this girl? Tommy was unaware of her existence.

He stopped at the room, straightened his shoulders, and walked inside. The bed held a slim girl lying prone her eyes were open. No movement, only exposed and vacant.

Tommy eased closer to the bed. He stood there looking down at her. She had not responded to his presence in any way. What was he to say? He cleared his throat, but still, she did not acknowledge him.

She was a pretty girl — the way her long hair fanned out on the pillow in a curly mass of silvery blonde hair. The same long tresses wrapped around his brother's hand, according to the nurse. Why? What was the story here? The girl had a bandage on her forehead and her arm. Some cuts were visible similar to the ones on Ted's body. Was the injury on her head the reason for the vacant look? She looked so lonely, lying so still and silent. He cleared his throat again only this time he spoke.

"Hi Emma, I am Tommy. Tommy Maxwell." He hesitated. No sound or acknowledgment came from her. "Ted is my older brother.

He is worried about you. He is concerned, wanting to know how you are. Anxious, in fact." He paused, waiting. He stared intently, but there was no movement or change in her expression.

When he sidled closer, he was able to observe her eyes better. They were staring and sad looking. What possible explanation for her car's journey over the cliff? She had so much of her life ahead of her. Tommy could only surmise what must have happened, although neither of them was divulging any crucial details so far.

His assumption naturally came from the officer's description of the burnt car at the bottom of the deep gully. He knew it was impossible to ever run that far off the road by accident. Nor could the car accidentally progress as far as the waterfall, no matter how fast or reckless you drove with the rocky terrain and distance. *It had to have been deliberate.*

Chapter Four

Why would this pretty girl be at Ted's place? It was a dead-end road. She looked maybe twenty or twenty-two. She couldn't have seen enough of life being so young to want to leave it this soon. But why else was her car at the waterfall? This puzzled him greatly.

Tommy decided to try to get her attention by shouting a bit. "EMMA, I HAVE A MESSAGE FROM TED FOR YOU..." He was embarrassed. The nurse had walked into the room.

"Is she responding at all?" she asked as though it was perfectly natural to be yelling at a patient. Which only made Tommy more embarrassed for some reason.

"No."

The nurse was taking the girl's blood pressure. He hoped the nurse wouldn't throw him out for yelling at Emma.

"Do you think she hears me? She has her eyes open, but she has such a vacant look. I would rather see her with her eyes closed then you can assume she is sleeping." Tommy stopped speaking. Did he leave or stay? Was there any point in all of this?

Emma had barely opened her lips in response to the nurse's putting the thermometer in her mouth.

The nurse asked, "what did you call this girl?"

"My brother told me her name was Emma, but that is all I know. He asked me to visit her, but she doesn't seem to be responding to anything I say, including the yelling," Tommy said categorically.

"The fact that she responded to the thermometer near her lips means she is aware. But I think she has closed her mind to her surroundings. She has been like this ever since she came in." The nurse was straightening the covers. "Just keep talking to her. You might say something that will make her react. If not, I guess you might as well leave." Her expression showed deep concern.

He eased back over to the bed. He just stood watching Emma with interest. With the likelihood the car incident was not an accident, why would this girl try to commit suicide? Ted must have thwarted her intent of self-destruction. The only explanation for the 'I hate you' comment to his brother that he had witnessed. He must have saved her against her wishes. The fact that Ted seemed to get the worst of it was immaterial to Emma. Why would Ted say he loved her when the girl was saying the opposite?

"Emma, I have a message for you from Ted. Please tell me how you feel about it. He will be waiting for a reply." Did she move, or was it his imagination? He stared intently but perceived no further movement.

"The message is 'Tell her I love her and I hope she is okay.'"

Emma blinked her eyes but otherwise did not move. At last, she closed her eyes. A movement of her lips was not more than expelled air. "No." had escaped. How could he explain that to Ted? Was there any point in trying again? Then he thought maybe she had trouble speaking as his brother had. He went around the bed to the side table. He picked up the cup with a straw. He held the straw to her lips. Emma was not cooperating.

"Come on, Emma. Just take a little sip. I know you need it."

The girl did not open her lips. He pushed the straw more firmly against her lips while tilting the cup. Water wet her lips, then trickled down her chin to her neck. The tiny droplets pooled there. Tommy put down the cup. He was ready to give up in defeat. He heard a weak voice. "Is Ted okay?"

He eased back towards her hopefully. "Yes, he is okay. How are you doing? Did you understand Ted's message?" Tommy was optimistic for a few seconds.

Then much to his surprise, her voice came strongly. "You must tell him I do not love him. I hate him." Emma stopped speaking, closed her eyes and lips firmly. He knew it was pointless to continue standing there.

* * *

Tommy went back to Ted's room. McNally was questioning him. But from the expression on the officer's face, he was pretty sure Ted wasn't being cooperative. The officer looked up as Tommy walked in. "I understand you were up visiting the girl that came in with your brother. Did you get any response from her?"

"No," replied Tommy. "She wouldn't talk to me at all, nor acknowledge I was there."

"Well, you are not alone. Your brother isn't talking either. It is like a conspiracy between the two of them." Officer McNally flipped his notebook closed with some disgust. His body showed his disappointment as he sauntered to the door. He threw over his shoulder. "Ted, if you feel like talking later, I will be waiting near the nurse's station. The doctor is supposed to be coming to see you, the nurse mentioned. I want an update from him too." He shook his head, continuing out the door.

Tommy walked over to the bed. Ted lifted his head to glance at him questioningly. "What did she say when you gave her my message?" asked Ted intently.

"I'm sorry, Ted, she expressed 'she hates you.' She was rather emphatic about it." Ted was not surprised at the response from her. He twisted his head away and gazed out the window.

Tommy came to the bed, staring intently down at his brother. Ted was usually the one in command of things. This unknown girl had changed things. Why was the girl heading for the gully? Why the secrecy between the two of them? Could Ted have known this girl before today?

Tommy went around the bed to get some water to offer to Ted. He drank greedily. Then Tommy sat down so he could be on Ted's level. "You know you have to say something about what happened out at the waterfall. That car didn't make its way into the gully by itself. The police will piece it together from the tire tracks. Then they will be back until you give in. You know that, don't you?" Disturbed, Tommy sat back in the chair. He could see the stubbornness in Ted's face. "She did ask how you were, but I told her very little." Ted's eyes held sadness.

"Why does this girl mean so much to you? Did you know her before? How can you love her when she says she hates you?" Tommy waited. "Talk to me, Ted."

Ted went on, gazing at Tommy, should he tell him. He had to tell him something after all he had come to his rescue immediately. Besides, Ted did not usually have secrets from his brother.

"When you leave here, will you go to my place to close it up? I have a feeling I am tied to this bed indefinitely."

"Okay."

At last, Ted came around to the accident but thought he would gloss over some of the details. "I heard this scream but never thought much about it at first. The second scream held terror. I dashed outside to an unexpected sight. In the distance, I could see a car sitting its nose precariously into the waterfall. Not exactly sitting but partway suspended into space seesawing back and forth. The water was pounding down on the hood of the car, causing the rocking motion. The wedged car was on a rock, trapped there. I knew it would only be a matter of time before the torrential flow of water would force the car-free from its precarious position. There was no way I could move the car, so I concentrated on removing the girl. I smashed the back window."

His voice had been getting weaker as he talked. Tommy wasn't sure whether it was the magnitude of the memory or just a dry throat. He held the straw as Ted took a drink. Then Ted just lay there, not talking, looking distant.

Tommy still held the straw within reach. "Drink your fill, and then I will leave. I will go to your place to close up." Ted sipped the water, gathering his thoughts. Tommy was rising prepared to leave, dropped down again at the sound of Ted's voice.

"I climbed on the trunk, easing inside that is how I got the cuts and glass embedded in my bare skin from not clearing shattered glass from the window frame. Emma pushed herself up. I tried to reach her.

But she gave up because of her injured ankle. The car started to slip forward. She had hurt her ankle, so she couldn't put her weight on it to push herself up far enough with her arms held out. When I tried to climb inside further, the car slid forward on the rock."

The terror of that moment refreshed in his mind. The almost tragedy that could have happened if he had given in to her wishes.

"So, I grabbed her hair and tried pulling her out, forcing her arms up and hoping she would put enough pressure on her foot to push up. Although I had pulled on her hair a lot, her removal wasn't successful."

Ted went on. "The car was trying to free itself from its wedged position on the rock with the forceful water. My weight as I pushed in further, was helping the car in its journey. I had to release her hair slightly then tightened my grip, forcing her to think about the hair pain and forget her painful foot. She pushed up her arms, to grapple with my hold on her hair. I grabbed her hands and eased back out of the vehicle dragging her with me. Her good foot anchored itself on the window as the car started forward in earnest. The rock had released its steely grip of control. The car started screeching and scraping over rocks on its way over the cliff to its destination below. By this time, my feet were on the ground. The momentum of the car and the wedge of Emma's trapped foot was dragging us with the car. In desperation, I must have given a frantic tug because her foot slipped free of its restriction. Emma landed back on top of me. She was flailing around trying to get off me, only to cause the rock I had fallen on to drill into my back jaggedly deeper. I knew I was bleeding quite badly and was afraid I would pass out, but my prime concern was Emma. I was afraid she would go into shock. We managed to roll away from each other. The difficulty in standing I am not sure how I did it. Then I picked her up and carried her into the house. That was when I called you."

Tommy was confident there was more to this story than Ted was telling. "Why didn't you talk to the police if that is all there was to the story?"

Ted said without a pause. "I hated to relive the horror as to the car's trip into the gully nearly terminating our lives. You heard the officer talk about the burnt-out car from the explosion. It was frightening, as I wouldn't let go. The car was dragging us, in its last death throes. Besides, I felt I needed to give you the explanation first. I will tell the police eventually. I want some of the horror of the event to recede. I know once I give in to their questions, they will harass me for more information, I don't have. Please hold off for a while, telling the officers."

Tommy got up. "I'm glad you wanted to tell me. I will leave now so you can rest. I will go to your place first. I will take care of everything. Is there anything I can bring you?"

"Yes, I will need a robe, slippers, shaving gear, and clothes. I am supposed to be on my stomach for a few days until the skin graft mends. Then I will be able to get out of bed hopefully. I guess I really did a number on my back."

Tommy winced remembering, the size of the torn and stitched wound. "Okay, I will bring your things next time I come. I won't be back now until tomorrow because I have to work late to make up for what time I missed this morning." He started around the bed.

Ted offered. "I know you think there is more to this story. This morning was the first time I set eyes on Emma. It is bizarre. I fell in love with her. I looked into her eyes, and this weird feeling came over me. Like, I needed this girl in my life, believe it or not."

"I know you believe that, but love doesn't happen that way." Tommy disputed.

Ted knew it was ridiculous too. "But that was the way it happened strangely enough," replied Ted. "I didn't understand it either. Maybe it was her helplessness. I have to continue this relationship somehow, or I will always be alone in my life." His voice held conviction.

Tommy, who had paused when Ted denoted his belief, continued to the door saying. "I will be back tomorrow evening. Maybe I will have Sally with me." He exited the door and traveled down the hall toward the elevators.

The nurse seemed to be lying in wait for him. "The doctor would like to meet with you in his office. It is on the main floor, Room 102, in the Administration Offices, which is in the wing opposite the emergency room. If you follow the signs, you can't miss it."

Pressing the down button, Tommy thanked the nurse. The elevator trudged in an upward voyage from the lower floors, pinged and noisily opened its doors. He stepped in pressed the M for the Main level. The doors slide closed. The elevator shuddered, then a jolt. Tommy tried not to look apprehensive as the ancient elevator descended downward.

It stopped on the third floor. The doors grated back to frame Emma in its opening. The buttons were askew in her haste to leave. When she saw Tommy, the frenzied look on her face clued him in that she was trying to escape. She half-turned but couldn't run because her hobble indicated excessive pain.

Tommy stepped out quickly, grasping her arm. "Where do you think you are going?" he asked in a concerned voice. The elevator continued its journey without them.

Emma said emphatically. "Let me go. You can't stop me. Keep your hands off me." Emma was struggling to extract her arm from his grip, but he held on tightly.

"You are not going anywhere on your own. Do you hear me? So, quit struggling." Tommy's voice tolerated no resistance. He pushed the elevator button again. He was trying to figure out what his next move would be. There was no point in returning her to her room. She would probably try to leave again as soon as he departed.

The doctor waiting for him in his office, just possibly, wouldn't recognize Emma if he hadn't seen her at the time of her admission.

The elevator arrived vacant, thankfully. Tommy dragged Emma in with him.

"Now we are going down to Administration as Ted's doctor wants to see me. You are going with me." Without thinking, he reached over and redid her buttons on her blouse. She didn't even flinch.

"I can't possibly go with you. The doctor is sure to recognize me," Emma said pleadingly.

"No, he won't. This doctor was the one that operated on Ted's back, so I doubt he would have occasion to see you. I am going to pass you off as my wife so behave, or I will blow the whistle on you, that will curtail your escape." He smiled at her in the hopes of winning her confidence after his threat.

"What do you intend to do with me?" she asked beseechingly.

"That is a good question, but you are not leaving here alone. Ted would never forgive me. Decide, either come with me or go back to your room. You will no doubt, be strapped to the bed on your stomach, helpless and humiliated. It is not comfortable, I hear." He eased his grip on her as the door opened slowly. She must have decided to cooperate because she didn't resist as they exited the elevator.

Emma had decided to wait until they were clear of the hospital fearful of his threats. Hospitals were not her favorite place. Tommy was busy looking for the sign to indicate where he could find Administration. He finally found one as he took another corridor.

She was making slow hobbling progress. Tommy slowed down to accommodate her painful gait. He was anxious to get away from the hospital, now that he had Emma in tow. If this meeting weren't significant to him, Tommy would have avoided Ted's doctor. They paused in front of 102 with Dr. D. L. Murray on the door. He knocked. A voice loudly invited him in.

He entered the room, noting the doctor was on the phone. Tommy helped Emma to the chairs across from the desk the doctor indicated. She kept sneaking looks at Tommy, but he was staring out the window, hoping the doctor's conversation would end soon. He was trying to think about how best to explain Emma. At last, the doctor terminated the call.

"Thank you for coming, Mr. Maxwell. I wanted to talk to you about your brother." Although he was talking to Tommy, his eyes questioningly were straying in Emma's direction.

Tommy observed this byplay. "Oh, I would like you to meet my wife, Sally. I had her here to see Ted, but she couldn't walk that far, so she waited down here in the lobby." Reaching over to rest his hand on her arm in a husbandly fashion. "Are you okay now, dear?"

"Yes, dear, I am fine as long as I am sitting and off my foot," Emma said sweetly, too sweetly.

Tommy turned to the doctor. "What did you need to see me about?"

"The reason I wanted to talk to you is that I am getting the feeling that there is more to your brother's accident than Ted is admitting. I could not find any other injury or explanation for his hazy recollection of the accident other than a slightly bruised eye. The police have been questioning me about Ted's physical condition. They want to know if there was some head injury or reason for his avoidance in talking. Do you know the story?" Dr. Murray inquired.

"Ted told me he saved some girl from a car that eventually went over a cliff into the gully at the back of his place. Other than that, I don't have any other details. No explanation as to the girl's identity or how the car got there. He didn't appear to know anything more."

Dr. Murray shifted in his chair. "I would like to keep your brother in for at least a week to make sure the skin graft heals properly. The wound may still contain fragments of rock, although I hope I got them all. We will know if he gets an infection in the wound caused by a foreign entity. It was impossible to see clearly with all the blood. He had already lost too much blood, so I didn't like to delay closing."

Dr. Murray continued. "I asked you about the details of the accident because I don't like having problems with the police if I can help it. Nor do I want any reason for a delay in Ted's recovery. Are you and your wife coming back tonight? The reason I am asking, it is not easy to lie on your stomach when you're not used to it. Visitors help to alleviate the boredom and discomfort. I don't want any pressure or pulling on that skin graft, so he must stay on his stomach."

Tommy shifted in his seat. "My wife has a bad ankle. I was going to stay home tonight to help her put the children to bed." Tommy looked at Emma with a concerned expression. She piped up. "Tommy if you feel you would rather be here, I can cope with the kids alone," Emma chirped playing along.

Dr. Murray was looking from one to the other thinking, what a caring couple. He stood up, coming around the desk, as they stood too. Tommy stuck out his hand. "Thank you, Dr. Murray. I will try to get back tonight if things go well at home." He reached over and helped Emma to the door. She tried to disguise the extent of her injury because she didn't want the doctor to know it was new.

"Mrs. Maxwell, what happened to your ankle?" He asked kindly, also noting the cuts and bandage on her face.

Tommy said quickly. "She fell over one of the boys' skateboards left at the bottom of the stairs. She had dirty laundry in her arms at the time. It happened last week."

"Oh, I am sorry to hear that. Take care of that ankle." He held the door open while they made slow progress to the door.

"Thank you for your concern. She is improving every day." He was cringing inside. He hated to lie, but he felt he had no choice while the police had an interest in Emma. "Thanks again."

Helping Emma, he kept heading to the nearest exit. His truck was back at Ted's. So, he looked for a phone to call his friend, Steve, who he knew was off today. He had talked to Steve last night. Tommy envied him his rotating days off. He wouldn't mind shift work, but Sally didn't feel the same way.

He found the phone after he placed Emma in a chair near the doorway in the visitor's lounge. The phone was within twenty yards of the bench. He tried to be firm and threatening before he left her. He had visions of Emma escaping him, which he tried to ignore.

Steve answered his call and offered to come right away. All the while Tommy was phoning, Emma was trying to figure out how to get away from him. But she knew he was watching her too closely. Soon there would be just the two of them. Escape would be impossible.

Tommy reached Emma. "Darling, I think we should wait for Steve outside. I need some fresh air. I'm sure you do too." He half expected to hear voices, requesting them to halt. They cleared the entrance without mishap.

There were benches against a wall along the sidewalk at a separate entrance from the emergency exit, so Tommy headed there. Emma was walking slower now, as her efforts in front of the doctor to walk normally had caused her horrific pain. He put his arm around her and took her weight against his body to help. He was tempted to pick her up and carry her. He was anxious to put space between the hospital and them.

Emma said through gritted teeth. "What are you going to do with me?"

"I honestly don't know. Maybe I can come up with something while Steve drives us to Ted's."

"I am sorry about your brother's back. I didn't mean for him to get hurt, but he wouldn't believe me. He insisted on helping me out." She stopped talking when she realized what she was saying. She shut her mouth, hoping Tommy hadn't noticed her slip of the tongue.

Tommy took in what the girl had said. He figured out then that this girl had wanted to die. Ted had forced her to live. He didn't know whether to get mad at her or feel sad. He decided on being sad. Because if he thought the other way, he knew he would be furious at her for risking Ted's life.

Emma knew she had let the cat out of the bag by Tommy's stern look. What will happen now? Will he turn her over to the police? Would he hate her for endangering Ted? When she felt ready, she would have to apologize to Ted. It was very gallant of him what he had risked for her. Why couldn't she just have been grateful, instead of telling him she hated him.

Tommy was having similar thoughts. Why did she hate Ted? If he saved her, why wasn't she grateful to him? Why did this young girl want to die?

Chapter Five

Now Tommy knew why she was leaving the hospital the way she did. She was avoiding the police. He was beginning to see things more clearly.

Steve showed up then. She wanted to get into the back seat, but Tommy leaped over the side into the back. He thought the trip would be jolting enough from the front seat as Steve had picked up his ancient jeep from an Army Surplus place. No extra comfort here, but Steve loved it.

Steve was curious but didn't question the girl's presence. "How's Ted?"

Tommy replied, "his back is pretty bad. He has to lie on his stomach. That is definitely not his favorite position. He has heavy sedation for pain and discomfort. They had to give him a blood transfusion." Tommy stopped. He noticed Emma was shifting in her seat. He didn't know whether from guilt or discomfort. He hoped it was from her inflicting injury on Ted so severely.

Steve didn't know what was going on, but he knew something wasn't quite kosher here. Why, when Ted is so injured, would Tommy be with this girl? He wasn't the kind to play around. He had tried several times to get him to go out for beers, and some hanky panky for fun. But Tommy would only drink two beers then go home to Sally. It just didn't make sense. Besides, how could Ted have just happened to be injured in the first place? Tommy wasn't explaining the situation appropriately. Steve kept looking at the girl out of the corner of his eye. She was staring straight ahead, but he would swear she wasn't observing the scenery. It was more like she was going over something in her mind. Do I ask now or later? Tommy was usually an open person, but Steve knew he wasn't this time.

The trip continued with Tommy and Emma deep in thought. Steve was more intrigued than ever. Tommy finally said, "what's doing? Why weren't you at work today? Last night, you mentioned you might go in for some overtime."

"I was hungover after a snout full last night down at Kelly's. There was this blonde. She kept getting up and dancing on the table. Finally, her clothes started coming off provocatively as more and more guys were giving her money. She was dressed for the occasion, as she had several layers of clothes on. It turns out she was nothing but a tease. She left with one of the bouncers at closing time." Steve's voice was one of disgust. "So, our crowd got quite drunk, and the bar got wealthy."

Steve looked at the girl. She showed no reaction to his story. "So, Tommy, how did Ted get hurt?" Steve asked, taking the bull by the horns.

"Well, I am not quite sure he seems to have had an accident out by the waterfall. You know the place. You have been out there." Tommy's voice was clear and seemed to hold no hidden meaning.

Sally would be unhappy with him when he arrived with Emma. But what else could he do with her? She was the clue to this whole mystery. He wasn't about to let her go until he had the full story for Ted's sake. He knew she was the key. Ted wasn't taking the wrap for her. The police were being pretty persistent.

Steve pulled in beside Tommy's truck. Tommy jumped out and opened the door for Emma.

"Thanks, Steve. I owe you for this." He dragged her away with him. Steve knew he was dismissed. "Yo," He said and swung the jeep in reverse and executed a turn in the wide laneway. He headed back up the lane with spinning wheels.

Tommy helped the girl towards the house. She moved reluctantly. He went up on the veranda. He parked her there in a chair. She was still limping badly. He felt she wasn't going anywhere, so he headed for the door to Ted's house. "I'll be right back."

Emma sank into the rocking chair. Her ankle was swelling. The bandage was getting too tight. She would have to take her boot off to ease it. But that was easier said than done. The foot was encased inside even though she tugged and tugged. Her face distorted in pain. She knew she had been foolish to walk on it. But she had no choice. She couldn't stay in the hospital to be questioned by the police. She was sorry about Ted. After all, he had saved her. When the car exploded in flames, she knew she didn't want a fiery death.

What was Tommy going to do with her? How could she get away from him? How could she explain the missing car to Daddy and Jimmy? They would want to know where it is. She certainly couldn't give any explanation for what happened. Emma tried again to ease for boot off. But there was no way she could pry it loose.

Tommy was tramping through the house, checking everything. He finally checked the fridge, knowing it would be a few days before his brother's return. He went to the cupboard to grab a large paper bag. He started putting vegetables and meat into the bag along with the milk. Ted believed in cooking healthy meals for himself as he preferred that instead of eating out. He removed everything he didn't think would keep.

Ted was crazy to live way out here. It was a pretty spot. Ted was quite the outdoors person. He was always trekking in the woods or checking out the valley below. He frequently climbed down the cliff.

Checking out the bedroom, he grabbed the sheets from the bed where Ted had dripped blood. He cleaned the drips of blood from the floor in the bedroom and hall as best he could. Tommy headed to the front door with the bag of food, and the rolled-up sheets, under his arm. What was he going to do with Emma?

Emma looked over as the door opened. What was his reaction now? He didn't seem angry, but his face wasn't pleasant either.

He came over to her. She must have had a distressed look because he asked, "are you all right? How is your foot? Can you walk to the truck?"

Emma frowned. "It is swelling. My boot is too tight." Emma put her weight on her foot, squealing with pain.

"If you can make it to the truck with my help, I will take off your boot there before you get in."

Tommy put the food and sheets down and lifted Emma into his arms. He started to the truck. She tried to pull away. He wasn't taking any nonsense from her. He just hiked her up higher and headed for his truck with decisive steps. Putting her down, he opened the door. Tommy lifted Emma by her waist and set her on the seat sideways so he could remove her tight boot. "If I had my knife with me, I'd cut it off. As it is now, I'm going to have to hurt you. But there is no other alternative."

He placed his hands on the boot, then he tried wiggling it, but it wouldn't move. Then he positioned one hand on the bottom of the boot and one on the back. He pulled firmly. The boot was starting to move, but Emma pulled away, squealing in pain.

"Close your eyes, then you won't know what I am about to do until it happens," he said, trying to be helpful. He certainly didn't want to hurt this girl, but the boot had to come off. Should he go back and get a knife from Ted's house? It did seem a shame to destroy these expensive designer boots that probably cost a week's wages for him.

"You know it would be easier if you wiggle your foot. I know it must hurt like the devil, but I think it is the only way we will get the boot off."

Emma wiggled her foot, trying to help. The boot started to move, as he pulled. It released like suction had been holding it in place. Emma cried out, in pain and relief. He quickly put the boot down on the floor and helped her turn around on the seat. He went back and grabbed the bag and sheets, stowing them in the back of the truck. Then he ran around the other side and opened the door to slide inside. He hoped Sally would know what to do with Emma.

Emma managed to engage her seat belt. She hadn't felt safe in the jeep without one. So, I really didn't want to die, or I wouldn't be thinking of protecting myself. What have I done? If only I had thought this through properly. Ted wouldn't be in the hospital. I wouldn't be in this predicament.

Tommy arrived home in record time. Sally, hearing the truck, was standing at the door. He went around and helped Emma out of the vehicle. He decided the best way to get her in the house quickly was to carry her. He walked to the back door, where Sally was standing, watching his approach with interest. Emma seemed to be avoiding bodily contact with him.

"Open the door. We need to get her inside," he said to his wife. "She has an injured ankle, and she is having difficulty walking. Perhaps we should put her in the living room on the sofa."

Sally asked calmly, trying to contain her curiosity. "Who is she? What happened to Ted? I have been waiting for some news since you called. The radio revealed nothing about an accident. I have been listening."

"When I get her into the living room, I will explain about Ted. Will you make her a cup of tea first?" Sally headed to the kitchen stove to make the tea. She was anxious to get to the living room. She could hear Tommy talking to the girl. Their voices weren't clear enough for her to hear them. She was impatient with the kettle. Hurry and boil were her silent plea.

Tommy had placed Emma on the sofa.

"What does your foot feel like now? Are you feeling okay otherwise?" He was anxious about her condition since he had rather strong-armed her at the hospital.

Emma was hesitant to answer. She had stayed silent in the truck. Tommy had finally given up questioning her. Emma knew she must say something, but she knew when the questions started, it would be about Ted and her. "Yes, I am okay. My ankle is very painful, but it is feeling a bit better with elevation." He had put pillows under her foot and propped her up in the corner of the sofa.

"I need to contact my family. They will be wondering where I am." She tried to ease her foot to the floor, but Tommy stopped her.

"I will bring you the phone but have your tea first and catch your breath before making the call. You don't want to frighten them, you know." She settled back with relief. It was then that Sally appeared at the door with the tea on a tray. She placed the tray on the coffee table.

He reached for one of the cups, laced it with sugar, asking. "Do you need milk?"

"No, but that amount of sugar is too much. I can't drink it that way."

"You have had quite a shock to your system today, from what I can gather." He looked at Sally. He could tell that she was buzzing with excitement wanting to know what was happening.

"Emma, I would like you to meet my wife, Sally. Sally, this is Emma, the girl Ted was helping when he became injured. They operated on his back, which took the brunt of the fall, requiring a skin graft. He has to lie on his stomach. Ted certainly is not thrilled with that."

Sally inquired, "a back injury. How?"

"He injured it on a sharp rock, which dug into his back, leaving rock fragments embedded there."

"What was he doing to get that kind of an injury? There is something you're not telling me isn't there?" Sally said in a perturbed voice.

Emma said, ever so flatly. "It was because of me. Ted saved me from tumbling over the cliff in my car."

"What? What do you mean going over the cliff? What was your car doing near the cliff? It is a long way from the road."

"I know. I was trying to go over the cliff with my car, except it got caught on a rock at the waterfall." Emma had finally confessed and told it like it was.

"You were going over the cliff, whatever for?" Sally exclaimed.

"Well, I have a problem... and I thought that was the only way to solve it," Emma said evasively.

"But that still doesn't explain why Ted got hurt," Sally said determinedly. She had always liked Ted. He was the one she had initially met. But before they had developed a more meaningful relationship, Ted had introduced her to his brother. Tommy swept her off her feet, and before she knew what happened, she had said, 'I do.'

He let Sally ask the questions because at least she was getting some answers.

"Emma, why was Ted hurt?" Sally questioned her again. "I don't quite understand." Looking at Tommy as if he had the explanation, but he was looking at Emma, waiting with interest for an answer.

"You will understand if I tell you what happened." They deserved an explanation after all Ted had landed in the hospital because of her.

"I have an unfixable problem, so I was going to end my life. When the car didn't go over immediately, I screamed. Ted must have heard me scream. He came running to the tipped car hung up on a rock. The water was pounding down on the hood that was protruding under the waterfall. Ted couldn't get either door open, so he had to break the glass in the rear window to climb in. He couldn't get in too far as the car was rocking precariously forward between the pounding water and Ted's added weight."

Emma took a breath and drank some tea with a shutter as it was far too sweet for her. It had made her feel better somehow.

"Do you want more tea?" Sally hadn't touched hers nor Tommy his.

"Yes, please. But not so much sugar this time," replied Emma, dragging out the story by drinking tea, knowing they would hate her with the next part of the story. Emma took a couple of sips. "Do you think Ted will be okay? I didn't mean to hurt him. I was desperate." Emma was feeling really bad about Ted now.

Tommy wanted to hurry the story along. Surely this wasn't all. "Ted should be okay. The doctor felt sure."

Emma took another drink, pausing. Then she started in again.

"Ted had trouble reaching me as the car was slipping forward off the rock, with his added weight. So, he tried to get me to push myself up, so he could reach my hands. But I decided I still wanted to go down with the car, now that it was freeing itself from the rock. So, Ted grabbed my hair and pulled tight, trying to force me to help him. He pulled my hair so hard that strands were coming out by the roots. Ted kept pulling so tightly, that I put my hands up to stop him. He grabbed my hands and dragged me out, just as the car freed itself with the fast movements of their bodies."

"Ted fell backward on the ground I fell on top of him. I turned over and started hitting and pounding him. Telling him, I hated him for saving me." Emma said adamantly, getting caught up in her story. She took another drink of tea. They were looking at her in horror.

Now that she had calmed down a bit, there was remorse in her voice. "We almost went over with the car as my foot had caught on the window frame, pulling us along with the car. Ted really yanked to release my foot. We fell back towards the ground with considerable force. I knocked his breath out of him when I landed on top of him. I'm sorry, I didn't know about the rock piercing his back. He was only trying to get away from my flailing fists."

Emma let out a sigh at the horror of the memory, now that she was safe. She was glad Ted had saved her, but her problem was still there. She would put it away for later. She sat there looking sheepishly at them.

Sally expressed her anger. "How could you hit him and hurt him after he saved you? Are you crazy?" Sally was feeling very indignant towards this girl.

Tommy was more matter of fact. "You should be in jail. Why would you hit him after he saved you?" He was yelling at Emma.

"Because I was desperate, I can't explain further," Emma said pitifully.

"Are you pregnant?" questioned Sally.

"No. It is nothing like that. I don't even have a boyfriend."

Tommy threw up his hands in disgust. Here his brother had risked his life for a flake. He was mad. He spewed out at her, "For the love of God, why?" Emma cringed as he yelled at her.

"I can't explain any further than I already have. I knew I shouldn't have told you." Emma turned her face away, with a stubborn expression.

Tommy stormed out of the room. He wanted to throttle the girl. He slammed the back door and stomped into the back yard. "Jesus Christ." Stomp, stomp. "Jesus Christ."

Sally, meanwhile, although angry, was suggesting to Emma to drink the rest of her tea. She knew Tommy was mad, so she thought she should stay here with Emma until he worked off some of his anger.

"What are you going to do now?" Emma questioned. "Are you going to tell the police?" she asked with some dread.

Sally said. "I don't know it's up to Tommy. He is pretty mad."

Emma cringed down on the sofa more. What would she do if Tommy turned her in to the police? Emma asked in a meek voice. "Can I have a telephone now?"

Chapter Six

Sally went to get the telephone for Emma. She handed her the phone after plugging it in near the sofa. Then she walked out. Sally wanted to give her privacy, but her curiosity kept her close by.

Emma dialed a number.

"Put me through to my father, Matilda." There was a pause. Sally strained to hear. "Daddy, could you come and get me?" Emma called out to Sally. "Where am I?"

Sally stepped into the room. "You are here in town on Bush Street number 64 off-Broadway near Shuter," Sally said helpfully. Emma repeated the information as Sally was giving it. Then there was a pause.

"Yes, Daddy, I am okay. I need a ride, that is all. Can you come and get me now?" "No, I don't have my car." "I am at a friend's house." "I left my car at another friend's house because this couple brought me here." "No Daddy, it is not that way. I have not been drinking. I just came here for a visit."

Sally knew Emma was lying to protect herself. However, it was her life. Tommy might not want her to go yet, so Sally decided she better follow him into the yard as she had heard Emma say, 'Daddy, please just come and get me.'

Tommy was still stomping around the backyard.

"Are you okay? Emma made a phone call to her father, asking him to come and get her."

Tommy neared the house. Reaching the little porch, he hopped up to where she was standing. He put his arms around her hugging her and placing his chin on her head. He looked towards the house. "I guess we can't stop her. I don't think Ted would appreciate us turning her into the police. Not the way he has been protecting her from them so far. Besides, he gave me the strangest message for her, tell her I love her."

Sally hugged him with her arms linked around his waist. "Why are you helping her if you are so angry with her?"

"Because of Ted and only Ted. Otherwise, I would turn her in."

"I wonder what her father is going to be like."

"We will just have to wait and see," Tommy replied.

"I had better get back inside." Sally hugged him tightly.

He looked down into her eyes, "Sally, I am so grateful to have you. I love you. Have I told you lately?" He kissed her lightly. She went back into the house with Tommy trailing behind her. He entered the kitchen, and Sally continued to the living room. Emma was reclining on the sofa with her eyes closed, indicating she wanted no conversation. Sally sat down on the chair opposite the sofa. Emma must have heard her, but she kept her eyes shut.

Sally wanted to know why she was trying to kill herself. But she knew she probably wouldn't get an answer. So, she asked the one question that was still bothering her. "What about Ted, Emma? Are you walking out of our lives and forgetting Ted?"

Emma just fidgeted a bit but didn't say anything. Sally continued. "You know, Ted is a happy, caring guy. Even if he is a bit of a loner as his place indicates. He is a gentleman. He respects women. So, if he has clammed up about what happened, he will stay that way. But he is the one in the hospital. He can't get away from the police. You are the mystery person in all of this. If you disappear, they will keep hounding Ted. Are you going to let that happen?"

Emma shifted a bit but made no reply. Sally got up with disgust and walked from the room into the kitchen. Tommy was sitting at the table, staring out the window with clenched hands. He must have heard their conversation.

* * *

Ted was being washed by a young nurse, which was difficult the way he was lying. She rubbed lotion on his body. He felt useless in this awkward position. The nurse's ministrations to him were soothing. His mind began to wander.

The police had just left before the nurse came in. But the story he told them was about the rescue, successfully getting the young lady out of the precariously positioned car. He avoided mentioning any dialogue that had gone on between them. He was disappointed to hear that she had left the hospital somehow, without a trace. He wondered if he would ever see her again. Will she try again? Had she learned her lesson with this failed attempt?

Ted knew as soon as he looked down into her face that this girl was for him. But now he would never know, she was gone. He was a loner, quite happy with his life, wasn't he?

The nurse tidied up the bed with fresh linen. The actions made his back start throbbing, pushing the painkiller button. He was soon groggy as the painkillers kicked in.

* * *

Sally lifted her head from Tommy's chest. She listened, had she heard a car. She walked to the front door without looking into the living room. The man who knocked on the door was a big man. His height and stature were impressive. His suit spoke of quality. His complexion was rugged and tanned. He had a concerned look, but a smile that never reached his eyes that were gray. Sally stared at him, waiting to hear him speak. Was he an involved father or just a father figure as many fathers are?

He asked, "is Emma here?"

"Yes, she is waiting for you in the living room. Come in, please." Sally's voice was noncommittal, so he had no idea what to expect. But he got the feeling this pregnant young woman was not a friend of his little Emma. He stepped into the hall. "Is Emma all right? Did something happen here?"

"I will let your daughter explain. She has hurt her ankle and needs carrying. Come right this way."

Sally walked towards the living room. He followed her, his footsteps firm, the steps of a confident man. He stopped at the archway and looked over at Emma. She was looking up at him, helpless. "Daddy, you're here, that was fast."

Emma's father crossed the room to stand beside his daughter. "Are you sure you are okay? I hear your ankle is hurt. What happened?" He noticed that she had some miniscule cuts and a couple of Band-Aids on her. One larger bandage on her face and one on her arm. The closed expression on Emma's face, let him know that no quick explanation would be forthcoming.

"Not now Daddy, I will tell you when we get in the car. It is too long a story." Emma had been frantically trying to figure out a plausible story to tell him. Although the truth would be best, she had discounted that immediately. She didn't want to have to explain her attempted trip into that deep gully.

Emma's father turned to Sally, waiting for her to enlighten him, but she wasn't talking either. "Thank you for taking care of my daughter. I appreciate the concern you have for her." Something wasn't quite right here, but he couldn't quite put his finger on it. There seemed to be animosity between the two women.

Sally politely said, "you're welcome. If you lift her, I will go ahead of you and open the door."

Sally watched as the big man leaned over and picked up his daughter with ease. Emma wrapped her arms around his neck. "Oh, my boot, it must still be in Tommy's truck."

Sally called, "Tommy, will you get Emma's boot from the truck, please?"

Emma's father heard the back-door slam as someone went out. "Who is Tommy?" Emma's father enquired.

"Tommy is my husband. He brought Emma here from the hospital, where she had her ankle and cuts attended." The father looked closely at his daughter, but Emma didn't respond.

"Tommy was visiting his brother Ted, who is in the hospital also. He ran into your daughter at the elevator. Emma asked him to help her with a lift into town." Sally opened the front door.

Emma's father looked toward Sally. "Thank you for taking Emma in and helping her."

Tommy was coming from the back of the house with the boot. His expression was not friendly either, the father noted, just polite. Something was wrong here. There was more than just giving his daughter a lift into town.

Tommy followed them out. Emma's father placed her inside the open limo before turning to the young man. "Thank you. Do you know what happened to my daughter?" He thought he would try once more. But before Tommy could say anything, Emma spoke from the backseat. "Not now, Daddy, I will explain later." Her voice was pleading, and firm at the same time.

"Well, thanks again." Emma's father stuck out his hand, and Tommy shook it lightly, then quickly dropped his hand. Suddenly realizing he still held the boot in his other hand. He placed it in the father's outstretched hand. The father ducked his head and got in beside his daughter. She had scooted over, grimacing with the pain in her ankle. She was trying to lift her leg onto the seat in front of her. The father leaned over to help her. The chauffeur closed the door and walked around the car to the driver's seat.

Tommy glared at Emma as the limo moved. Her face colored with guilt.

* * *

Ted was feeling unhappy with his situation. Why had Emma escaped? Where was she? When would the police give up? Ted knew he couldn't keep up this pretext of being groggy from the medication much longer because the painkillers were removed from his IV pole. The police would find out soon. He usually was an honest man. He was finding it difficult to handle being evasive. Were the police still trying to find her? He was just ready to consider spilling everything to the police when he heard the sounds of someone entering the room. Surely not the cops already. The nurse had already been. The doctor had been in also to check his back.

The feet approached the bed. They sounded like male feet. "Tommy, is that you?" The feet had stopped short of his vision near the bottom of the bed.

"No. It is Emma's father," the voice said. "I came to see how you were. Emma told me how you saved her from going over a cliff." The voice paused.

So, this was Daddy, Emma's Daddy. Ted liked the sound of his voice. Would he give his name? Ted was relieved it wasn't the police.

"I am feeling okay. How is Emma? I can't help but worry about her. Do the police know where she is?"

The voice answered in a wary voice. "No, I won't let her tell them yet. She won't tell me the full story. Can you fill me in?"

"No, that story, she must tell you herself. Besides, I know very little of the details." Ted sighed in relief. She was okay. The police had not found her.

The voice continued. "I am sorry you were hurt and got the brunt of the injuries. Emma is all right. I am Malvin Gibson. I don't know if you know or have heard of me in regards to my owning a shipping company." He paused to find out if Ted knew of him.

Ted's interest right now was solely on Emma, so he wasn't concentrating on what the man was saying as he asked, "how is Emma? Is her foot okay? Did she get home without too much difficulty? The police said she had left the hospital, but gave no details. I got the impression that she just disappeared."

"Your brother Tommy helped her. He found her trying to leave the hospital. He took her to his place. I met both Tommy and his wife, Sally. They seem like a very nice couple." Malvin paused. "I know you are still in pain. I conversed with the nurse. She said you were healing nicely, so they are assuming that all the rock fragments were removed. Emma asked me to come and see you mentioning the rock incident. She is sorry about your back." He hesitated. "She sent a strange message, 'she doesn't hate you,' whatever that means."

Ted digested this last bit then said, "tell Emma to think nothing of that." Ted quickly went on, "I will be glad to get off my stomach. I must say it is very unpleasant for me. Just as long as Emma is okay, I will be fine." Ted finished lamely.

"Yes, she is okay," Malvin assured Ted. "Her ankle is still keeping her from being mobile. Otherwise, she is okay. If you could call trying to kill herself, okay, that is." Malvin felt dejected. Why was this strange man protecting his daughter? What did he know about her? Emma had always been open with him. He was feeling baffled about the reason for her vulnerability in wanting to take her life. Why won't Emma tell me the truth? What more could he say to this young man, other than to thank him again?

"You aren't going to tell me anything, are you? I need to know what happened to her so I can help her. Why did she try to drive her car over the cliff? I get the feeling you haven't told the police everything either." Malvin's voice was weary and sad.

Ted held his peace and said nothing. The story was not his to tell. Ted was only concerned about Emma. Hoping she was feeling better and had no intention of doing something foolish again.

Her father continued. "Emma is sorry for what she did. Mostly about injuring you. That is why I'm here. You are evading telling me the truth, as is Emma." The voice was becoming sadder each time he spoke.

There was a long pause, where neither spoke as they both had their thoughts consuming them. The feet shifted forward into Ted's vision, a pair of shiny shoes. He tried to raise his head to get a full view of him. But the man placed a hand on his shoulder and held it there as if to comfort himself somehow.

"Thank you for Emma's life. I don't know what I would have done if she had been successful in her death. I understand the car exploded on impact." His voice, stricken at the thought.

Ted said sadly, "I'm sorry that Emma found it necessary to take that action in her young life. But I can't help you. I know by your voice you feel appalled about the situation. I would too if I was her father. But she must tell you herself. All I can do to help is to be evasive, with the police,"

Malvin responded. "Emma knows she will eventually have to go to the police. They will be able to trace the car when they get their experts working on it. I'm just giving her a little time before I put her through that, time to review what happened. Then she must do the right thing. Well, I'd better get going. Thank you again." The pressure on Ted's shoulder lifted as the voice stepped away from the bed heading for the door.

* * *

Emma was relaxing on a chaise lounge by the pool. She had her clothes on as this was not a sunny day. She was waiting for Jimmy to come home. She hoped he would get here before father returned. She eased her foot around on the pillow. The pain had lessened, but it was a reminder of what had almost ended in tragedy. Was Ted all right? Were the police still harassing him? Tommy hates me for what I did to Ted. I could see it in his eyes, standing there watching me leave. Sally had made it plain how she felt about the situation too.

Emma looked towards the door of the solarium, where it opened onto the pool area. Jimmy stood framed in the doorway. Does he know that she discovered his secret?

Other than he was broader and taller than she. It was a similar likeness to her standing there. They weren't identical twins, but the similarity was striking.

"Emma, how are you? What happened?"

Jimmy came over, perching on the edge of the chaise lounge. After giving her a hug and a kiss, Emma started to cry. The incident with the car and the aftermath of the almost tragedy was still devastating to her. Jimmy pulled her into his arms. Emma clung to him, her sobs deepening. "There, there, Emma, tell me what happened?"

She just cried all the more. The tears were soaking his shirt. But she couldn't stop. He was getting worried. What could be that dreadful that she would have broken down like this? Something was drastically wrong.

Chapter Seven

Emma finally stopped crying. She had the hiccups. Her eyes hurt from her tearful sobbing. She knew she had to say something as her father would be back from the hospital shortly.

"Jimmy." Emma sobbed and hiccupped. "You have to tell Daddy what you have done. I can't protect you any longer. I tried to do this for you, but it didn't work. Besides, Ted made me realize it would have come out anyway even if I had been successful."

"What are you talking about? Successful in what?" Jimmy pushed his sister away from him to get a better look at her. "I don't know what you are talking about, no idea." His voice held such amazement.

Emma almost believed him. "Jimmy, I keep the books for Daddy. I found out you have been embezzling funds from the shipping company."

He grabbed her arms and shook her lightly. "What are you saying? I have never embezzled anything, particularly from the shipping company. Did you try something because of me?" His voice held utter amazement.

"Jimmy, I know what the records are saying isn't the truth, but the records have your signature on them. I know it is you that has done this. It has been happening for over six months that I am aware of." Emma trailed off sadly.

"I don't know what you are talking about. If someone is robbing the shipping company, it isn't me," Jimmy said in a hurt voice. "We are twins for God's sake. Have you no more faith in me than that?" He was horrified.

"But Jimmy, all the records have your signature on them. I recognize your signature."

"Sis, I am sorry you did whatever you did for me. Can you really believe I could embezzle funds from my father?"

"If it isn't you, Jimmy, then tell me who could be doing this?"

"That is what I have to find out. Now tell me what you did. I get the impression that it was to protect me." Jimmy pulled her back into his arms. Emma went willingly.

"Oh, Jimmy, I should have told you before ..." Emma paused.

"Before what?" Jimmy asked.

"Before... I tried to drive my car off the cliff." she wailed.

"A cliff? Is this the accident? Did you try to drive over a cliff?" Jimmy's voice held utter shock.

"Yes, I tried to drive my car over the cliff on Old Canyon Road. But it got caught up on a big rock. Some man got me out of the car before it went over into the gully. Ted is in the hospital. He got injured when he fell, pulling me out through the back window. Jimmy, it was terrible. The car started moving. We were being dragged forward with it because my foot caught. Ted wouldn't let go of me. He kept pulling until my foot released. And then I fell on top of him." She omitted the part about hitting him and hating him. She knew his injury happened by forcing him to move his back around on the jagged rock. That guilt would be with her forever.

Jimmy pushed her away from him but still held her arms. "What are you saying?" He was having difficulty taking this in. "Tell me everything."

"I drove out to Old Canyon Road and deliberately tried to drive the car over the cliff. But I guess the rocky terrain was throwing the car about so much that the car ended up precariously caught up on a big rock. But the front end was suspended over the cliff under a waterfall. The water was pounding on the hood of the car and causing it to seesaw." She shuttered. "I knew it was just a matter of time before I went over into the deep gully below. I started screaming."

Jimmy pulled her against him, his hand rubbing her back, comforting her. "Go on."

"Well, this man came running towards the tipped car. I guess in my agitated emotional state. I hadn't even noticed the house." She paused, took a deep breath. She put her arms around Jimmy as an anchor against the factual memory of almost going over.

"Ted couldn't get the door open. So, he broke the glass in the back window, and that is how I got the cuts on me from flying glass particles. I injured my ankle when I got it twisted on impact under the brake pedal. When I couldn't get free, he tried climbing in after me. His added weight was causing the car to slip forward off the rock. He was a big man, much bigger than his brother."

"Was his brother there?" questioned Jimmy.

"No, I met him later at the hospital." Emma continued her narration. "I was not able to push myself up on my injured ankle. Ted wasn't about to let me go over the cliff either. So, he grabbed my hair and tried pulling me out until he was ripping my hair out by the roots. That caused me to lift my hands to relieve the pressure, which made me forget the pain in my ankle, pushing myself up backward. Ted grabbed my hands and pulled me out. But my foot got caught on the back-window frame. Between the movement of my body and the pounding of the water, the car broke free of the rock. We were being dragged over the cliff, but Ted just wouldn't let go of me. I can't believe his persistence even with the movement of the car towards devastation. He just wouldn't let go. My foot came free, finally. Ted fell back onto the jagged rock. I landed on top of him. The serrated rock he landed on plus my added weight on top of him caused punishment to his back. He had to have an operation to remove rock fragments. I discovered from Tommy, his brother, that they had to do a skin graft, his back so severely ripped." She paused.

"He is still in the hospital, and now the police are looking for me." Emma's mind was jumping around. "The car exploded when it landed at the bottom of the gully and burnt, so I don't know if the plates are legible or not. I am sure it is only a matter of time before they find me." Emma stopped. She hadn't told Jimmy about begging Ted to let her die or her escaping the hospital.

"What am I going to do when they find me?" asked Emma.

"I don't know, but I will think of something. Where is Dad?"

"He went to see Ted for me. I wanted Daddy to find out if Ted is okay. He has gone to thank him for saving me." The heavy-handed knock on the door traveled to where they were sitting at the poolside. Her worst dread had arrived. Emma squeezed her brother tightly as though in fear, the police would take her away from him.

They both knew it must be the police. Cops were notorious for being heavy-handed, when on police business. Jimmy thought quickly. "Emma, we will say you were having a breakdown and that we are going to seek medical attention for you. Stick to that story, no matter what they ask. Keep saying you can't talk about it. Say it is too horrible and cry a lot." Emma was looking at him helplessly.

"Emma, I know this is deceitful and against your nature to lie. But we can't let the police know about the embezzlement. Not yet. I want to do some investigation on my own since someone is trying to frame me." She continued to look at him, slightly stunned. "Please, Emma, agree to this?" Jimmy looked towards the solarium door.

Matilda was there announcing. "The police are waiting in the library."

Jimmy helped Emma up from the chaise lounge. But when she tried to walk, he noticed her deep pain. He lifted her into his arms and passed through the door that Matilda had left open. He entered the library where the police were standing and walked over to the sofa. He placed Emma down gently, pulling the pillow up behind her. Then he put a couple of pillows under her ankle to elevate it. Then he straightened and looked at them. There were two of them. One was tall and thin. The other was medium height and stocky. But both wore suits.

"What can we do for you, gentlemen?" he asked politely.

The tall one had already stepped forward with his hand out. "Detective Harding and this is Detective Davies." The other man nodded as Jimmy shook the first detective's hand. Detective Harding stood back and eased out a notebook from his pocket and handed it to his partner. "You record everything that is said here."

Jimmy invited them to sit in the chairs, across from Emma. Then he sat on the arm of the couch and held his sister's body against him.

Detective Harding asked, "are you, Emma Gibson?"

"Yes."

"Did your car go over a cliff into the gully up on Old Canyon Road?"

"Yes."

"Why? Tell us in your own words what happened?"

Emma looked up at Jimmy as if looking for permission to speak.

Jimmy quickly intervened. "My sister hasn't been well, so can we keep this brief?"

Detective Harding didn't acknowledge Jimmy just looked towards Emma and waited.

"Well," Emma, licking her lip. "I went for a drive. I seemed to have a lot on my mind, although I can't recall for the life of me what. I think the close call..." Emma's voice trailed off. She noticeably swallowed.

"Well, the next thing I remember, I was in my car hanging over a cliff under a waterfall with the water pounding on the hood. I guess the shock of nearly dying has made my mind hazy. So, I don't quite remember too much. I was so deep in thought that I don't know how I got in that position in the first place. I have never been to that area before." She paused, then slowly continued. "I don't know where I was even now." She was being vague and shaking her head as if in wonderment and quite dazed.

The two detectives looked at each other. Either this girl was a good actress or she was mentally disturbed because her dialogue seemed irrational. "Did you have a destination in mind when you got in the car?"

Again, Emma shook her head and looked puzzled. "I think I was driving to the store, but I had no idea how I got so far out of town. Maybe in my confusion, I lost control of the car," Emma said weakly.

"That cliff is pretty far off the road. Rocky terrain should have brought you to awareness," Detective Harding said gently.

Emma shook her head. "Maybe I panicked and stepped on the gas instead of the brake." She started to cry. In a shaky voice, she continued. "The horror and terror with the car rocking over the edge of the cliff, and the water was pounding on the hood." She shuttered and turned her head into Jimmy's arm and started sobbing almost hysterically.

"That is enough. Can't you see how distraught she is? How can you keep questioning her? We have an appointment with the doctor in half an hour. We will have to leave now. She needs time to recover before you ask her any more questions." Jimmy turned back to his sister to console her.

"There, there, Emma." Jimmy patted her back. Emma continued to sob loudly.

The two detectives stood up, as they doubted, she would impart with any more information. "Will you call us when your sister feels better? We still have more unanswered questions to clear this matter up?"

Jimmy nodded but still sat holding his sobbing sister.

Detective Harding stopped. "There is just one more thing. Emma, how did you get here from the hospital?"

Jimmy replied, "someone phoned my father. He went to get her," which was half true. The detectives met Matilda outside the door, ready to show the two men out.

Jimmy eased himself down behind her body. She was sobbing deeply. He rubbed her back soothingly.

"You know Emma. I think you should see a doctor. I think you need something to help you calm down,"

A disturbance at the front door generated by their father's blustering voice, inquiring for his daughter from Matilda. "Both Emma and Jimmy are in the library." Malvin Gibson strode into the library.

"I just saw the police leaving here. Did Emma tell them anything? Is she okay?" Malvin saw his daughter was crying in her brother's arms. "Thank heavens you were here. Did she answer any of their questions?"

"Calm down, Dad." Jimmy looked at his father. "No, she didn't tell them much. She was too upset, but she did tell me. I think we had better get her to a doctor. I think she's on the verge of a breakdown that can be the only explanation for what happened to her." Jimmy looked down at his sister lovingly, holding her close. Her tears had dissipated.

Malvin went out into the hall and picked up the phone. He quietly asked to speak directly to Dr. Brown. The nurse replied that he was busy. He asked for a return call as soon as the doctor was free, giving his name. He re-entered the library.

"Jimmy, how is she? Is she calming down yet? I can see that she has stopped crying, at least."

"She'll be okay, Dad, after the doctor gives her something. She has been through a lot."

Emma lifted her head from Jimmy's chest, looking at her father.

"I'm sorry, Daddy. I didn't mean to upset anyone." Then her voice faded away. How would she get out of this dilemma? Why couldn't Ted have let her die?

Her father was standing watching her. Why would a girl try to commit suicide when she has everything going for her? There has to be an explanation for her unwise venture. He knew Emma was avoiding the truth. Why would she be out on Old Canyon Road in the first place? He slipped his eyes to his son. Jimmy knew more than he was letting on protecting her as usual, having that unique understanding of twins.

When Dora was alive, she had noticed it too. But she had just accepted the special twin bond. Malvin had always been jealous of their closeness. He had consistently tried to overcome this feeling by calling her Daddy's girl. So, at work, Daddy's girl is what he openly preferred rather than 'bookkeeper.' He realized it was a silly notion.

Matilda came to the door. "Mr. Gibson, there is a Dr. Brown on the phone." Malvin headed down the hall away from his children.

"Hello, Gary, Malvin Gibson here."

"Hello Malvin, what can I do for you?"

"I have a little problem that could become a major problem. I hope you can handle it for me." He paused, took a deep breath, then continued. "My daughter was in an accident early this morning. Now the police are questioning her. I believe it was no accident. But that she tried to take her life." Again, he paused. His body physically shuttered.

"My son will be bringing Emma to the office. I need you to take her under your wing and treat her for depression or something. Let the police know you will be treating her if they contact you, but no time frame. She is pretty distraught right now. She needs something to calm her. Will you do that for me? Then when she gets back to normal, we will have to address the situation more thoroughly with the police." He stopped as if he had realized he was pleading for his daughter's life. What would he have done if she had gone down with the car? Malvin winced.

Dr. Brown was saying. "She should come in right away by the sounds of that. I'll let my nurse know they are coming. I will see her as soon as she gets here. You're not to worry we will get to the bottom of this. From what you have told me, it sounds serious. Of course, I'll keep the patient's confidentiality by answering with no more than a vague timeline should the police arrive. I will fill my nurse in as to patient confidentiality, although I will probably offend her. She is an excellent nurse, efficient in all matters. Bring Emma in immediately. I will certainly take care of her."

"Thanks," then he added, "Gary, I knew I could count on you." Then he headed back to the library. Jimmy was still holding Emma. She had her eyes closed as if she couldn't stand the situation and was closing it out.

Malvin felt they had been talking while he was gone. But the two of them were playing possum now. He wished his wife was here now to help him. He ran his hand through his hair in agitation.

"Jimmy, I spoke to Dr. Brown. You need to take Emma over to see him right away. He realizes that she has had an unusual accident. He will help her. It would be better if I went into the shipping office. That way, the police won't be suspicious of my concern for her when they come to ask me questions."

Jimmy eased up off the sofa then bent down, picking Emma up and carried her towards the door. He looked sad as he passed his father.

Malvin led them to the side door. "Take care of her son and drive carefully."

He closed the door behind them. What was so horrible in Emma's life that she would do this? Was there something that I could've done to avoid this? Self-doubt started to eat at his insides.

Chapter Eight

Ted was trying to eat something, but not effectively. The nurse had put a towel folded up on the bed to catch the drips. She was feeding him a thick soup. His neck was hurting, trying to hold his head up. The nurse wasn't too worried as he was still on intravenous. Her goal was to help him eat. The nurse put another spoonful to his lips. "You would probably do better with a thick straw. I should have realized that and brought one with me."

Ted was feeling ridiculous as he was drooling his soup rather than swallowing it. He was not happy about the situation. "Don't feed me anymore," he ordered, then he tempered his anger. "Please, and thank you for your efforts. I am just not in the mood for food."

The nurse got up, putting the bowl back on the tray. She whisked the towel away and straightened the covers, taking the tray and headed out of the door. "You rest now, Mr. Maxwell."

Ted knew there was no rest, for his mind was churning. Why did Emma want to die when her brother was the guilty one, not her? Where was Tommy? He said he would be back with Sally. I need Tommy to try to find Emma. But how could he when I don't know where she lives.

Just then, the phone rang. Ted put out his arm with some difficulty, managing to grab the phone. "Hello."

"Hello, Ted. It's Tommy, how are you?"

"I am worried sick about Emma. I heard she disappeared from the hospital and you helped her. I need to find her. But I don't even know her full name or where she lives." In his concern for Emma, Ted hadn't absorbed her father's name.

"Yes, I helped her into the elevator. I was leaving, so I took her with me as I knew you seemed to care a great deal. She called her father. He came and got her. He didn't offer his name or where they live, but he came in a limousine. So, he must be some bigwig." Tommy's voice trailed off.

"Why didn't you ask him?"

"Because I was so furious with Emma at the time. I just wanted her gone. I'm sorry." Tommy felt terrible. "Maybe she will call you," he said lamely.

"No, she won't call." There was silence on the line for a while. "Tommy, thanks for helping her. She has a real problem that she is trying to handle — a very unpleasant problem. I feel sorry for her, that is why I would like to find her. Don't be angry with her for what happened to me. I was playing Sir Galahad when I accidentally slipped and fell landing on a sharp rock. That is all."

"I will take your word for it. I must admit I was somewhat mad with Emma, and she knew it."

"Thanks, Tommy, I am okay. I feel sorry for Emma, as her life is in profound turmoil. She has to deal with it all on her own."

"As long as you're okay, that is the important thing to Sally and me. The police were here, wanting to know if we knew Emma. I told them I had no idea who she was, which we don't really. So, I didn't lie. I just said I helped her with a ride."

"I owe you. Thanks again. I am going to hang up because I have some thinking to do. Thank heavens, they should allow me to turn over tomorrow or the next day for sure, as the doctor said my back was looking quite good."

"Bye, brother, take care, Sally and I will be in to see you tomorrow."

"Bye, Tommy, don't worry about me. I'll be fine." Ted fumbled the phone back on the cradle. His arm was going numb from the awkward position. He was trying to shift it up and down to relieve the odd feeling.

Maybe Emma would phone. Thank heavens, Tommy helped her. I wish I were out of here. Perhaps I could find her. How many limos can there be in this area? I could get my friend Colin to check for me.

* * *

Tommy and Sally showed up at visiting time the next day, but Ted was still on his stomach. Poor Ted to be like this, for someone who hadn't even been grateful. Emma didn't deserve Ted's attention.

He put a smile on his face, guiding Sally with him to the window side of the bed. The chair was oversized, so Tommy and Sally shared, as he was lean in stature. It would be easier on Ted's neck to see them that way.

"Hi, buddy. How's it going?" asked Tommy, trying to be cheerful. "Look at my girl's belly. Isn't she beautiful?" He rubbed Sally's budding stomach. He did love the look of her carrying his baby.

Sally giggled. "Tommy cut it out. Ted doesn't want to see you feeling me up. Do you, Ted?"

Ted frowned. Would he ever be in a position to experience parenthood? "Sally, Tommy is a lucky man. I don't blame him for being proud that you are carrying his baby."

She reached over for Ted's hand and squeezed it. "Ted, how are you doing really?"

"Okay, I guess. I'll be so much happier when I can change my position, which won't be for a couple more days. The doctor wants to make sure there are no more rock fragments in my back. I guess I was jumping the gun, thinking it would be sooner," he replied dejectedly.

Tommy eased forward and patted Ted's shoulder. "You want to be sure, don't you? Can I help move your arms and legs to keep the muscles toned?"

"Yes, I would appreciate that. My arms and legs get numb and tingly," Ted replied.

Tommy got up and started massaging Ted's arms and legs and also bending them up and down as best he could. Sally had brought some lotion with her, so she took over, creaming his skin where they were coming in contact with the rough bed linen.

"Don't get too used to that as Sally is only on loan until you are over on your back. Then the pampering stops," Tommy said jokingly.

Ted wanted to ask. Had Emma talked to the police yet? Was she okay? Will I ever see her again?

Tommy inquired, "have the police been back?"

"No, they seem to be leaving me alone. I guess I convinced them I didn't know anything, or else the police have found Emma."

Sally said, "she didn't seem very happy about the situation when she was with us. She wasn't talking either. She never said anything to her father when he came to get her unless she said something to him in the car. You know, I think I recognized him. I think I saw his picture in the paper once, something to do with some shipping company."

"Shipping?" Ted remembered. "Could it be Malvin Gibson? No wonder Emma was afraid of him. He is quite a blustering bullheaded man." Ted's memory was clear at last, remembering Gibson mentioning his shipping company. "He calls her Daddy's girl. Can you believe that? She must be about 24 years old, and he treats her like a little girl," Ted said astonishingly.

"Why would anyone who is Daddy's girl want to kill herself?" Tommy asked.

Ted clammed up. He wasn't about to explain why Emma had felt she had reason to die.

Tommy tried again. "Did you think there was just cause for her to do what she did? Did you get the impression she needed help? She was definitely escaping when I found her on the elevator. The doctor had asked me to call into his office. I took Emma with me and passed her off as Sally. I hope Sally doesn't run into the doctor with me. He will be wondering who this pregnant woman is," Tommy said laughingly.

Sally hit him jokingly. "Fine, you have a harem, do you?" She was trying to lighten the situation. She had never seen Ted act this way. Emma had gotten under his skin in more ways than one, looking at his bandaged back.

Now Ted knew her name at least, Emma Gibson.

Tommy clutched at Sally in such a way that she knew he wanted to go. She said brightly. "Ted, we had better get going. We need to call in on my mother on the way home."

Tommy jumped up. "Yeah, we need to stop at Mom's place. She wants to see how big Sally is getting," he said lightly. "Goodbye, we'll be back tomorrow night, or I will come at least. Maybe I will stop on my way home from work." Tommy squeezed his shoulder.

"Goodbye, Sally, take this lummox home with you, and love him for me." Ted wanted to let them know that he felt their caring, and also their support in his feelings for Emma.

Sally and Tommy left the room, stopping in the doorway and looked back at Ted. Tommy yelled from the door. "Watch out for the nurses wanting your body. There are some pretty cute ones, I noticed." A grunt occurred as Sally gave him an elbow in the ribs. Then they disappeared from the doorway.

* * *

Ted was thinking of 'Daddy' as Emma called him. He remembered meeting him once when there was some trouble down at the docks. Gibson squashed the crisis quickly, with a few well-placed words, and a heavy hand on the instigator. He wasn't a man to take any guff from anyone.

Ted was surprised that Emma was Daddy's girl. Gibson didn't seem the type to treat girls that way or women either with his gruff manner that Ted had witnessed. Ted's view of him was bullish and rather crass. He now understood after Malvin Gibson's visit, that he was a caring man where his family was concerned. Perhaps that is why Emma feared for her twin. Jimmy's guilt would disappoint their father. But would that have stopped Jimmy maybe it would have if his twin had died? But only if Jimmy had figured out why she had committed suicide.

Emma Gibson sounds like a nice name. It goes well together. If only she cared enough about him to call. During the father's visit, it didn't seem like he wanted their connection to go any further.

* * *

Dr. Brown was examining Emma. "How are you feeling, Emma?" She was sitting on the side of the examining table.

"Not so good, my ankle hurts and keeps swelling, and my wrist and hand hurt too occasionally. I think I wedged my ribs into the steering wheel, they feel quite bruised also," Emma replied, sadly.

"Do you want to talk about the accident, Emma?" Dr. Brown had been her doctor since her birth. He and Mal took to the golf-links now and then.

"No, I don't. I can't." Shaking her head. "Not yet, no, maybe another day."

"Well, Emma, you know I love you like a daughter. I have been friends with your family for a long time. I will listen to you, and I will try to help you. You know that, don't you? Concerns sometimes are better shared," he said kindly.

"Yes," Emma said weakly, but she hesitated in saying more.

"Well then make an appointment for a week. In the meantime, I'll give you some pills to help you with the pain and some to help you relax until you start feeling better. If you ever want to talk, call me or drop in and I will see you. I am a good listener." He patted her hands that were tightly together in her lap.

"Your ankle is going to be a problem for you for a while, as you have put your weight on it too soon after injuring it. That is why your ankle keeps swelling. You will need crutches. I will speak to Jimmy to fit you with them. You should use them for a week or two. As to your hands and wrists, they will take time until the bruising goes away. The cuts should heal without scars. Now, wait here until I get Jimmy. He can carry you until you get functioning on crutches." He went to speak to Jimmy.

On the return down the hall towards the examining room, the doctor said, "Emma is going to need a lot of tender care and pampering. She is quite disturbed about something. Be sure to get her crutches to help her get around. I want her off that ankle, so carry her until then. Also, make sure she takes these pills faithfully for a few days. She has had a traumatic experience, which might cause her to have nightmares. More important is to try to get her to share her problem with you. She is welcome to come to me anytime. I know how close you are. She may share sooner with you."

He thanked the doctor as they arrived at the door of the examining room.

"Hi, Sis, ready to go?" Jimmy walked over to her. He lifted her off the table.

"Thank you, Dr. Brown," said Jimmy pretending to be falling with her weight. "I will take care of my baby sister."

"By two minutes only," she glared as she squeezed his neck with her uninjured arm. Dr. Brown laughed to see their good rapport. Hopefully, Jimmy would be able to reassure her enough to get to the bottom of things.

* * *

Reaching for the phone, Ted knew Colin would probably be at the local bar. He would try his home first anyway. He had nothing better to do now that visiting hours were over. He punched in the number and waited. On the fifth ring, a girl's voice came on the phone. "Hello."

"Hello. This is Ted. Is Colin around?"

"Yes, he is in the kitchen. I will call him just a minute. Oh, Colin, phone." The girl's voice indicated that Colin was entertaining at home. He was divorced. His ex, Judy, was long gone.

"Hello, Ted. According to the scuttlebutt, you are in the hospital."

"Yes, I am in the hospital. I had a slight accident but nothing serious," Ted added quickly.

"You sound funny. What's the matter?"

"I am on my stomach, so it is difficult to talk normally. I injured my back."

"How did you do that?"

"I fell on a rock which gouged my back, so it was necessary to have surgery and a skin graft."

"It must have been quite a fall," said Colin. Ted heard a voice in the background telling him to hurry up.

"Tell you what I need," said Ted. "I need you to check up on someone named Gibson owning a limousine. Your brother still works down at the motor vehicle place, doesn't he? I need to know the name and address and telephone number."

"Why do you need that kind of info?" Prompting Colin's curiosity.

"I will tell you after you get me the information. It sounds like you have a hot date there. If she wants you to 'hurry up' is any indication." Ted heard Colin drag in a breath like he was sexually encouraged.

"Ted, you know how it is Buddy. When you got it, you got it? You should try it sometime." Colin's voice went up a few octaves as he drew in a deep breath. Was someone embracing him or even more? "I better go." Again, Colin's voice was expressive as a dial tone sounded in Ted's ear. Probably with good reason knowing Colin the way he did. Hopefully, Colin absorbed the information he needed before his girlfriend distracted him. Ted would try to trace Emma if only to make sure she was all right. Why didn't she at least call to see how he was faring?

Ted groaned. Would he ever get off his stomach? He was uncomfortable. They had shut down his sedative medication, so he wasn't sleeping as much. Their reasoning so that he wouldn't become dependent on the drugs.

Chapter Nine

On the way home from the doctor's, Jimmy reconfirmed to Emma mentioning. He was not the embezzler. If it wasn't him, who could it be? That was what was bothering him so much. He had to find out. Someone was forging his signature on documents. He was deeply troubled that anyone involved with the family, such as their employees, could do such a thing. The first place he would have to start with was in Emma's records.

They agreed that Emma should stay home for a few days. Jimmy would work on her accounts. The idea was to deter their father from knowing what was going on. Because Jimmy never went near Emma's books usually.

Upon arriving home, Emma walked to her house on crutches. She had trouble manipulating the stairs, so Jimmy lifted her. She lost her grasp on the crutches. They fell to the steps with a loud clatter. Emma grabbed Jimmy around the neck. He carried her into the library.

He came in with her crutches saying. "Hadn't you better call the hospital and thank the fellow, who helped you? After all, he is the one who didn't fare too well as a result of your irrationality." Jimmy paused, letting that sink in. "You owe him your life, Emma. I want to shake his hand. I am glad he saved you. How could you think I would do something as unspeakable as to steal from my father?" he asked in a hurt voice.

"I'm sorry, Jimmy. I know I should have trusted you, but I thought the evidence was pretty incriminating. I should have known you wouldn't steal from Daddy. Please forgive me."

Jimmy went over and sat beside her. He pulled her against him tightly and kissed her temple.

"I know the evidence is against me. But it did hurt that you didn't have faith in me. But I can never stay mad at you. Just believe me when I say I didn't do it."

In the evening, Jimmy said, "I'm going to the office to see what I can find out. I don't even want to wait till morning."

Emma hoped she was doing the right thing by letting him go to the office at night without her. She was worried that their father would pick up on their deception.

"I am going to take you upstairs. Then I will send Matilda up to help you get ready for bed. But first, I am going to give you two pills to help you relax. Then you should be ready to sleep, which I think is important right now."

Jimmy went over to the small frig under the liquor cabinet. He took out a bottle of water and poured some in a glass. He retrieved the pills from his pocket. Flipping two into his hand, he picked up the glass heading back to Emma. He watched her drink them down. The doctor had warned him that Emma's sleep might be disturbed by nightmares reliving the trauma of her near death. He was hoping the pills would put her into a deep sleep and no nightmares.

Picking Emma up, he headed out to the stairs that led to the upper-level bedrooms.

Malvin thrust the front door open and entered the hallway. He glanced at Jimmy and Emma. He was upset to know that his daughter had problems. Let's hope he could get to the bottom of things tonight so that he could let Ted know something positive. It wasn't fair for Ted to be kept in the dark and have the police bothering him when he had saved Emma. Looking at his daughter closely, he could see the direction that Jimmy was taking her was upstairs.

"How is she? What did the doctor say?" Malvin paused. He rubbed his finger against her cheek.

"Daddy, I am okay. The doctor said I would be fine in a week or so. I have to stay off my ankle and rest it so Jimmy is going to take over the bookkeeping until I can get around better." Emma plunged ahead.

"He knows how to do them."

"Yes, perhaps you should have some time off. Now up to bed and rest. Did Gary give you any pills to make you sleep?"

Jimmy replied before Emma could. "Yes, I just gave them to her. So, I better get her upstairs before she falls asleep on me. Can you ask Matilda to come up and help her?" Jimmy continued towards the stairs.

"Goodnight, Emma," said Emma's father turning toward the kitchen.

Jimmy was glad his father had accepted the fact that he was going into the office to work on the accounts for Emma. Although he omitted that he intended going tonight, so his father couldn't say don't go. It could wait until Emma was feeling better.

"Dad took that better than I expected, but it could still become a sticky situation. So, I had better find out something quickly. He is still going to probe into why you were out on Old Canyon Road, hanging over a cliff." He squeezed her as though he was getting a better grip. He was so thankful that she had not succeeded.

Emma knew he was trying to hide his distress. That horrible thought plagued him as it did her. She couldn't believe how she had berated Ted for saving her. She felt guilty about that now that she was safe in her brother's arms. She really should consider calling Ted. But no, it would be best that he forgot her.

Her thoughts leaped back to Jimmy. He couldn't have done the embezzlement she realized, not her Jimmy. Why had she even considered that he was an embezzler? True explanations for Daddy would have to come later, much later, as her lids started to droop.

* * *

Jimmy reached the office of Gibson & Gibson Shipping Lines, founded by his great-grandfather. It was in darkness as he expected. He had a better look for Charlie the night watchman to let him know that he intended to be working for a while.

Charlie, previously a cop, had left the force after a scandal. His partner had taken graft and had named Charlie in betrayal to cover himself. Although cleared, he had lost heart. He had been working for

Jimmy's father for seventeen years. Emma and Jimmy knew him well, as they were allowed to hang around the shipping office constantly after their mother died. Jimmy found Charlie at the guardhouse, having a tea break. Charlie was known as a 'tea granny' but took that jokingly.

"Hi, Charlie."

"Hi, Jimmy, what are you doing here at this time of night? I haven't seen you around here much lately."

"I have moved up in the world. I now handle shipping contracts and spend most of my time on the road or overseas."

"But still, why are you here at this time of night?"

"My sister, Emma, has had an accident, so I have spent the last couple of days with her. She asked me to check up on somethings in the office. Tonight is the only time I have free. If you see the light on in the office, it will only be me. I will let you know when I leave."

"Okay, Jimmy, don't work too late." Charlie chuckled as though he had made a joke.

Jimmy headed back to the office. He took out his keys to open the door. He put on lights, heading for Emma's office. He threw the keys on the desk, not knowing where to start. That was the big question. How do you find an embezzler?

Jimmy got the keys for the filing cabinets from the secret place. He took out the ledgers from the bottom drawer and went over to the desk. What inaccuracies did Emma find that twigged her to the embezzlement? Damn, he should have asked, but she was still too upset with the accident, and her belief that he was guilty.

He glanced through the ledger. He knew most of the accounts as he set up the shipping contracts for the past three years.

His father had Cliff, a long-time worker and close friend teaching Jimmy when he joined the company. Cliff was his father's right-hand man. Jimmy tried to do it right the first time. Cliff was a hard taskmaster. Jimmy proceeded to rise into a position working with customers and getting contracts that relieved his father from traveling.

He knew Cliff, as well as his father, would take this hard if they learned what Emma had discovered. He had to find out first and correct the matter as soon as possible before it became public knowledge.

He was scanning the ledgers looking at the names and transactions. He also turned on the computer and opened up the program where Emma recorded the information. Emma had told him her password to access her accounting program.

He started comparing with the shipping records, recorded on the ledger by hand by the front office clerk, Alan. The ledger was passed on to Emma each night. There were two sets of books, one for alternate days. So, Emma could work on the accounts without holding up Alan. It worked best with the ledger books moveable to the dock area. Bills of lading that were stuck to the containers, as mostly found on overseas shipments, were easily recorded. Follow up bills of lading arrived by mail. Proper identification of the stock at arrival was important.

Jimmy kept scanning the ledger and the computer coinciding account records. At first, he found nothing missing or out of the ordinary. It was several hours later when he started seeing a pattern in the second ledger. Jimmy went back to the beginning of the second ledger and started inspecting the accounts more closely. About a third of the way through the book, three companies started appearing that he didn't recognize. At first, it was just the one then another was added a few weeks later, then the third appeared too.

He went to the file cabinets and started pulling invoices. He had never had any dealings with these companies. Then he looked for the original contracts signed with these companies. Sure enough, the signed contracts were there. They had his signature on them, but not quite identical. The signature didn't have his natural flow or added bold stroke at the end. Someone was falsifying his name, disconcerting him. Who could have done this?

Jimmy was getting too tired. He decided to call it a night. Thinking Emma might need him with the potential of nightmares.

But first, he copied some of the file's transactions to a disk so he could look more thoroughly at home on their computer. Then he put everything away and locked up the records, shutting down the computer. Shut off the lights on the way out.

He would ask Emma to help him go through the accounts tomorrow if she was feeling better. To think she would have driven her car over that cliff for him. The appalling thought wouldn't leave him, although gratified that she loved him that much.

* * *

Ted was beside himself. The police were here again trying to confirm Emma's story, but he kept on repeating the facts of the rescue, leaving out the dialogue between them. The doctor had arrived, delaying the questioning. Ted expected him to say that he could turn over at last. But instead, he was being scheduled for more surgery at ten. The doctor had found evidence that the wound was starting to seep pus, which meant more rock fragments must be deep inside. The nurse would be here shortly to prep him. His disillusioned look made the police vacate the room quickly.

The phone rang. Ted reached for it with difficulty.

"Hello."

"Hello, Ted. How are you?" The voice belonged to Emma.

"Emma, how are you?" Ted's exhilarated voice asked.

"Ted, I asked first."

He wondered, did he tell her about the second operation or not. He just had to keep her on the phone. Maybe she would care enough to come. "Emma, I am scheduled for another operation in an hour."

"Oh, Ted, no." Emma's voice held shame.

"They think there are more rock fragments in my back. Will you come to see me?"

"Oh, Ted, I am so sorry." She felt guilty.

"Emma, how are you?" Ted interjected.

"I am feeling better. I have good news for you. Jimmy didn't do the embezzling. He says he is being framed. He is attempting to find out who set him up."

"Emma, that is good news for you. Aren't you glad now I stopped you?"

"Yes, Ted, but at the time, I thought it was my only solution. Jimmy said the same as you that it would have come out anyway. Then I would have died senselessly."

"Emma, will you come to see me?" Ted pleaded again.

"Ted, I can't."

"Why, Emma? I need to see you."

"Ted, there is no point. We can never do anything to erase what happened. I just phoned to say thank you for saving my life. I will phone you after your operation to find out if you are okay."

"Emma, just come once, that is all I ask. I want to see you one more time to see that you are okay." Ted tried to keep the begging tone out of his voice, but he wasn't successful.

Emma knew that it was her fault that another operation was necessary. "Ted, I am truly sorry, but I am off my feet for a week, doctor's orders." Emma's voice trailed off. There was silence at both ends of the phone.

Ted finally said, "I am glad you have your father and brother Jimmy to help you. I will be okay."

Silence once more, then Ted said, "Emma, promise me one thing, call me if you ever need me. If you can't reach me at home, you can call me through Tommy, promise me?"

"Ted, what good will that do? Everything will be fine now. I think the police finally believe my story that I was distraught and under doctor's care. That is why I have to stay home for a week or two."

Ted was perplexed. "Emma, please promise me that you will call me if you ever need me? Ever?" Ted repeated.

"Okay, I promise even though I don't see any point in saying it."

"I have to go now, the nurse is here, but you did say you would call back, right?" said Ted hopefully.

"Ted, I will call after you are out of the recovery room. I am praying for you."

"Thanks, Emma, I needed that and the promise. I can go to my surgery in a better frame of mind now." Ted smiled. The phone line went dead.

She was crying again. What had she done to Ted? He didn't deserve this. He was the injured party, not her. All he was guilty of was saving her. She had willfully hurt him more when she had hit him and kept striking him and yelling that she hated him. She was on top of him, weighing him down on that offending rock.

Emma was sobbing so badly that she didn't hear Jimmy come in. He quickly came over to the desk where she was sitting with her head encircled in her arms. He bent over her, grabbed her shoulders, and hugged her, saying. "Emma, you will be all right. We will get through this together. I found something last night. I downloaded information on a disk so we can check it."

"Jimmy, Ted is scheduled for another operation at ten. They figure his back still has some rock fragments under the skin, and it isn't healing. So, they have to go in again and probably do another skin graft." Emma started weeping again loudly.

"Now, now Emma, that isn't going to help. Do you want to go to the hospital? I will take you."

"Oh no, I don't want to go anywhere near him. He is better off without me. I have hurt Ted too much already." She could hardly speak for crying. He reached down and picked her up and carried her over to the sofa sitting down beside her, easing her into his arms to better comfort her.

"Emma, you can't keep crying like this. You're going to make yourself depressed. I know he probably wants to see you as I know I would if I was in his place," he said to her gently.

"I did call Ted, only to find out that because of me, he needed further surgery. I will never do that again," she said with a shudder.

"Emma, I know he wants to see you," he said candidly.

"Jimmy, it is best left this way. Ted doesn't need a screw up like me in his life." Emma tried to look positive.

"Did you sleep alright last night? Did you dream at all?" Jimmy was probing her face intently.

"No, the pills knocked me out. I still feel slightly groggy. Do you think Daddy has left yet? He will be unhappy with me crying again."

"Emma, let's go get some breakfast. Matilda will tell us if Dad is still here." Jimmy eased out from behind her, picking her up to head for the breakfast room.

"Just think, Emma, if I keep trekking you around like this, I won't have to exercise for months to keep in shape."

Emma hit him playfully on his shoulder. A half-smile appeared on her lips, which pleased him.

"That's my girl. Smiles are the order of the day. After breakfast, we will head for the computer. I want to get to the bottom of this embezzlement as soon as possible. I want to clear my name and clear your mind at the same time," Jimmy said optimistically.

When they entered the breakfast room, their father was sitting there. They both showed looks of guilt. Had he heard them?

Chapter Ten

W hat's this about clearing things? Are you all right, Emma? Did you mean you talked to the police? What are you two talking about?" Malvin asked quickly.

"Daddy, Ted is having another operation. I just called the hospital," said Emma in an attempt to distract him.

"What do you mean he is having another operation? Why?"

"He has more rock fragments in his back. The skin graft isn't healing."

Jimmy put Emma down in her chair as Matilda came in with omelets. Jimmy went around to his seat, saying, "I offered to take Emma to the hospital, but she won't go. She says that Ted will be better off not ever seeing her again."

"Daddy, you know, he must resent me putting him through this ordeal because of my thoughtlessness." Emma hoped that he wasn't in agreement with her twin.

"Well, I do think someone should call into the hospital after the operation if you don't feel up to that, maybe Jimmy will go."

"Okay, Dad, I'll call into the hospital sometime this afternoon. He should be out of recovery and back in his room by then."

"Daddy, does anyone have to go?" asked Emma pointedly. "I want to drop the whole thing. Then he will forget me sooner."

Jimmy said, "it doesn't work that way, Emma. The man is going through another operation. He will be in considerable pain for a while yet. He isn't about to forget you anytime soon."

"Oh, dear, I guess you are right. I know I can't go back there." She shuddered at the thought.

"Emma might be right. The police may be snooping around. We don't want to trigger any inquisitiveness towards her." Malvin pointed out. "Emma, I want you to stay close to the house for two weeks, as the doctor suggested. Jimmy has offered to do some of your work in the office to keep you up to date. And you could use the computer here which is linked to the office remember. You don't have to do that if you don't feel up to it." Malvin looked at his daughter, thoughtfully.

Malvin pulled his napkin from his lap and rose from the table. "We are going to have a serious talk tonight when I get home about your accident. I want the whole truth this time. Something you should think about is confessing everything as I don't want any more half-truths or evasions that you both are so good at." Malvin's voice was gruff but firm.

Jimmy and Emma looked at each other guiltily. Malvin was heading for the front door knowing the chauffeur would be patiently waiting with the car.

"Good morning, Roger, I want to go directly to the bank this morning before going to the office." He ducked, entering the limo.

"Yes sir," Roger said as he closed the door with a slight thud. He quickly went around to the driver's side.

Malvin sighed with resignation, knowing the twins were hiding something from him. It hurt that he wasn't included in their hidden information. Why were they keeping this from him? His shoulders slumped a bit.

Malvin had always done what was best for the twins. Jimmy had fit in quickly with Cliff's tutelage after finishing his schooling. Emma had fit in also, but she had not been easy to convince. She had a desire to be an interior designer. She finally relented after he had forced her into taking the accounting job for a trial period of two years. However, Emma had just stayed much to his satisfaction.

Now Emma had a problem which she was keeping from him. Could she be pregnant? No, she does have friends, but she didn't have a steady boyfriend, at least not to his knowledge. Nor had Jimmy ever indicated that she was seeing someone in particular.

Of course, Jimmy was a different story. Jimmy was not a stay at home kind of lad, with the number of girls he was seeing. His latest girlfriend, Beth, was a hopeful. When would either of them get married and settle down with a good spouse?

Malvin realized that the car had stopped in front of the bank. Roger was opening the door for him. "Thank you, Roger. I should be approximately an hour or hopefully less.

"Fine, Mr. Gibson. Roger thumped the door behind him then sprinted across the sidewalk, to open the bank door for Malvin. Crossing the marble floor to the bank manager's office, Malvin knew he had to shelve his problems because he needed to deal with his bank business with an unsullied mind.

* * *

Sally was getting ready to go to the hospital. Tommy had gone to work but was meeting her at the hospital on his lunch hour. They both wanted to be there for Ted after his operation. She was worried about Ted, but she was concerned about Tommy too. He cared for his brother. For Tommy's sake, she hoped Emma stayed away, but she also knew that Ted was wishing that Emma would come. With slow steps, she headed out the door.

Ted was in the recovery room. He was still on his stomach. He had not come out of the anesthetic yet. A nurse was checking his vital signs. "Mr. Maxwell wake up, come on Mr. Maxwell, it is time to wake up."

Ted's eyes flickered open for a second, then closed again. "Mr. Maxwell, try again, wake up." The nurse paused, waiting for a reaction. "Some people are waiting to see you. You need to open your eyes and keep them open."

Ted's eyes flipped open with a wide stare. It registered that he was still on his stomach, with a slight groan his eyes closed again. There was pain in his back and areas of numbness. The operation must be over.

"Am I in my room?" asked Ted.

"No, you're in the recovery room after surgery. You are going up to your room soon."

"But I'm still on my stomach," he said groggily.

Ted opened his eyes; he was not pleased. More days of being on his stomach were imminent. Would he ever get out of here? Would Emma come? His mind flashed in hope then disbelief, knowing that would be too much to be true.

"Nurse, I am awake. Can I go back to my room now?" Ted didn't want any more prodding at him. He just wanted to suffer in peace.

"Soon, Mr. Maxwell, we need to make sure you are properly awake. You will go back to your room shortly."

The nurse went over to his chart and recorded her findings for his pulse and blood pressure. She walked away to attend another patient knowing full well that she left a discontented man behind.

Finally, Ted was wheeled up to his room. He was glad he could brood in peace. When he was near the room, Sally and Tommy's voices reached him. Tommy was keeping pace with the stretcher. "How are you? How do you feel?" He needed to hear his brother's voice. That was all.

"I'm okay. At least that is what the nurse tells me. The nurse said the doctor would be up to see me." Ted's voice was sort of garbled as the stretcher wheeled along quickly.

Tommy patted him on the shoulder then walked back to Sally to wait until they settled Ted.

"Tommy, what about some lunch? I grabbed a Big Mac on the way over."

"Thanks, that will suffice. I want to be here for Ted as long as possible before I have to leave."

The attendant and stretcher exited from Ted's room, along with the nurse. She gave Tommy a half-smile, saying, "You can go in now. He is still groggy, but he should be able to talk. If you feel he needs water, then give him sips."

Tommy and Sally headed into the room. Ted was looking shrunken under the covers. This latest setback had taken a toll on him. They looked sadly at each other.

Circling the bed, Sally and Tommy sat in the big chair. "Hi, big guy. I'm glad I was able to see you before I had to go back to work." Tommy was trying to be cheerful.

Distinct footsteps were approaching the door. They looked that way, hoping it would be the doctor.

The doctor came into the room, followed by a police detective. Tommy and Sally recognized Detective Harding. He was one of the detectives that had interviewed them at their home. The doctor came around the bed after they both moved out of the way, as Ted was looking in that direction.

"Well, Ted, I have good news and bad news. The good news is, I feel very confident that we got all of the fragments this time. The bad news is because we had to do the skin graft over again, you will be on your stomach much longer. I'm sorry there is no other alternative. I know it is uncomfortable, but healing is an important issue here. We found two small pieces that we missed the first time due to excessive bleeding and the depth of the wound. I'm confident that every piece is gone. Everything will be okay this time." Dr. Murray looked at Tommy, indicating with a tilt of his head, he wanted to talk to him.

Before leaving, he indicated to the police detective. "Mr. Maxwell may not be too clear-headed for a while yet, so go easy on him." The doctor left the room with Tommy ahead of him. They went down the corridor a little way.

"I am not happy with your brother's present condition. He seems depressed due to this latest setback. If you can think of anything to pull him out of it, I would appreciate it. We have done our best, but it may take someone like you to help him. The operation was a success, but the depression is the concern now," Dr. Murray intoned.

"I understand. Ted hates being on his stomach, but I realize it is a necessity. But even more, he wants to see the girl again. He saved her life. Ted wants to know that she is okay. I think that is why he is so anguished," Tommy said with concern.

It suddenly dawned on Tommy that Sally was with him, not Emma. But the doctor didn't acknowledge this in his concern for Ted's recovery.

Tommy didn't want anything more to do with Emma, but he knew Ted still did. She was the cause of his discomfort now. She probably wanted to give her family a scare. Somehow it got out of hand. But Ted needed this spoilt girl to come and see him for his speedy recovery.

That was what was important right now, not his feelings or Sally's or Emma's.

"Dr. Murray, I don't know where this girl is living. I have no idea of her last name even. However, I will look for her if it will help Ted's recovery."

The doctor walked away as soon as the goodbyes were over, leaving the problem of Ted with his brother. Tommy cared and would do what was best for Ted. Sally could tell from his face he wasn't happy about what the doctor said. He was about to be less than pleased with the detective's persistent questioning of Ted. Not that Ted had been answering many of his questions so far.

He interrupted, "Look, my brother has been through a lot today. Added to that is your constant questions over and over, which are getting you nowhere but upsetting him. Why don't you find the girl? She has the answers, not Ted. All he did was save the girl's life. So, I am politely suggesting you look for the girl." Tommy's look signified no more.

"We found her, but she is very distraught and didn't help us much. We didn't find out many of the facts other than a doctor is involved in treating her condition. We have two people unwilling to say anything of value," the detective replied unhappily. "The girl's name is Emma Gibson. I think I can tell you that much. That was not a normal accident. We need answers, that is why we are so persistent. I'm only doing my job here. The location of the accident and the explosion of the car something is fishy. I need to know more." Looking from one brother to the other, the police detective walked out frustrated.

Harding stopped at the door. "Until we get to the bottom of this, I will be back. You can be sure of that." He walked away unhappily.

Tommy looked down. "Ted, how do you feel? Is there anything I can get for you or anything you want attended to at your place?"

"No. I don't need anything. Why can't the police drop it? She is under doctor's care. I wish I could see her," Ted murmured.

Tommy said, "I have her name now. I will try to find her even if I have to phone every Gibson in the phone book."

Ted replies, "I phoned Colin to find the limo so he will find her address and everything. He should be getting back to me soon."

Tommy shifted into the seat with Sally. Ted was not faring too well with this latest operation. Why didn't Emma have the decency to come? Personally, he wished she would stay lost forever, but that wouldn't help Ted.

The phone rang. Tommy got up to answer it. It was from Colin. He had the information Ted needed. "The limo is registered to a Malvin Gibson, at 1040 Knoxville Drive, Sussex Place, San Anjani, the phone number is 555-1206." Tommy thanked him and hung up. Sally had been recording the information as Tommy repeated it after Colin.

"Ted, we will go and see her this evening after we have dinner. Sorry but I have to get back to work. So, I will see you later. Sally, why don't you stay for a while longer," he said as he bent down to kiss her.

Ted mumbled, thanks. Tommy patted his shoulder.

Sally watched him leave the room with loving eyes. She patted her stomach at the baby's kick. Ted must have noticed her hand movements.

"Sally is the baby, okay? Do you feel all right? Maybe you had better leave. You should be resting, shouldn't you?" Ted's voice wasn't its usual robust tone. "Can you give me a drink before you go, please?"

Sally jumped up. She held the bent straw to his lips. "Not too fast. You have lots of time. I won't be leaving yet. The baby is fine. I hope it is a girl. Tommy wants a girl to be his 'Daddy's girl' you know that's what they say." Sally paused.

Ted took another drink, but his mind had zoomed to Daddy's girl, Emma. Why does this girl mean so much to me? Why don't I hate her as she hates me? The pain in his back became so intense as the numbness was disappearing.

Sally was talking, but Ted appeared to be deep in thought. He finally became aware of what she was saying.

"...and we will find Emma for you. You must concentrate on getting better for your own sake and Tommy's. That guy sure loves you. You are his hero, and you always will be."

Ted loved Tommy too. He had more or less raised him from a youngster even when his mom and dad had been around. His parents were so taken with each other that he and Tommy felt like interlopers when their parents were together. It wasn't that the parents didn't love them. It was just that they loved each other more. Their parents had died in an accident while on a driving vacation. It was only natural that his younger brother had turned to him after his parent's death.

Ted was sorry he had never found a girl that he could feel that way about himself. But he was glad Tommy had. Sally was perfect for him in their love for each other.

"Sally, will you promise me something? I know you are deeply in love, but this promise will be a benefit to you both." Ted paused, waiting.

"What, Ted?" Thinking he was going to ask about Emma. "I hope it isn't something Tommy's going to disapprove. I couldn't promise then."

"Will you promise me when you have your baby that you will still love Tommy but at the same time include your children in your love for each other. Children are important and need to be openly loved. Promise me?"

Sally knew right away what Ted was saying. Tommy had told her how his parents excluded the boys in their tender love.

"Yes, Ted, don't worry, Tommy would never let me make that mistake with our baby. I sometimes think that is why he wants a girl so much because he thinks boys aren't as lovable," Sally replied.

"Good. I'm glad you know why Tommy looks up to me. Don't ever be jealous of me either because you come first with him always. But please include your baby in that love."

"That is not the way Tommy and I love each other to the exclusion of others. You must know we both love you very much. I hope you find a girl to share your life. You stay alone too much. There are some nice girls out there. One for you is just waiting if you would only look." Sally took Ted's hand, holding it tightly.

Ted's mind jumped right away to Emma. He had never needed anyone for a long time. Why now?

Sally said she thought she should be going, placing a kiss on his cheek. Their hands disengaged after a loving squeeze. "Don't worry about me. I will be okay now, you'll see." Ted watched her leave.

Then he turned his eyes scanned the window. His mind shifted to the girl plastered against the window of a car precariously rocking back and forth, hanging over towards death. He was so glad he had saved her even though she had fought him bitterly right to the end. Ted shuddered as he realized how close it had been when he finally felt the release of the car's clutches on her. He hated being on his stomach but felt glad because his back injury was a reminder of his successful fight with death. Will Emma get over her dance with death?

There was a noise at the door a cheerful voice said, "how are we feeling now, Mr. Maxwell? Are you completely recovered yet?" The nurse asked, bustling around him. "Do you want a sponge bath? Would that make you feel better?" She prattled on with a cheery voice as she took his blood pressure and temperature. "I will fix you up as soon as I get some water and towels. You will feel like a new man. Is the pain too much? If it helps, I can increase the dosage now that you have recovered." She walked away as if no answer from him was a regular occurrence for her. That nurse's cheerfulness was driving him crazy.

Then he heard another sound. He turned his head on the pillow to see with his limited view of the door. A man stood barely in range, looking at him. He seemed very familiar, somehow. Ted was wondering why? He knew he had never met this young man.

Chapter Eleven

The young man started walking towards him. There was something familiar about him. Ted lifted his head to see him.

"Hello. You don't know me, but I have come to see you after your latest operation. To find out its success." Ted knew who he was immediately. The man came closer. Emma. He was her twin brother. Then his eyes leaped to the door with hopeful expectation. He was disappointed by Jimmy's words.

"Emma wanted to come, but she isn't getting around too well. The doctor wants her to stay off her foot." Jimmy wanted to tell him the truth. After what this man had gone through, he deserved it. "I am Jimmy, Emma's twin brother. You have guessed by the expression on your face. Also, you know why she was in the car, clinging precariously to the cliff edge." Jimmy paused with trepidation.

Ted seemed to care for Emma, the way he kept glancing towards the door, hoping she would appear. What had gone on between them? Why did Emma hate him? Emma's feelings were irrational.

"Firstly, thank you for saving my sister. I don't know what I would have done had she gone over with her car. Secondly, she would have died in vain, because I did not embezzle any money from the company. I would never do anything like that. I know that it looks bad for me, but I didn't do it. Now I have to try to find out who set me up. It hurts that she didn't trust me to believe in my innocence. Why didn't she come to me first for verification?"

Ted liked the look of this young man and was hoping he was

telling the truth. "Are you fully aware, what your sister was trying to do for you, right up until I dragged her out. She hated me for saving her. I was bound and determined that your sister was going to live. I hope you understand how much she loves you. Emma was hurt by what you had done. She wanted to keep it from your father."

"Yes, I know, don't you realize I love Emma as much she loves me. I would never hurt my father in that way. I will find the answers. The files show my signature. They are an excellent forgery. So, I understand how she could have misunderstood." Did Ted believe him?

Ted finally said after a lengthy time. "Jimmy, I believe you. Now come over and sit in the chair. It is easier for me to see you from this ungodly position I have to stay in."

Jimmy headed around the bed with a sigh of relief. Ted didn't even know him, but he just needed Ted's approval.

"How is Emma? Is she okay? Why didn't she come with you? I know you said she was at home under doctor's orders. I also know her true feelings for me. So were the doctor's orders just an excuse for her not to come to see me?" Ted stopped before he got angrier than he already was.

Jimmy hesitated. How could he tell this man the truth? The anger Ted contained showed.

"Ted, may I call you Ted?"

"Yes." Ted waited to see what he would say.

"Ted, Emma is at home under a doctor's care, but I have to be honest with you. She would defy orders if she wanted to come. But somehow, she has pegged you as the villain in all this. For the life of me, I can't think why." Jimmy sought Ted's understanding.

"I don't understand, but I am also worried about her mental state. Does she believe you? Are you really innocent and not conning me? I don't want her attempting something like this again."

"Honest, Ted, I need you to believe me. I wouldn't do something like that, not ever. I know I can prove that I was out of town when some of these transactions happened with my signature."

"You are positive that the signature is a duplicate of yours," asked Ted.

"I spotted the difference immediately. I doubt anyone else can.

But I can, that is not my signature. I've don't know how else I'm going to prove things." His voice held his dejection.

"Are you the shipping Gibson's?" asked Ted.

"Yes. It was my great-grandfather that founded the company in 1837. He was a captain of a crawler, but he wanted a better life for him and his family. He started the shipping lines, importing goods from the Middle East and beyond. When my grandfather was old enough, he went into the business too. Later my father joined him, and now Emma and I."

"When your father came in to thank me for saving Emma, I was not in the best of moods."

Jimmy shifted guiltily in his seat.

"I hear you are still having problems. Did the latest operation bring success at last? I am truly sorry you got hurt."

"That's okay as long as I was able to save Emma, that was the important thing to me. How does she feel about me? Did she send you in her place?" Ted waited expectantly for answers while trying to ignore the pain that was getting out of hand.

"Sorry, Ted. It was my father that insisted I come. Emma is still not feeling too kindly towards you. Other than she is sorry, you had to have the second operation."

Ted knew the answer before Jimmy acknowledged it. He was hoping he was wrong, and Emma forgave him. Being detained in this bed in such a manner was difficult, mainly because he wanted to find her and talk to her instead. But now he knew it was hopeless. Jimmy had just confirmed that for him.

Jimmy had been waiting for his response, but there was just silence. He could see this man was hurting in more ways than one. Jimmy contemplated whether to leave. So, he sat waiting, feeling guilty about Emma's decision not to come.

Ted shuddered opened his eyes, fixing Jimmy with a stare. "Make sure you get to the bottom of the embezzlement issue. I don't want to hear of Emma's death in her caring for you. Tell her I hope her future brightens up. Jimmy, take care of my Emma for me." Jimmy stood now. He felt dismissed. He would get to the bottom of the problem that was still facing him. The speech had definite overtones of the demise of a relationship that had never been.

Ted said one final thing. "I have no time for Daddy's girl. You can tell her that for me." He closed his eyes, and Jimmy made a hasty exit.

* * *

That night Tommy and Sally went to visit Emma at the address given by Colin. They found the house without difficulty. It had a very commanding look, set back on a hill through the iron gates. A winding driveway meandered through a row of majestic trees. Tommy spoke into the black box, giving his name only. The gate swung open. He edged his truck inside, trapping them to the sound of the closing loud clang. They proceeded up the paved driveway. They soon came into a circular drive set between colorful flower beds and shrubs.

They sat gazing towards the house, which was like a setting from an English Novel. The front door was massive, with a bronze lion's head door knocker.

They looked at each other with a little dread of the occupants within. Sally took Tommy's hand tightly after he helped her from the truck. Their steps brought them to the impressive entrance. Before they could knock the door opened, a motherly looking woman stood in the doorway, emitting friendliness.

"Good Evening." Matilda held out her hands. "I will take your coats. Will you come into the parlor? Right, this way." Her arm swept, indicating the direction after she quickly disposed of their coats.

Tommy took Sally's hand. They followed Matilda to the parlor door, which she opened with a flourish. "Wait here. I will call Mr. Gibson." Matilda swiveled away before they could turn.

Tommy whirled around. "Oh, no, ma'am. We want to see Emma Gibson."

"I am sorry. I have instructions Emma isn't seeing anyone right now. She is temporarily incapacitated. I will get Mr. Gibson." Matilda scurried away.

Sally said, "let's leave. This is useless."

Tommy replied, "no, Sally, I am going to speak to Emma before I leave this house." Tommy was quite adamant about his position.

"I don't think so," stated the gruff voice as the imposing gentleman filled the doorway. He was the mature man of daunting height that came to their house to pick up Emma.

Tommy tried to look taller as he drew himself up straight. "Mr. Gibson. I want to see Emma. I am Tommy Maxwell, Ted's brother, and this is my wife, Sally. You came to my home to pick up Emma. You were concerned about your daughter at the time." Tommy trailed off slowly.

"Yes, Mr. Maxwell, I am fully aware of who you are. No, you may not speak to my daughter. She is unavailable right now."

"After all the problems that Emma has caused my brother, I think she should at least hear what I have to say."

"Emma is lying down now in her room. I don't want to disturb her. She still hasn't recovered from her ordeal."

"Mr. Gibson, I am not leaving until I speak to her even if I have to wait all night." He thrust his chin out for emphasis. Sally was pulling at his arm, but he shook her off.

Jimmy walked into the room. "Is there a problem here, Dad?"

"No, this young man and his lady are just leaving."

Tommy turned towards Jimmy, noting the strong resemblance to his sister. "I have to see Emma. I have to get her to see Ted. The doctor says Ted isn't doing well mentally, and it will delay his recovery. The reason I feel is his concern for Emma. He wants and needs to see her. Surely he deserves that much."

"Have you seen your brother since three o'clock?" asked Jimmy inquiringly.

"No, I saw him this morning after his operation," answered Tommy.

"Well, three o'clock was when I left him. Ted adamantly stated at that time, he was never going to see or wanted to hear from Emma again. So, I think it would be best for you to leave," Jimmy said firmly but kindly.

Mr. Gibson came forward and held out his hand. "I am truly sorry for what your brother is going through. If there is any way I can help with the bills or his recovery, just let me know. I want what's best for Ted considering what he did for Emma."

Tommy looked at him. Then he looked down at his hand. But

he did not grasp it. Mr. Gibson dropped his hand and stepped back, ignoring the affront.

Jimmy said, "I am truly sorry too. I will tell Emma you were here, but I think it would be pointless to speak to her, especially now that Ted has expressed no wish for any more contact with her."

Mr. Gibson stepped back and swept his arm out as if to indicate they should leave.

Tommy clasped Sally's hand, glared at the two men, and headed for the door. "You haven't got rid of me yet. I will be back to see Emma another time. And when I do, she better be available." Tommy stomped out, pulling Sally behind him, with disgust.

Matilda was standing by the front door with their coats as if she knew that their exit was imminent.

"Thank you. We will be back," Tommy alleged as he accepted their coats. He helped Sally with hers and then looked back at the two men standing just outside the parlor. They were like a steel wall. The way they stood, their legs spread, feet planted, determination reflected on their faces in response to Tommy's anger.

Tommy heard a disturbance at the top of the stairs, and there stood Emma with a frightened look on her face.

He stepped to the bottom of the stairs. But Jimmy quickly grabbed him.

Tommy railed at Emma. "I hope you're proud of yourself. You didn't deserve saving at the cost of what Ted is going through. I came to beg you to see him, but the more I see of you and your family, I realize I don't want you to have any further contact with my brother. You are not good enough for him." He threw her another look of distaste then turned to the door, taking Sally's arm.

There was a gasp from upstairs and a cry of 'no.' But Tommy kept going as Jimmy was heading upstairs to comfort Emma.

Tommy was shaking with anger as Sally embraced him on the stone steps, soothing him through his rage before he drove the truck.

The door opened. Jimmy appeared. "Wait, I want to talk to you."

Tommy didn't turn. He just stayed in Sally's embrace, but his shoulders stiffened.

"Emma is sorry Ted is hurting. She never meant that to happen.

My sister is under a great deal of stress right now. After talking to Ted at the hospital, I think it is best for everyone if you forget about us. I know it is hard with Ted still recovering from the second operation. But I still think it is best," he hesitated. "I am truly sorry. I don't want you to leave engulfed in anger against us. We are nice people, and we certainly didn't want this to happen. Please understand." Jimmy stood, waiting to see what response they would give.

But Tommy stepped back from Sally, saying, "are you ready to go, I am?" Tommy looked at Jimmy, gave a shrug, and then walked the rest of the way down the stone steps. He was not happy but knew there was no point in arguing.

Jimmy wasn't happy with the situation either. To think it was all happening because of someone else's nefarious exploit that was the part that was difficult to accept.

Tommy looked at Sally as they cleared the gates. "What can we do now? They are protecting her too much. We will never get past that gate again."

Sally hesitated then replied consolingly. "Tommy, maybe it is for the best. There will only be more heartbreak for Ted if we continue. Whatever Jimmy and Ted discussed this afternoon seems to have made Ted say he didn't want to see Emma ever again. It is still early enough. Let's call by the hospital and see how Ted is faring," said Sally hoping to bolster Tommy after his defeat in convincing Emma.

"All right, but we won't tell Ted what happened at Emma's," said Tommy straightening his shoulders. He would have to shrug off his resentment.

Entering Ted's room, they could tell he was in a sour mood. Whatever was said this afternoon, Ted wasn't in total agreement despite what Jimmy had said.

"Hi, good buddy, how's it going?" asked Tommy. His false, cheerful face was for his brother's benefit.

"Hi, Tommy, did you bring Sally?" Ted questioned, moving his head in the general direction of the door.

"Yes, she is right here." Grabbing Sally's hand and dragging her forward. "Look at this beautiful girl who is pregnant with my baby."

"Quit that. You are always saying things to embarrass me." Sally rebuked.

"You do look beautiful, especially your round pot belly. You look like you have swallowed an enormous watermelon," Ted said, trying to be jovial.

"Thanks, you're as bad as Tommy for trying to embarrass me. A watermelon, just how romantic is that? Couldn't you have come up with something more flattering? Perhaps something akin to blossoming motherhood." Sally said, sitting on Tommy's knee, no easy feat in her advanced condition.

"How are you feeling, Ted? Is it hurting as much now?" asked Tommy with concern.

"No, it isn't hurting, but I don't know how many more days I can stand this position. I will never lay on my stomach again." Ted's voice was adamant.

"Do you think they will let you turn over soon if it doesn't hurt anymore," asked Tommy philosophically.

"The doctor wants to be sure that it heals properly. He wasn't happy that it was necessary to disturb the first skin graft."

Sally wiggled on Tommy's lap as he was tickling her. She started to giggle.

"Tommy, stop, behave yourself. Ted isn't enjoying this at all."

Ted said lightheartedly, "Don't mind me, go right ahead and enjoy yourselves. Tommy, you need to phone my work and tell them I won't be in for possibly a couple of weeks. I doubt I could lift anything."

"OK, I will call them. I will also call Colin and let him know," said Tommy helpfully.

"Do you think you will be able to go back to your job that soon?" asked Sally tenderly.

"I hope so because I don't want to be lying around any longer than I have to." Ted tried to shift his weight to ease his arms.

"Can I exercise your arms and legs for you?" Tommy inquired as he pushed Sally up off his lap. She grabbed the lotion and started in on Ted's arms, while Tommy massaged his legs.

Ted remained quiet as they attended in his outer body, enjoying the feeling of being cared for by loved ones.

Chapter Twelve

Ted was able to finally turnover on the fifth day after his second operation. He would be released soon if all went well. But first, they had to get him up and walking before he could leave.

He was feeling like getting up right away. His diet had been, mostly liquids, to ease his stomach. Soups, sloppy stew's, jelly, or ice cream. The food of kings, yeah right. His spirits were very low at the moment. Jimmy had called to inquire how he was but no word from Emma. I guess she got my message, 'No time for Daddy's girl.'

Ted knew it was time to get out of bed and try to walk. He had to get out of there and pick up his life again.

He needed a shave. The nurses weren't pleased about shaving him while he was in the face-down position. It wasn't too easy. He didn't like a beard, so he felt quite uncomfortable.

He placed his feet firmly onto the floor. He felt shaky. Was it the food he mostly ignored? Maybe it would be best to wait until a nurse came. No, he would do it himself. He wanted to get as far as the washroom, at least. He preferred to do that on his own without an audience. He eased his weight off the bed. At first, his legs didn't feel a part of him as though separated from his body. He was still holding onto the bed.

Communication between his brain and his feet apparently was in slow motion, as he seemed rooted to the spot. He finally slid a foot forward, but his knee didn't want to bend, definitely harder than he had initially thought. It had only been a little over a week, and he felt powerless.

Still balancing with his hand on the bed, he eased his other foot forward. It moved slowly, but it moved, progress at last. Now, he was going to have to slide his hand while he was still leaning heavily.

Slipping it forward slowly, he tried to put his weight more on his legs as they were becoming a part of his body again. They were tingling and weak. Maybe this wasn't such a good idea after all. He seemed suspended in time. What do I do now? Get back into bed or keep trying.

"Quit being such a wimp." Ted berated himself, talking out loud.

"I can do it, I know it." That's right. Be positive.

"Push your foot forward," he ordered. Ted eased his foot forward again, this time his knee bent. He felt relieved, but the washroom still looked far away. On top of that, he had gotten out of the wrong side of the bed and now had that added distance to cover.

"Dumb, dumb, buddy." At least that's better than wimp, he thought. "Get some backbone. You can do it, stand tall and walk." He eased the other foot forward and found he wasn't leaning so heavily on the bed with his hand. "I guess my pep talk is working. Hand forward only lift it this time, wimp." He said out loud, back to wimp again. Oh well, if it works, why not?

His hand lifted this time, he teetered and quickly put his hand down forward on the bed. It was time for the foot again. "Foot forward, stride out, and give it your best." His voice firmer. His right foot moved more positively. He was going to make it. He straightened his body and reached for the railing on the foot of the bed. "Foot forward, bring the other foot, slide the hand no lift the hand, that's better. Now march."

He finally made it around the bed. His legs were getting steadier. Now the real test, he had to let go of the bed. Now, if only he could reach the washroom. Although he felt steadier on his feet, he was feeling the strain was exhausting him. The distance still seemed insurmountable. Where was someone when you needed them? They are always poking and prodding when he wanted to be left alone. Come, someone, it must be time for more poking.

Come on. You are almost there. Yeah, right, disheartened again.

"Foot forward one two three four steps. You will be halfway there. Halfway there? Must be an easier way." Ted commiserated.

He took the four steps in a wavering manner, feeling that he could topple any moment. Soon he could reach for the wall to stop himself from tumbling. He commanded his feet to move faster, and they responded. Then he was falling towards the wall, putting his hands out to save himself. Guess he wasn't quite ready for a marathon yet as the wall stopped him from falling. He leaned his forehead on the wall. The sweat was beading on his body.

On top of this, 'Nature' was advising him that the trip better be continued. He lifted his head. He forced himself to step towards the door to ease inside.

Success. Now you just have to get back again, buddy. He felt refreshed after he washed but wasn't happy about the beard, but his shaving gear was in the cupboard provided for patients. So near but too far at the moment. Ted decided he would sit on the toilet for a while. He was dreading that long trip back to the bed. He had to improve on the way back if he wanted to leave the hospital. After sitting for a while, he felt he was ready for the next challenge. He straightened his back to stand, causing a stab of pain that made him gasp.

Walk and walk smartly. You can do it. A small room isn't going to defeat you. Think positive. Ted squared his shoulders and started moving his feet. They were much stronger. His feet were moving. Wouldn't you know it pep talks work every time? Then he faltered. Oh well, most of the time. He righted himself and kept putting one foot in front of the other, heading for the nearest side of the bed. He had made it back.

Ted tumbled thankfully onto the bed, sliding himself forward towards the headboard then lifting the covers to slip in. His gown twisted, but he didn't care.

The door exploded; the cheerful nurse came inside.

"Well, we can get you up now, Mr. Maxwell. Aren't you happy about that? We are going to the washroom for your first walk so you can wash."

"Been there, done that," said Ted in a belligerent voice. "Where were you when I needed you?" He glared at her and her cheery manner.

He wasn't budging from that bed.

"Oh, so you did some walking, did you? Did you find your feet, okay?"

"What kind of a dumb question is that?" Ted did not feel the least bit accommodating.

"Now Mr. Maxwell, we will have none of that. You have to get out of bed so I can help you walk," she said ever so pleasantly as she whipped the covers back. Ted wished he had straightened his gown as he was exposed.

"You're not to be embarrassed. I have seen lots of men in the bare necessities in my nursing career."

"Well, you are not going to see my necessities." He yanked down the gown.

"Feeling a bit shy, are we? I better get you a housecoat, or you will accuse me of indecent looking." She looked at him with a broad smile. The nurse was driving him crazy. She quickly came back with a housecoat from his locker and slippers too.

"Mr. Maxwell, we will get up and walk. So, you might as well resolve yourself to the fact, up a daisy."

"I am not a kid."

"No, but you are certainly acting like one," she said more cheerfully if that was possible.

Ted figured he had better give in, if for no other reason than he did want to get out of here, the sooner, the better.

"Why are we uncooperative, Mr. Maxwell?"

"There is no we here, there is only me, and I am ready." Ted pulled his housecoat around him and belted it.

The nurse took his arm and helped him stand. "Now we will try walking to the door and back." She eased her foot forward, waiting for him to step forward too. Ted didn't want this to drag on, so he stepped out rather lively, considering he had arrived back to the bed exhausted.

"Now, Mr. Maxwell, teeny steps to start with."

"Teeny steps are for babies," Ted said surly. He took a longer stride, then another.

"Well, this is going better than I thought, isn't it, Mr. Maxwell?"

Her arm entwined in his.

Ted's stride was improving. Maybe it was the fact that he didn't want to show weakness.

"That's it one foot then the other. We will have you dancing in no time." She was easing him into a quicker gait. The door seemed to appear in no time. Why was the washroom so far? This door is twice the distance. Ted felt better now that he had mastered walking. The nurse turned him. He strode back to the bed more confidently.

"See Mr. Maxwell. It was a piece of cake, wasn't it?" Ted did feel stronger.

"In under the covers. I will bring you a treat for being such a good boy. Now, I will be back in a moment with your treat." She bustled out of the room. Ted smirked. He felt better already, although tired and his back was complaining.

She was back in no time with the drink of juice for him and a muffin.

"What no lollipop? I thought that is the standard treat for good boys." Ted smiled.

"Mr. Maxwell, you are more cheerful. That is pleasant to see." Then she left with a cheery goodbye. Ted sank back into the pillows sipping on the juice. He would try again later on his own. He had to get out of here.

* * *

Sally was cleaning the stove when Tommy arrived. He came up behind her, placing his arms around her. "How are my loved ones?" He kissed her neck.

"Fine, let me finish. The pudding I was making boiled over. There is nothing worse than burnt milk."

"I'm early. So, take your time. I want to get to Ted as soon as we finish eating. He phoned to say that he could be released anytime now. I told him we would be there shortly after dinner. I would have gone right from work, but I wanted to get cleaned up first. I will have a shower while you quickly throw something together."

"It's almost ready. I have a casserole in the oven. The salad is already in the frig. The pudding is cooling on the counter."

"Oh, yummy burnt pudding my favorite," he cajoled.

"It is not burnt. It just boiled over," said Sally laughingly. She did so love this man as he went whistling down the hall. She was glad Ted was finally coming home. He was coming here overnight, and she would take him to his place the next day. Tommy felt Ted was strong enough. It was his mental attitude in question. He wanted to observe Ted, getting a clear picture.

"Do you know where my gray cords are?" Tommy asked.

"Yes, they are folded in your third drawer." She eyed his legs appreciatively.

* * *

The dinner was soon over. Tommy and Sally headed for the hospital. The truck was doing a little bit over the speed limit as if it was anxious to get there.

Ted awaited their arrival. He was all dressed and had finally shaved all traces of his beard. It felt so good to have a smooth face again. He was practicing his walking regularly since he first got up yesterday, and he was back to normal. Well, almost he concurred. He walked around the bed to get his things off the side table and pack them in the bag.

He had apologized to the nurse for being such a jerk. She took it okay, explaining when people have a weakness, they hide it with grouchiness. She accepted his apology.

Ted was all for walking out of there and waiting downstairs at the front entrance. But the nurse was adamant that he couldn't sign out until someone was there to pick him up. His back was not bothering him anymore. He was ready to pick up his life, where it was before all this folderol happened. Who was he kidding? Emma kept popping in and out of his mind.

Had Jimmy had any success in finding out who framed him? Why did he care so much about them? He would have to forget this girl who came creeping into his heart and nestled there.

* * *

Emma was showing Jimmy the list of transactions that didn't jibe. He was checking the dates. "Bingo. There are at least three entries here, that were signed while I was in Paris. How could I possibly have put my signature on these documents? Now, we will have to find out who is doing this."

Emma watched the happy face of her twin. He had been wandering around gloomy ever since this happened. They took longer than expected to check the disk because their father had said no computer until she was ultimately better. They had submitted to the off-limits order of no computer to hide their devious activities.

"You're not going to show Daddy, are you?"

"No, not yet, he will blow his stack. I would rather try and find out what's going on quietly, as they used my signature to frame me. Emma, I am so glad you didn't go over with the car. Why didn't you come to me? We are so close, or at least I always thought we were."

"We have been over this several times since it happened. You were my first concern. I didn't want Daddy to be disappointed in you. I hoped my death would make you mend your ways. I know now, it was ridiculous. The discrepancy would have come out anyway." She shuddered at her near demise.

Jimmy hugged her. "Well, sweetheart, it is over now. We have evidence that it couldn't possibly be me. So now you have to get your ankle better." He kissed her forehead and squeezed her tight. He couldn't imagine life without her.

"I think Daddy would like to know Jimmy. I think he will be more upset if we don't tell him." Emma was saying.

"Emma, let me handle this for a few days, and then I will tell him."

"Is Beth coming over tonight, or are you two going out? When are you proposing to her? She will love the beautiful ring you bought her." Emma was pleased that her twin had found such a wonderful girl.

"I just thought I would wait until this mess is all cleared up."

"No, don't do that, it would be better if you are engaged. Then no one will suspect that you are on to them."

"I am taking her to the Country Club Dance. I had originally planned to give her the ring while we were dancing. I told Dad I was going to pop the question, and he seemed pleased with my choice of Beth."

"Beth is a lovely girl, sincere, and she loves you. You can see that, the way her eyes follow you everywhere when you're together."

"I am pleased that you and Dad care for her too. It has taken me a long time for this to happen. There was something about her that drew me to her when I first met her at Luke's party. Now we have to find someone for you, Emma." He gave her a final squeeze.

"You know me. I never get serious about anyone I meet." Emma sat down with a sigh as much for herself as her now aching ankle. Emma looked at her brother with envy that he had Beth.

* * *

Ted wasn't pleased when he ended up at Tommy's house. He didn't want to watch the loving way that Tommy and Sally had with each other. He was too jealous. At home, he could return to his solitary life.

Tommy put his arm around him. "Come on, buddy. We will get you into the house."

"Tommy, I can walk. I have been practicing since I turned over two days ago."

Tommy dropped his arm, falling back and let Ted walk in front of him into the house.

"Well, aren't you the independent man walking so sprightly," Sally said.

Ted mastered the three steps to reach the door. He did it with ease, or so it would seem to others. I guess I am weaker than I thought. He went into Sally's arms to be hugged and kissed. He felt her budding motherhood against him. Would he ever have a wife that would carry his baby?

Tommy watched the two of them together and knew instantly there was a change in his brother, and not for the better. Why did that girl have to pick Ted's place to stage her great exodus from life? He wanted his brother back. He had been his best friend all his life.

"Come in, Ted. We will have something to drink in the kitchen. If you are up to it?" Sally encouraged.

"None of that," said Ted jovially. "I will not be treated as a patient."

Sally proceeded them into the kitchen. "What would you like to drink?"

"Just a cup of your great coffee, thanks. They do not serve good coffee or food in that place."

"Good, I made some just in case. Sit down in your usual spot," Sally said with a smile.

"Tommy, will you get the cups, while I get the coffee and cream."

Tommy leaped sprightly. "Yes, dear, your bidding is my command." He took down the cups and swung back towards the table. He noted Ted was trying to put on a cheerful attitude but not succeeding.

The next day Ted was adamant that Tommy drive him home before he went to work, even though it was out of his way. He had to get away before his change in attitude destroyed everything between them.

When Ted, neared his place, he looked to the waterfall in the distance behind his house. It all came back to him. The car under the falls with Emma's face pressed against the window. Emma, why did you come into my life and leave again? Will I ever get you back? Will I ever get back to a normal life? The answer was no.

Chapter Thirteen

Emma asked Jimmy if he had found out anything yet. She was bugging him to tell Daddy. But Jimmy was persistent in doing it on his own. He had traced the activities to the one recording the waybills, Alan, who had access to the computer and files, but he knew this was not the person perpetrating the actual crime, the act of pocketing the money. Alan did not have that kind of mind. He was a follower who took orders.

"Emma, it is coming into place. I have set a trap for them. Whoever them is. I have told the computer to accept the transactions, but not to print cheques on that account without a keyed in authorization. When the cheques stop, there will be some questions asked. I should get wind of them. Alan is not capable of keeping his cool if he thinks that there are problems anywhere. I am watching him like a hawk."

"This is not going to be easy, is it, Jimmy?"

"No, Emma, it may get quite ugly before finishing. I hope it comes to a head real soon."

"Daddy's going to guess because I'm just about better and should be going into the office," Emma said plaintively.

"You can play your cloudy mind and your ankle by limping more. The experience was traumatic for you, play that angle. Anything to give me a little more time please sis, for me. I don't want you in the office until this over. It is likely to become dangerous."

"You are not the one sitting around bored to tears. Why can't I help?"

"Because it may get nasty, and I don't want you involved. Please, Emma, do this for me?"

"OK, but I will give you until Monday. Then I am going into the office regardless of whether you find the answer or not," Emma said firmly.

He was heading for the door, talking over his shoulder.

"Keep the home fires burning. I am going into the office. Hopefully, today will be the day things will start happening." Jimmy looked back at his sister and gave a wave. When he started looking for answers, he thought it would be simple. But it was taking longer than he had hoped. Who could be doing this, and why? Here was the question that plagued him. He was no closer to the answer, much to his aggravation.

* * *

Jimmy arrived at the office early. Alan wasn't there yet. He went into Alan's work area and looked around. Nothing was leaping out at him. No clues as to the identity of the guilty party. He was heading back to Emma's office when Alan shouted out.

"Hi Jimmy, you're in early today," said Alan looking guiltily towards his desk.

"Hello Alan, I thought I would print the cheques for the accounts due to be paid as we haven't done any since Emma got laid up. I am not as efficient as Emma, but I'll do my best."

"Well, I'm going to the wharf. I need to get information off the containers from the freighter Belle Star," Alan said, grabbing his book.

"OK, I will see you later." Belle Star rang a bell with Jimmy. Several of the false invoices were connected to that particular freighter he recalled. Things may come to a head yet. He would double-check all transactions pertaining to the bills of lading for this ship and its many containers. The very break he was looking for, maybe. He wanted this over.

As he entered Emma's office, he noticed the phone was indicating a message. He checked while waiting for the computer to boot up.

The message was from one of the Companies in question. The gruff voice was asking about payment of invoice. Jimmy stopped the machine then rewound it, concentrating on the voice rather than the message this time. But he didn't recognize the voice at all. The telephone number was given. He recorded it on pad on the desk.

The computer was ready, and the printer setup the way Emma had told him. Jimmy went into payables. He started calling up cheques for printing. As he proceeded, he found he was getting faster, which eased his mind because he wanted to get down to the docks and check on the Belle Star's cargo himself. He also wanted to make sure the accounts that he had highlighted did not produce cheques. The program completed producing lists of all transactions.

Good no cheques for the bogus accounts printed, the list showed asterisks beside these accounts. Things were going as planned.

Now to get down to the docks. Jimmy would get Emma to do the cheques in envelopes and stamps for mailing to give her something to do. He put everything in his briefcase and locked it up. He grabbed the clipboard and headed for the docks. He quickly spotted Alan. He was talking to a couple of the ship's handlers of the cargo.

Jimmy decided to see if he could speak to the Captain. He wanted to feel him out on the bogus account names.

"Captain Jorgensen, how are things, did you have a good sailing?"

The two of them had formed a relationship over the years, which Jimmy was thankful for, because now he might need that friendship, provided Jorgensen wasn't involved. Let's hope that was the case.

"Hi, Jimmy. Things are great. The sailing went well, but there was one bit of weather we ran into that was nasty, but didn't last long. How are you?"

"Fine. I want to inquire about a couple of accounts. I am not familiar with them. They seem to be on your manifest each time your ship comes in. They are the Sentinel Transport of Import and Export Goods, and the other is the International Corp. of Goods for Import and Export."

"What do you want to know?" Captain Jorgensen asked cautiously.

"Well, I am not familiar with the names. I wondered if you could recall anything about them?"

"Yes, they have been shipping with us for a considerable length of time. I seem to recall these companies use us quite a bit."

"That's strange. I thought I knew all our accounts, at least by name, if not personally. These two are entirely new to me?" A question in this voice.

"Well, I don't know why you don't recognize them as they are quite familiar to me. These companies have containers with us regularly. Do you think you have forgotten?" The Captain expressed, trying to be helpful.

"No, I think my memory is quite good. I think I will check on them when I get back to the office. I'll check the bills of lading from the containers on your ship while I'm here," Jimmy said.

"Why is that necessary, isn't your regular guy already doing that now? I saw him a minute ago checking everything with the help of my deckhand. The forklift guys are moving the smaller containers already," he added lamely.

"Well, I want to check things for myself, that's all. Thanks for your help." Jimmy said in a friendly voice.

"No problem anytime." Captain Jorgensen replied as Jimmy went down the ramp.

Captain Jorgensen knew the jig was up. Jimmy was becoming too nosy. He bustled back up to the ship's quarters and called to a couple of big bruisers of men. "Chuck and Steve get down on the dock and steer Jimmy back on the ship. He's the guy in the suit. Detain him in the empty cabin nearest mine. I don't want him leaving this ship. No rough stuff unless it is absolutely necessary. We will get rid of him when we are out at sea." The men were looking at him questionably.

"Quickly now before he gets too nosy and comes up with what he is looking for, which shouldn't be too difficult."

The two men looked like ruffians rather than deckhands headed for the dock. They could see Jimmy talking to some shipment handlers. Jimmy would have to be separated from them before they could take him.

After chatting for a while, Jimmy was heading towards Alan when two men fell into step with him. He didn't like the look of them.

"What do you want?" Jimmy asked apprehensively.

"Captain Jorgensen sent us to get you. He asked that you be brought back on the ship," the burly man said.

"What does he want?" Jimmy was getting a bad feeling.

"He didn't say he just said bring you back. He wanted to talk to you," the second man said forcefully.

"Tell him I'll be back, I just want to speak to Alan for a minute," said Jimmy walking away.

The first man grabbed his arm, replying. "I can't let you do that. Captain Jorgensen said to bring you back right now. The Captain was quite adamant about needing you." He was tightening his grip as he spoke. Jimmy knew this was not going to be a friendly talk this time, as the second man grabbed his other arm.

Jimmy called to Alan, but he didn't respond. Jimmy thought he probably didn't hear over the noise caused by the hydraulics for the lifters that ran along the tracks beside the ship.

He was contemplating pulling away from them, but they were now holding him too tightly. What if he just yelled for help would someone come to his rescue? Maybe he could reason with Captain Jorgensen, as the burly thugs steered him along.

But he wasn't to see Captain Jorgensen after all. Before they got to the Captain's cabin, the two men opened the door of the nearer cabin, projecting him inside without ceremony. He heard the door decisively lock behind him. Then he knew that this involved more than the two persons as he initially thought. What can he do now? Would someone miss him and come looking for him before the ship sailed in four days?

He looked around to see if he could find something to jimmy the door. But after a thorough search, he knew there was nothing to do but wait. He wasn't the patient type. Again, he looked around for something to use as a weapon but to no avail. The cabin was an unoccupied one.

Jimmy finally sat down to think and hope that someone would miss him enough to come looking for him. Had Alan noticed him on the dock? Would Alan tell someone, or did he know that Jimmy knew he was part of the scam? Would anyone think to check the ship before it sailed, or would they assume he had left the dock? Beth was expecting him to take her out for dinner tonight. Would she think he had stood her up? Would Emma wonder why he didn't come home first?

Could he possibly overpower someone that came for him? He had kept in shape at the local gym. He could maybe if there was only one of them. The element of surprise would be the only way. Not that he was that strong compared to the two bruisers that had apprehended him.

Please someone, come and help me. Why was he being detained here? He must have been closer to the truth than he had been aware. Who was involved? It confirmed Alan wasn't alone in this.

If only I had told father what was going on. Emma had begged me to say something to him, but no, I was adamant. I wanted time to do it on my own. Now I am sorry about that decision. Should I pretend I know more than I did, or should I play innocent letting them think I know less than I do? Which was the best route to take? He couldn't just sit here and do nothing, but what choice did he have. Why didn't he tell his father? Would Emma tell Dad?

These questions were running frantically through his mind, causing his mind to go into overdrive. It was an exercise in futility. He sat down, defeated.

* * *

When Jimmy did not come home by 6 o'clock, Emma started to wonder where he was. She wasn't too worried because she thought he might have needed to work later for some reason.

Beth had called because Jimmy had said he would pick her up at 6:30, and she was running late at the office and might not make the 6:30 deadline. She felt she could be ready by seven. Emma said she would pass the information on to Jimmy when he came in.

"Daddy, do you know why Jimmy is late getting home?" She looked up at her father inquiringly as he stepped into the room.

"No, I don't. I called in at the office, but Jimmy wasn't there. The funny thing is his briefcase was sitting on the floor by your desk. It is unusual for him to leave that there. He usually has it glued to his side. I asked Alan if he had seen him, and Alan said no."

Emma looked hesitant, then decided to tell her father about the bogus companies. Jimmy's remarks about it may get dangerous, concerned her.

"Daddy, I have something to tell you. I don't want you to be unhappy or mad with Jimmy and me." Pause. "Last week, when I tried to drive my car over the cliff, it was because I found out Jimmy was embezzling money from the company."

Before she could continue her father bellowed. "WHAT?" His face was turning red with anger.

"Calm down, Daddy, it isn't like it sounds." Emma took a deep breath. "When I confronted Jimmy after Ted saved me, he adamantly denied responsibility for the embezzlement. Jimmy took the opportunity to go into the office to check when I was laid up. He found out that he couldn't possibly have signed them, he was away, when the contracts were approved. He didn't want you to know until he could verify the dates and the actual signatures. They are forged." Emma looked at her father, sadly then continued. "I wanted to tell you, Daddy. I really did because of what I had done on Old Canyon Road. But Jimmy wouldn't hear of it. He wanted to investigate first." She stopped and looked at her father to see how he was taking her confession.

"Yes, go on." Her father said sternly but with steely control in his voice.

"Well, Jimmy went into the office and found the information I had discovered on the computer. He checked the contracts. Sure enough, it was his signature..."

"HIS SIGNATURE! You said Jimmy didn't do it," Malvin blustered.

"Just a minute, the signature wasn't his. Jimmy said it was almost perfect, but he could detect a slight difference that only he would recognize because it was a good forgery. The stroke was there but not bold enough, which was his trademark." Emma saw her father relax a bit.

"Go on."

"Well, he downloaded the information onto a disk and brought it home. We have been compiling activities of those bogus transactions. The data shows that it couldn't possibly be Jimmy because he was away in France on some of the dates and somewhere in the Orient on the others. But not all were when he was away." Emma paused. She thought her father didn't seem quite so angry.

"We have been working on this here together whenever you were not around. We had enough evidence to know that Alan is involved, but not alone in this. Jimmy didn't want to confront Alan until he knew who else was."

"Today, he went into the office to see if he could find any more clues. He phoned to say that he found something he wanted to check further. He didn't say exactly what. He did say before he left that he felt things might get dangerous before this was over. That is why I am worried that Jimmy hasn't come home yet. Particularly because he promised that he would pick Beth up by 6:30, he is never tardy."

"You mean to say he went down there, and you didn't think it was necessary to tell me until now?" Malvin said with a gruff voice.

"Daddy, I wanted to tell you. I kept trying to get Jimmy to change his mind and let you in on the embezzlement. Part of my avoiding telling you the truth about my car mishap was my thinking Jimmy was guilty in the beginning. Daddy, I know he must be in trouble. What do you think we should do?" Emma asked with real concern.

"Now, we know Jimmy must be near the docks somewhere. If only we knew what he discovered today. I think I will go down to the shipping office and recover his briefcase and see if that tells us anything. Why didn't you go over Jimmy's head before now? We might not be in this position. We know he found something out, but we don't know what, why, where, or who is involved. That gives me a good starting place," Malvin said sarcastically.

"Daddy, I said I was sorry. I didn't want to hide it from you. Where is his car?" asked Emma, suddenly curious. "Did you see it near the shipping office if you say his briefcase is still there?"

"Funny, you should say that. Yes, Jimmy's car was in the usual parking spot. Not expecting problems, I never thought about it at that time. Besides, when I asked Alan, he said he hadn't seen him. I should have checked further," Malvin said with self-disgust. "He must be near the docks. If only we knew what he had discovered today. Hopefully, his briefcase will tell us something."

"Daddy, be careful, won't you? What about Cliff? Can he go with you?" Emma said hopefully.

"Yes, I'll give Cliff a call." Malvin went to the phone. "Hi, Cliff, could you meet me down at my shipping office on the docks?" Malvin had to explain because he had another office downtown.

"Why? Is there a problem?" asked Cliff in response to the gruffness in Malvin's voice.

"I'm not sure, but I think there might be as Jimmy is missing. We know he went to the shipping office."

"What do you mean Jimmy is missing?" Cliff inquired.

"Well, he hasn't come home, and that isn't like Jimmy when he has a date with Beth for dinner."

"Maybe Jimmy went directly to Beth's house when he couldn't make it home on time. Did you call there?"

"No, Beth called and said she would be home late, so she hadn't seen him."

"Well, that doesn't mean Jimmy hasn't gone directly there since, call her,"

"All right, I will call, but I've got this feeling something's wrong, and he won't be at Beth's place. I will call you right back." Malvin hung up the phone and looked at Emma.

"I want you to call Beth and say Jimmy's running late too. She may say he is there. We don't want Beth upset at this point."

Emma walked across the room to the phone. "Yes, that is a good idea."

"Beth, Emma here, Jimmy said he was running late. As it is almost seven, I thought he might go directly to your place." "No?" "I guess he will be truly late."

Beth said with relief. "Good, that will give me extra time to get ready. Thanks for letting me know. Goodbye."

"He's not there, Daddy." Emma's voice held a frightened tone.

"Give me back the phone. I'll call Cliff and let him know." Cliff picked up the phone on the first ring. Having picked up on Malvin's urgency on his first call.

"Cliff, Jimmy isn't at Beth's house, so would you meet me down at the docks?"

"I'll be there in fifteen minutes. I'm heading out right now." Cliff looked at his wife. "Sorry, dear, I have to leave, but the dinner was great, as always."

He came over to Tina and kissed her. She looked up at him with concern.

"Problems," she asked.

"I don't truthfully know. Jimmy seems to be missing." Cliff grabbed his keys and headed out the door. "Be careful," Tina yelled after him.

Chapter Fourteen

Emma was walking back and forth, worrying until she felt her ankle throbbing. She sat down gingerly on the sofa but wasn't in the right frame of mind to be just sitting. She was too anxious about Jimmy.

When he finished his call with Cliff, her father raced out of the house at a fast gait unusual for him because he walked with a purposeful stride and rarely went beyond that. He must be concerned too. I knew I should have given the truth to Daddy, regardless of what Jimmy thought. Emma started to cry as Matilda came into the room.

"I was coming to call you for dinner. There, there, dearie, what is it?" Matilda sat down and gathered Emma in her arms.

"Oh, Matilda, Jimmy's missing. We don't know where he is," Emma said in a tearful voice. "I didn't tell Daddy about the embezzlement, and now I am sorry. I knew it was seriously wrong. I listened to Jimmy instead of believing that Daddy would understand that it wasn't Jimmy's fault."

"Dry your eyes, and have some dinner. You don't know for sure he is missing. Come eat to pass the time to give your father a chance to find him." Matilda was drying Emma's face with the end of her apron. She hoped that Jimmy wasn't missing but rather that he was just late. She didn't think that was the case after Mr. Gibson had run out of the house so fast.

"Come on, lamb, come, and eat some dinner. You will feel much better. Jimmy will show up. You will have worried for nothing."

Matilda helped Emma up and walked with her arm around her waist.

"Matilda, I don't think I can eat anything," Emma said dejectedly.

"No, Emma, I am telling you to eat. If Jimmy is missing, I do not agree with that mind you. Then you will need food to sustain you," Matilda cajoled.

Emma sat down at the table. When Matilda returned with her dinner, she saw it was her favorite. It was veal cutlets, asparagus, and potato croquettes with a green salad on a side plate.

"Now eat the hot dish first. You can always eat the salad later," Matilda coaxed.

"Matilda, will you eat with me. I don't want to be by myself," Emma said hopefully.

"Why certainly dear. I will go and get my dinner and be right back. Now you start while it's still hot, that's a good girl." Matilda hadn't treated her like a little girl for many years now. Somehow right now, it felt good. Emma picked up her fork but skimmed over the food, not wanting any of it. She was just too upset.

Matilda was back in no time. "Use your fork to eat, not play. I made your favorite dinner," Matilda said kindly.

Emma was making chewing motions. She couldn't produce much enthusiasm. Not when she knew in her heart, Jimmy was indeed missing. She just hoped they were not hurting him.

She took another fork full of dinner. Three, four, and now five bites when could she stop? Matilda was eating, but her eyes never left Emma.

"Emma, you are not to think the worst until you know there is something to worry about."

"But Matilda, I can feel he is in trouble," Emma said positively.

* * *

Malvin and Cliff met in the almost empty parking lot. There were just five cars left beside Cliff's, Jimmy's and Charlie's, and three unfamiliar cars.

When Cliff went looking for the night watchman, he found that Charlie was standing watching the Belle Star. "Is there a problem?" Cliff asked.

"No, just watching the ship. There seems to be more activity than usual." Charlie gave his attention to Cliff. "What are you doing down here at this time of night?"

"Mr. Gibson is looking for Jimmy. His car is here. Have you seen Jimmy?"

"No, although I noticed there are extra cars left in the lot tonight."

"Mr. Gibson has gone in to see if everything is okay inside. Do you know if anyone left later than usual? Or do you know if anything is out of place?"

"No, Cliff, I haven't noticed anything out of the ordinary. I checked around when I came on duty. What do you hope to find here?"

"Anything that will lead to some clue as to Jimmy's whereabouts. Are you sure he is not around here?"

"I am positive I haven't seen him, but I did wonder about his car. I assumed someone had come by to pick him up."

"Did the other three cars come before or after your shift started?"

Two were here before then the last one that arrived went on to the Belle Star, I think. As I said, there seems to be more activity than usual on the ship, but nothing appears to be a problem," he finished.

"Well, I better get back to the office to see how Mr. Gibson is making out. Are you going to stay here?" Cliff inquired.

"Yes, I think I will just patrol a bit out here and keep tabs on the Belle Star." He looked up at the ship. The cloudy evening made it look more sinister.

Cliff walked to the office. He knocked on the door. He saw Malvin coming towards him. Malvin stepped aside so Cliff could enter. "Did you see Charlie?"

"Yes, Charlie says that he was aware Jimmy's car was here but assumed someone had come to pick him up. He also said two of the other cars were here when he came on shift. The other one arrived later. He must have boarded the Belle Star. By the way, Charlie is watching the Belle Star. He says there is more activity on it than usual, but nothing he feels to be concerned about at this point. Did you find anything?"

"No, I looked at his briefcase, but it was locked. There must be something important inside. I wish I knew for sure Jimmy's disappearance was real and not just a case of him going off with someone else."

Cliff went over to Alan's desk and looked around. "Do you think Alan knows anything?"

"I asked Alan if he saw Jimmy when I was here earlier, he said no. But Emma says he is part of the embezzlement. Jimmy was looking into something that involved using his signature to falsify records. A forged signature Emma mentioned," Malvin said.

"Do you think the Belle Star is involved? I can't help thinking about that extra activity on the ship that Charlie mentioned," Cliff pondered.

"Maybe, but I doubt we will get any cooperation from Captain Jorgensen if he is involved. However, I fully intend to board the Belle Star before I leave here. The only problem is I won't be able to search it without the police and a search warrant. I have no proof that they are involved. Besides, Jimmy won't be officially missing for 24 hours," he finished.

Cliff had his doubts. "Do you believe that?"

"No deep down in my gut, I feel somebody has Jimmy. Oh yes, by the way, I found out at the same time from Emma. The trip over the cliff by Emma's car was her way of protecting Jimmy. If she had thought it through properly, maybe I would have been told the details," he said in a strained voice. "Can you imagine Emma going over the cliff with her car if that guy hadn't pulled her out? That gives me real shudders up my spine, to think my daughter could be dead right now. Who can be doing this to my family?"

Cliff patted him on the back. "Emma's safe, and that is the important thing. Why wouldn't she come to you or me? I thought you two were close."

"Yes, so did I, but Emma was horrified when she thought Jimmy was involved. All we can do is board Belle Star and keep our eyes open. Then if that doesn't produce anything, I'll take Jimmy's briefcase home with me. There must be an extra key. Let's go look on the ship," Malvin said. "You go out and see Charlie. I will lock up here and put the briefcase in the car. I was so anxious. I just drove myself. You know Jimmy means a lot to me," Malvin stated proudly.

Cliff went out the door, saying, "I know he does, and he does to me too. Let's get onto the ship and see if we can find out anything."

Malvin went back to the light switch, glancing over at the credenza. There was a piece of paper that looked like a bill of lading. He walked over to get it. The bill of lading was from the Belle Star. Why was this here? They keep them in Alan's office. Had Jimmy found some reason? Malvin thought it was something significant and was going to treat it that way, sticking it in his pocket so he could look more closely later. He flipped the switch after giving the room another glance, grabbing Jimmy's briefcase as he passed Emma's office.

After locking up, he headed for his car. Malvin hastily opened his trunk, placing the briefcase inside.

He approached Cliff and the night watchman, who was talking to one of the deckhands from the ship. They seemed to be arguing about something. Charlie was flailing his arms and hands around as though describing something, and the deckhand was saying in a loud voice.

"Definitely not."

Cliff chimed in, "if that is the case, you won't be offended if we come on board to see." He turned to Malvin as he reached the trio standing not far from the ship's ramp.

"Malvin, Charlie is questioning the activity on board, but the deckhand says some are relaxing after a big dinner, but most have gone into town to a pub. I think we should board the Belle Star and check for ourselves, don't you, Malvin?"

"Yes, we can meet with Captain Jorgensen." He signaled for the deckhand to precede them. Malvin followed him up the boarding ramp.

The deckhand paused at the top before stepping onto that deck. He seemed to be peering around quickly as though looking for something. He must have been satisfied because he finally stepped down. He moved far enough away for Malvin and Cliff to enter onto the ship. They glanced around. No one was in sight. The deck looked normal other then it could do with a good scrubbing.

Malvin wasn't familiar with the Belle Star, which was Portuguese, according to its manifest. The deckhand was heading for topside to the captain's bridge. Usually abandoned at this time of night, except

Malvin could detect a moving shadow observing the dock and their progress on board. Then someone stepped out to confront them. Malvin could see it was Captain Jorgensen. He was looking downright unpleasant.

"Good evening, Captain Jorgensen," said Malvin pleasantly. "We came aboard because the night watchman, Charlie, has been observing your ship. He says that there seems to be undue activity on it. We thought we would check to see if there was some problem aboard."

Captain Jorgensen looked at the deckhand and said, "you can go below now. I will look after this." He gave the deckhand a glaring stare as if he was accusing him of bringing them aboard deliberately.

The deckhand returned the Captain's look with an aggressive look of his own as though to say it wasn't his fault and sauntered away.

The Captain turned back to Malvin and Cliff. "What can I do for you?"

"Do you mind if we sort of look around?" Malvin asked. "We are curious to see the men that arrived, where are they?"

"What men? I don't know of any men other than my ship's crew."

"Charlie says he saw at least one man arrive. He came on board this ship. The fact that there are three cars in the parking lot, I am assuming they are all on board," Malvin stated firmly.

"Well, that isn't the case. They must be somewhere else on the docks. A few of the crew are relaxing after a long voyage. The rest are doing the town tonight." Captain Jorgensen shifted his weight to put the light behind him so they couldn't read his facial expressions. "I must say I do mind that you have boarded us in an accusing manner. We have nothing to hide. You are welcome to look around within reason but not the quarters. My crew deserves their privacy."

The Captain walked around the upper deck with them. There was no one in sight. Then they went down to the next level and there again the vast expanse seemed to be bare of living beings.

Malvin asked, "don't you have anyone on night duty on deck?"

"Not tonight," the Captain replied. "I gave everyone the night off as it is such a quiet night, and I didn't think it was necessary."

Malvin looked at Cliff and noticed that he was looking around. Then they looked at each other. Cliff gave a slight movement of his head that Malvin would have missed if he hadn't known Cliff for so long.

Malvin glanced in the direction that Cliff indicated. There seemed to be piles of tarp shrouded cases that were half moved, by the looks of them. Why was it separate here and not in the cargo hold? Malvin wanted to look under those tarps. He steered the Captain nearby the shrouded tarps, engaging the Captain in conversation, so his back was to the tarps.

He was asking the Captain how long he would be in dock and where his next port of call would be as though he was passing the time of day. Meanwhile, Cliff was moving the tarp with his foot so as not to cause too much body movement. The markings 'fruit' on the cases, now that wasn't practical -- no doubt a camouflage for what was actually in them.

The Captain swung around as if he realized that Cliff was behind him, but Cliff was standing watching them the picture of innocence.

"Well, have you seen enough? I wonder why you are so concerned about my ship? Is there something you are looking for in particular? Tell me, and I will see if I can help you." The Captain was trying to sound helpful. Although until now, he had sounded quite belligerent and uncooperative.

"No, nothing in particular only that the night watchman seemed to be concerned about the ship's activity, which is usually quiet after a day of unloading and the crew in town." With little lighting, it was difficult to see. Malvin got the impression that individuals were lurking in the darkness on the captain's bridge.

Malvin then nodded to Cliff. "I guess we had better be going. There seems nothing out of place, don't you agree, Cliff?

"Yeah, we had better get going, my wife is expecting me home shortly," Cliff added casually.

The Captain was steering them towards the ramp. He was getting rid of them slowly but positively. There was no doubt in Malvin's mind things were not kosher here. But there was no point in staying, as the Captain was controlling their movements.

"Well, Captain, thank you for the tour of your ship. Enjoy your stay in dock." Malvin put his foot on the top of the exit ramp and turned. With the brighter light, he could see the Captain's face. "You say there are no extra men on board, and yet Charlie says he watched one board."

Captain Jorgensen gave a guarded look. "Well, there is no one that I am aware of, I will have to check with my skeleton crew. Goodnight, gentlemen," he said in a dismissing manner.

Malvin and Cliff headed down the ramp. Nothing accomplished here. They both headed towards the parking lot.

Charlie called to them. They waited. "Did you find out anything?" Charlie asked.

"No, Captain Jorgensen denied that there was anything unusual happening. Even denied that strangers were on board only crew," Malvin replied.

"Mr. Gibson, I saw a man go on board. I know something is going on. I can't explain it, but something is weird here. I'll keep watch for you. I'll let you know if any strangers go on or off the ship," Charlie said firmly.

"Be careful, Charlie, don't get too close. I don't want you disappearing like Jimmy." Malvin squeezed Charlie's shoulder.

"Goodnight, Charlie, be careful, do you hear?" stated Cliff.

The two men continued toward the parking lot and their cars discussing the fruit boxes under the tarp that held no helpful clues.

They reached Cliff's car. "What are you going to do now, Mal?"

"Go home and try to get Jimmy's briefcase open, hoping for clues inside. Then call around to see if anyone has seen Jimmy. We may be worrying for nothing. I wish he would be there when I get home." His voice trailed off in wistfulness.

"Me too, Mal me too." Cliff pulled out his keys. "Goodnight."

Malvin replied, "goodnight, say hi to Tina. I'll let you know when I find out anything." Malvin stood back and watched Cliff leave. With a heavy heart, he walked over to Jimmy's car, but it was empty. Malvin squared his shoulders and took out his keys.

He sped through the dark parking lot to the front gate. Cliff had left it open. Normally it was kept locked at this time of night. He got out to close it after he was clear.

He viewed the Belle Star with interest. There appeared to be decisive movements on deck. He had a bad feeling that Captain Jorgensen was into something ominous. Malvin sighed deeply, then went to lock the gate.

His car slowly entered onto the deserted street. This area abandoned at this time of night. During the day, traffic was usually an ensnaring mess with vehicles jockeying for parking spaces to a chorus of honking horns.

Chapter Fifteen

When Malvin arrived home, Matilda and Emma were waiting at the door.

"Did you find him? Did you find out what might have happened to him?" Their two faces held such expectation that Malvin almost felt like a cruel person, telling them that the news was not good. Their hopeful expressions turned to fear.

"Daddy, where can Jimmy be? Why couldn't you find him?"

"I looked, but I didn't find Jimmy nor any clues to his disappearance other than that his car and briefcase were still at the shipping office. I feel that it has something to do with the Belle Star. The ship that is in port at the moment. But when I boarded her, there didn't seem to be any evidence of him. I must say that Captain Jorgensen didn't let me see much, so I don't know for sure."

"Daddy, we have to do something. We can't just wait till he shows up. He may be injured somewhere and need our help," worry in her voice.

"I know darling, but you can't go unless we have a definite purpose. I have Jimmy's briefcase here. Do you know of another key to open it?"

"Yes, there is one on a key chain in his top drawer. He mentioned it to me one day when he thought he had lost his keys." Emma turned to get Jimmy's keys.

"I am going to phone around to some of Jimmy's friends." Malvin picked up the phone and dialed Jimmy's best friend, Coulter.

"Coulter, this is Mr. Gibson. I have some bad news. Jimmy is missing. No one knows where he is. That is why I am calling you, hoping that you have heard from him or know where he went?"

"No, I haven't heard from him. We were all supposed to go to dinner tonight. Diane and Beth are both here. Beth has no idea where he is either. We thought your call might be him. Is there anything I can do?" Coulter asked.

"You might try calling some of his friends. The ones that he usually hangs with in your crowd. I will try some of his gym pals," Malvin said.

"I don't know if I'll get many at home tonight. Most of our group will be out, as it is Friday night. But I will try Mr. Gibson."

"Coulter, be careful how you tell Beth, won't you?"

"Yes, Mr. Gibson. It is a good thing she is here with us. She has been worried although she tried not to let on. Apparently, Emma phoned her earlier and sounded rather funny. She half expected there was a problem."

Malvin hung up and tried another of Jimmy's friends. He wasn't home. The ones he did contact had not seen him.

Emma handed the key to her father. Malvin opened the briefcase. On top were the cheques for signing and mailing. He picked up the list showing the payables paid. There were two names highlighted, checking, but there were no printed cheques. "Are these the bogus accounts, Emma?" Holding out the list to her.

"Yes, Daddy, they are two of the bogus companies. He must have gone in and put an indicator to stop their printing. Jimmy must have found out something. Is there nothing else in the briefcase?" Emma asked.

"No, the rest of the information has to do with our regular accounts," Malvin replied.

"What are we going to do now, Daddy?"

"We have no actual leads other than these bogus accounts." Malvin walked over to the liquor cabinet and poured himself a drink. He took a drink of the scotch. He hadn't had anything to eat. The liquor hit his empty stomach.

Matilda must have been thinking the same thing as she arrived with a sandwich knowing Mr. Gibson would be too upset to sit down to a proper meal.

"Malvin, you need to eat this. You will find Jimmy. You will think better on a full stomach," Matilda said, giving him a look.

Malvin sat down on the chair by the desk. It was then that he heard the crackle of paper. It was the bill of lading that he had shoved into his pocket. He got up again, pulling it out. He went over to the lamp to have a closer look. It was a bill of lading for one of the false companies. It named the Belle Star as the shipment carrier.

This must be what Jimmy was investigating when he disappeared. "Look Emma, it is a bill of lading, and it has to do with the ship that is in the dock now that we boarded. Captain Jorgensen curtailed our inspection."

Emma was now looking at the bill of lading too.

"Daddy, that is one of the bogus companies. He must have figured out what was going on. Alan would know about this. Jimmy said he is involved. Can't we call him?"

"Emma, if Alan is in on this and they have Jimmy I don't want to tip our hand too soon. They might whisk Jimmy away, never to hear from him again." He heard Emma's breath catch.

"We can't just leave him there. He must be on the Belle Star. That is the only explanation," Emma said.

"I know, but we have to give just cause before we get a search warrant, and so far, all we have is suppositions. We'll have to check the cargo tomorrow more carefully. I'll get Cliff onto it. He can do it without Alan knowing as Alan often sees him on the docks checking on things." Malvin reached for the phone. "I'm calling Charlie. He is keeping an eye on the Belle Star. I hope he doesn't get into any trouble."

Malvin waited and waited, but Charlie didn't pick up the phone.

Emma gave a sob, then another only stronger this time.

"Emma, maybe Charlie isn't near the phone. He may be outside near the ship."

Malvin tried again, letting it ring about 12 times still no Charlie. He hung up and took another drink, then reached for the sandwich. Why didn't Jimmy call me with his evidence and let me know his intentions?

He put the half-eaten sandwich down and ran his hands through his hair in despair. How could he get enough evidence for a search warrant? One bill of lading wasn't enough. How could he get on that ship? Captain Jorgensen was never overly friendly on past occasions, but he thought that was the nature of the man. He straightened up. He had to be braver about this for Emma's sake.

He went over to her on the sofa, sat to pull her into his arms. Emma was crying in earnest now. Malvin was trying to console her. She feared for Jimmy, seeing her father's defeated attitude confirmed it. Her brother was not coming home tonight.

* * *

Earlier in the day, Ted was getting antsy to be back at work. The doctor said he could go back on Monday. He had the weekend before him.

In the afternoon, he felt like he should take the opportunity to be with nature and dressed for hiking and scaling the cliffs. His favorite pastime in his private valley as he thought of it. People usually entered by the lower canyon, quite a distance away. The odd time he would see hikers in the canyon below.

After he had suited up with a heavy shirt and pants, he put on heavy socks and special hiking boots. He went out to the shed and got his climbing gear, ropes, pulleys, and cliques. Today he would do the easier climb because of his back.

Ted walked towards the waterfall, prodding a memory of Emma and the car teetering on the edge, ready to go over. His back gave a twinge. A reminder of his stay in the hospital and the pain of his back embedded on that jagged rock. Emma on top of him, hitting him and yelling, 'I hate you! I hate you!' Again, he felt the twinge in his back and the pain of the serrated rock pressing there. It was only in his mind, but it felt real as he flexed his shoulders and back.

Ted moved to the edge of the cliff and looked down into the deep gully. Police removed the burnt car, but he could see the burnt and scorched shrubs and blacken rock where the car had exploded.

Then the memory appeared of her half out of the window with her foot still caught. He remembered his feet being dragged forward towards the edge along with Emma and the car. He looked around at the jagged rock. Yes, there it was. It still had dried blood on it and the ground. So, near the edge, so close to being dragged into the gully. The explosion would have meant a fiery death.

"Emma! Emma! Why did you want to kill yourself? You are too beautiful and innocent to contemplate such a thing," Ted yelled to the sky, his head back in anguish. Did he want to climb after all?

He looked down into the gully again. Something was glittering in the bit of sunlight escaping the clouds. Curiosity got him, and he decided to go down out of inquisitiveness. He attached the rope securely nearby with the prongs of the grappling hook holding well. He then started repelling the wall of the cliff. He had traversed about 3/4 of the cliff when he spotted a purse hanging by its strap to a bush growing out of the rocks in a crevice. He hooked it onto his belt, feeling it would turn out to be Emma's. Here was his excuse to see her again, he thought, with a light heart. Ted continued down the wall pushing out once again with his feet. He had done this same downward climb hundreds of times.

The waterfall was pouring thousands of gallons of water into the valley each day. He could feel the spray, a fine mist covering his arms and face. His shirt was getting damp but not wet.

Finally, he reached the ground. He released the rope and started walking to the area where the car had exploded. The severely burned shrubs and the rocks scorched to such an extent that the fire must have been very intense at the time of the explosion. Bits and pieces were scattered around. The police only took the main chassis and the larger pieces of debris.

Ted was looking around, trying to find what he had seen from above. The object that had been glinting in the sun. He raised his face towards the falls to feel the cooling moisture. As he did so, he saw something off to the left of the falls.

He could not reach it unless he crossed the water to the other side. He kept a raft that he had made for this express purpose anchored on shore not far from where he was standing. There was a long pole to control the raft across as the current of the fast-moving water. Otherwise, the swift current would quickly take him down the river. At this point, the river wasn't very wide.

He had perfected a method of digging in the pole and anchoring it midstream. Then he pulled with his weight until the raft was beside the pole then pushed his way to shore. An effective way to do this as the river was too deep to wade against the strong current.

Ted finally reached the other side. Then he twisted the pole until it came loose from the river bed. He jumped off the raft onto the far shore. He pulled the raft and pole onshore, tying them to a large shrub.

He started to climb over rocks and small shrubs towards the shiny metal object that had drawn his attention. He finally reached his objective. It was a hubcap from Emma's car. He discovered a pouch also. Ted wondered what the devil was inside. Did this belong to Emma? The string was hooked into the hubcap under the missing cap as though someone had put it inside for safekeeping.

He unhooked the pouch, opening it. To his amazement, some stones fell into his hand, glittering tiny rainbows in the sunlight. He couldn't be sure, but he felt they were real diamonds, many of immense size probably worth a fortune. Ted was no expert in gems, but he felt sure that they were worth maybe millions by the quantity in the bulging pouch. He stuffed the pouch into Emma's purse to keep it secure.

Did Emma know about the diamonds? Was Jimmy dealing in gems as well as embezzlement? Or was this put there for safekeeping by someone else? Was there more to Jimmy's story than Emma was aware? Was he using his sister to cover up for his nefarious deeds? Jimmy did sound so sincere, saying he wasn't involved when he came to see me.

Then his mind flew to Emma. Could she be in more trouble because of her demolished car? Would the person that put the diamonds there be after Emma, needing to know the details of her car's demise? Emma may be in danger and not know it. He was getting worried.

He checked the cliff and the surrounding area for any signs of movement by another human, but he saw nothing. Then he started scanning the area for more debris.

Ted found a wallet in his search, but when he opened it, he realized that it must have belonged to someone else. There were some pictures, but no identification, as though someone had emptied it. He shoved the wallet into his pocket. Ted hunted some more but found nothing more of interest.

The raft and pole were placed in the water to get back across the stream. This time the pole hadn't dug into the water bed securely. The raft sped downstream at a fast pace. He kept trying to dig the pole in, but he was going too rapidly. His arms were getting tired from his frantic jabs into the river bed. Where the river widened, the churning water was directing the raft towards the opposite side of the river. The raft bumped into a group of rocks protruding from the river bed. The speed of the current whirled the raft sideways towards the shore, throwing him off balance, but luckily with the help of the pole he recovered. The raft stayed anchored against a rock closer to shore. Grabbing the rope, he leaped off and landed in the water. He was close enough that he was able to take a couple of strokes to put him ashore.

He was now downstream by about 300 feet as the fast-moving water had quickly carried him away. He had lost the wallet from his pocket, but he didn't care. He reached in to check for his keys. They were still there. He was thankful that he had put the pouch in Emma's purse and not his pocket as it too would have been gone.

He pulled the raft and pole way up on shore then he removed his boots and socks. He wrung out his socks. He took off his pants and shirt, rung them out too. He would have to put them back on, but he wanted to get the excess moisture out. The cliff face was too jagged to ascend without the protection of clothes. That was why he was wearing such a thick shirt and pants on such a hot day.

He did not relish putting on wet clothes again, but he didn't want to wait around until they dried. He wanted out of that gully as soon as possible. He needed to hide the pouch in a safe place until he could find out what was going on. After dressing, he started hiking back towards the waterfall. He started into a half lope to get there sooner. When he happened to notice someone was standing on the cliff watching him. It was the detective again.

Ted pretended to stumble and fall as though he had stumbled by looking up. The purse was under his body as he rolled so that his back was towards the cliff, and he was up against a rock that had quite a crevice in it. He pretended he was hurt and was rocking himself.

When in fact he was getting the pouch out of the purse and pushing it in the rock crevasse. He would find the rock because he put a hanky that came from Emma's handbag into the crevice too.

Chapter Sixteen

Ted was still making a rocking motion and holding his arm as though injured. He dragged himself up with one hand protecting his other arm. He limped at first to slow his movements to give him time to think of a story. Reaching the base of the cliff where the rope was hanging, he yelled up.

"Can you hear me?"

A faint 'yes' came back.

"I've hurt my arm," he yelled louder. "Can you help pull me up?"

A louder yell came back. "Yes."

Ted was keeping up the charade to deter the detective. He grabbed the rope. Then he noticed that the line was slowly pulled upwards. He used his right hand to hold on and walked up the cliff with his booted feet. Like he was scaling a ramp rather than a jagged rock cliff. When he got to the top, he looked up to see two men there, the detective from the hospital and another man. That was why they had been able to pull him up so easily. He favored his so-called bad arm as they pulled him up onto the safe ground.

"Thank you," Ted said. "I don't know what I would have done if you hadn't been here. I hurt my arm when I fell looking up at you." No reply was forthcoming. "Well, detective, what are you here for?"

The detective pointed to the purse, "I see you found something."

"Yes, I think it is Emma's purse," Ted replied.

The detective inquired, "may I see it?"

Ted undid the purse from his belt. "I haven't had a chance to look inside yet," he stated.

"That's all right. We can look together." Ted handed the detective the purse.

Harding knelt and dumped the purse onto a vacant spot. Cosmetics, credit cards in a case, brush, comb, and change purse were on the ground. Also, there were some quarters, a lipstick, a notebook, and a pen.

The detectives seemed disappointed somehow as Ted started gathering things up, returning them to the purse. What were they hoping to find? Did they know about the gems? Did they wish to prove something about Emma with the contents of the purse? The purse was hers as the credit cards revealed. As he was putting things back in the bag, he felt a zippered pocket on the side of the purse, but he didn't let on.

"I want to return this to Emma, do you mind? She will probably be happy to have her credit cards and her makeup back."

"No, that's alright with me. How is your back now?"

"It still lets me know it was injured when I lay down. Otherwise, it is mostly fine. Come back to the house I want to get out of these wet clothes and put my arm in a sling." Ted started leading the way to the house. The two detectives looked at each other and followed him.

They had hoped the girl's purse would be more revealing as to what was on her mind that day with the cliff incident. They weren't buying her story or her family's that she was mentally disturbed.

Ted ignored the two men and went into the house and down the hall to the bathroom. He had taken off his boots and wet socks at the door and flung the socks over the back of a chair. He went into the bathroom and closed the door. He removed the rest of his clothes and climbed into the shower. He stood there, letting the water pour over him. They could wait until he was ready to speak to them. He was getting tired of their questions. He had said all that he intended to say.

The water felt good as it poured over his head and ran down his face. Ted finally shut off the water and dried himself. He slipped into his terrycloth robe then looked under the sink for a sling. He knew he had one in his first aid kit. After putting on the sling, he combed his hair and then tightened the belt on the robe. Opening the door, he could hear them in the living room.

Heading in that direction, Ted found the two detectives had made themselves at home. Harding was sitting on the sofa, the other in a chair. The one in the chair was smoking and flicking his ashes into a dish he had on the table for candies.

"Do you mind not smoking? I would appreciate it."

The detective ground out his butt in the pretty crystal candy dish, which was a keepsake from his mother. Ted was furious. He wanted to tell both of them to get out.

"What do you want?" He wanted them gone, so he curbed his anger.

"Well, Ted, we have a few questions. Do you remember any more details of the day the car went over the cliff?"

"I said no, and I mean no," his voice very firm.

"What were you looking for down in the gully?"

"Nothing I rock climb regularly. Then I hike the gully. I do it often. I just happened to find Emma's purse is all."

"Did you find anything else?"

"Yes, a hubcap, but I didn't bother bringing it up," he replied honestly.

"How did you get wet? I know you didn't go swimming."

"I was crossing the river when the raft got swept away in the fast current, and a boulder stopped the raft. I had to swim to shore with the raft rope in my hand. It was difficult to keep dry," he said coldly.

"Are you seeing Emma Gibson?"

"No, I haven't had any contact with her since the accident."

"I find that odd that you had two operations, and she never bothered to contact you?"

"You said, Emma. I have not seen nor heard from her. Her brother Jimmy visited me in the hospital and thanked me for saving his twin sister."

"Why wouldn't Emma contact you?"

Ted said, "Jimmy said she was mentally disturbed and under doctor's care. I accepted that, so I did not try to contact her." He rubbed his head like he had a headache.

"If you don't mind, I think I will take a couple of aspirin and lay down. I am still not up to par from my operations. And I don't feel well after the fall. My arm is paining me." He lifted the sling as though calling their attention to the fact that he was hurt.

The two detectives exchanged looks, then got to their feet as if they were resigned to his refusal to help. "By the way, Ted, when will you be going back to work?" The smoker detective queried, as though he had to justify his part in the investigation somehow.

"Well, I was going back on Monday, but now I'm not sure. It will depend on how badly I hurt my arm." Rubbing it for effect.

Ted was much happier after they had gone. What did they expect me to find in the gully? They asked questions, but they never gave back any clues.

Ted was surprised when they let him keep Emma's purse. Maybe they were hoping I would make contact. Perhaps they thought I was in on whatever was developing, after all, he worked at the docks too.

When he got ready for bed that night, he felt tired and used up. He hadn't completely recovered from his sojourn to the hospital. As he lay down on his back, it was throbbing. He got up and took two aspirins. He was never going to get to sleep if he didn't quit thinking about Emma, the car, the brother, or the diamonds.

The diamonds changed the whole picture. Someone must be looking for them. Were they aware the car was demolished by the explosion?

Ted turned over, putting on the lamp. He got up to get Emma's purse. He wanted to see what was in the zipper part. He brought the purse back into the bedroom. He dumped the things out on the bedside table. Then he looked through the notebook. It was messages of appointments, dinner dates, and significant occasions such as birthdays, etc. Grabbing the purse, he felt for the zippered area to find it contained keys, driver's license, and some pictures. There was one of Emma and her brother, Jimmy.

She was the picture of innocence. He found it hard to link her to all this intrigue. Jimmy looked too clean-cut to be involved either. There was a card noting an appointment at the dentist on Tuesday.

Ted scooped up the things dropped them back into the purse except for the picture of Emma and her brother. He leaned the photo up against the lamp. He laid back down again, looking at the picture with interest. Ted sighed. Despite all that had happened, he did want to see this girl again. He thought he would try once more when she kept her appointment on Tuesday.

He had to get back down into the gully and retrieve the gems. Someone might be watching the place he thought it best to wait. He wasn't about to tempt fate, so someone else could take the diamonds.

"Goodnight, Emma," Ted said as he looked at her picture then put out the lamp. The aspirins were working. He felt that he could sleep now.

* * *

Her father insisted she rest. Emma was having no success in sleeping. Where was Jimmy? What could she do? Why hadn't she told her father sooner?

She kept turning from side to side, but her thoughts were going with her. How would they find Jimmy? Could he be injured? Are they torturing him? Are they going to kill him? Is he already dead?

No, he couldn't be, they were too close. She would feel it, wouldn't she? This latest thought was making her lay there, concentrating on Jimmy. She lay there waiting. Emma didn't even feel a twinge. Either he is asleep, or else nothing is occurring at this moment.

* * *

Jimmy was not asleep. He was unconscious. Someone had put drugs into his food, unbeknownst to him. He was laid out on the bunk. Someone was rifling through his pockets. There were voices in the room murmuring about him, wondering just how much he knew?

"It was a good thing Mr. Gibson didn't know he was here," Captain Jorgensen said.

The other man said, "I've got to find the girl's car. It hasn't been in the parking lot for a week or more. I will have to go to her place if she doesn't show up soon." The plan was to recover the diamonds from the car when the Belle Star was ready to leave port. Then the money would change hands, but now he didn't even know where the car or the girl was. He had been keeping clear of the docks but watching the parking lot through binoculars. He had not seen the girl or her car recently. "I don't know why the girl hasn't been here. I could find out from Alan, he must know. But I don't want Alan to know any more than he already does. He is useful but not reliable. He is to be our patsy. I don't want him to spill anything under pressure. The less he knows, the better."

"You will have to go to her place. You know where. It is your friend's place," said Captain Jorgensen. "Come on. We better get out of here before he becomes conscious. We'll keep him drugged until we get to sea." He led the way out of the cabin and down the corridor.

Captain Jorgensen glared at the man, as he was not happy with the fact that he had lost the diamonds, a severe setback. "Can you guarantee you will come up with the lost merchandise before I am ready to sail?" asked Jorgensen angrily.

"I had better, or heads will roll, and mine will be the first. When can I get back to you without being seen?"

"The best time to come is midnight. The night watchman does his rounds about then. Park away from here and walk. Make sure you aren't followed, now that we have a hostage. I think the traffic here might increase," Captain Jorgensen said worriedly.

"Now that you have him, what are you going to do with him?" the young man asked with some guilt.

"That is for me to know, you will be in the clear on that account as you will not know what happens to him. Now try to leave after the night watchman walks away again."

* * *

Malvin was on the phone to Charlie again. This time he answered on the third ring.

"What's going on down there?"

"I don't know Mr. Gibson, but whatever it is, I don't feel right about it," Charlie said apprehensively.

"Has anyone left the ship or gone on it?"

"Not that I saw. But there is a lot of movement for a skeleton crew."

"Charlie, I have been thinking about the cars in the parking lot.

Can you go out and write down a description and take the license numbers? I am going to get Roger to drive me down to pick up Jimmy's car, so I should see you within the hour."

"Sure thing, Mr. Gibson, but there is only one left. Two left while I was doing rounds. I will go out right now. See you soon." Charlie headed over to the parking lot. He heard the sound of a car leaving. He ran to see if he could catch a look at it, but all he saw was the receding taillights, and the gate was open." He walked over to it. Whoever had left had broken the lock, which wouldn't make Mr. Gibson very happy.

* * *

When Emma got up the next day, she felt un-refreshed. The night had been extra long. "Jimmy, where are you?" she asked plaintively. She rose from her chair before the dressing table where she had sunk in despair. She had to have a shower, get dressed, and then look for her father.

Emma glided down the stairs and put her head into the breakfast room, but her father wasn't there. She quickly went towards the place her father used as his office. Approaching the stairs, she looked up and saw her father was descending. He looked like he had just come from a shower, his hair was still damp but combed back in its usual waves.

"Daddy, did you find out anything else last night?" she asked hopefully.

"No, Emma, Charlie was too late to get a description of the cars, that may be involved in this. I could kick myself for not paying closer attention yesterday when I was there."

"Daddy, when are you going to call in the police?"

"Soon, darling soon. It hasn't been 24 hours yet."

"Daddy, I have tried to detect any feeling as to whether Jimmy is hurt, the close twin connection. But I got nothing as though he is asleep."

"Emma, that probably is the case. It seems logical they drugged him. But I hope not for his sake. I brought home Jimmy's car and looked through it thoroughly with Roger, but we found nothing that would help. We're not going to find him by sitting here, but I think we should wait a little longer before we call in the police. I am going down to the docks to see if I can find out anything with Cliff's help. We can start by asking more questions. We have to keep searching. What are you going to do today, Emma?" Malvin queried.

"I want to go with you, Daddy."

"No, you're staying away from the docks until this mess is cleared up, and Jimmy is safely at home. You can phone around to Jimmy's friends and see if anyone has seen him."

Emma replied, "Coulter didn't have any success last night, but not too many were at home. Also, Beth phoned, she is pretty upset. I doubt that she will have gone to work today."

Emma hugged her father. He closed his arms around her and dropped a kiss on the top of her head. She had tears in her eyes but held back from crying.

"Daddy, what are you going to do if we can't find him?"

"Now, don't you even think that way. We will have Jimmy home in no time," he said although he did not believe that. "Emma come on, we better try to eat something or Matilda will be after both of our hides. Come with me." He put his arm around her shoulders so they could walk together into the breakfast room.

Matilda was waiting for them with a coffee pot in her hand. There was juice on the table and silver covered lids on the plates. She looked at both of them with sadness in her heart. They were hurting, and so was she. "Eat up both of you. I want to see both of those plates empty. You both ate like sparrows last night. You will find Jimmy. Nothing can happen to separate you, Emma." She was trying to sound positive to give them the courage they needed.

"Thank you, Matilda," Malvin said but couldn't bring himself to say more. He picked up his coffee cup. It was good and strong just how he liked it. He knew he had to make an effort to eat because Matilda was standing right beside him.

She had removed the silver plate warmers. "Now, eat both of you."

Emma looked at her father, then picked up her fork and started to eat from the plate. After she took a mouthful, she realized how hungry she was. She looked across and noticed her father was eating with gusto too.

Matilda was content to see that her words were obeyed. She left the room. When she got back to the kitchen, she stood leaning against the counter and flung out her hands in despair. "Where are you, Jimmy? Please come home," she whispered.

* * *

Ted was up, dressed with a purpose. He was going to go back down to retrieve the pouch. He couldn't wait. He would look around thoroughly before descending the cliff. He would take his backpack and sit on the rock beside the crevice and have his coffee. While sitting there, transfer the pouch into his knapsack.

He felt that he couldn't take the chance of leaving the valuables down there. He hoped the detectives from yesterday didn't arrive as he couldn't climb with a sling on, and they would know that he had only pretended his arm was hurt. He only used the fall as cover to put the pouch in the crevice undetected.

He had breakfast then made fresh coffee for his thermos. He got his backpack and packed it with a blue nylon bag that held a T-shirt and socks. He was going to hide the pouch in the bag. After his backpack was ready, he went out to look around. He sauntered down the drive as if he was out for a stroll. He stopped to pick some weeds. Then he picked up a small rock and threw it in the direction of the shed as if he was doing target practice.

He glanced around casually and discovered three little birds harassing a crow. The squawking was a piercing cry of anger as they swooped and dived.

There was no one in sight, so he walked back to the house. He heard the phone ringing. He went into the house, moving swiftly. It was Tommy.

"Ted, how are you? Are you recovering, okay? Well enough to be heading back into work?"

"Hi, Tommy. I am fine. I was getting ready to do some cliff climbing. Yes, I am hoping to go back to work on Monday, all going well."

"Ted, why don't you wait for me? I will go climbing with you," Tommy asked, anxiously. He thought it was too soon and Ted shouldn't be climbing alone.

"Look, Tommy, I am all ready to go, but come if you like. You can come down into the gully. I will be back to meet you by the waterfall at about the same time you should get here. I was climbing yesterday. I have the rope well anchored. You should be okay getting down."

"Why can't you wait for me? I will leave right away."

Ted didn't want Tommy around while he retrieved the pouch. He didn't intend to tell him about it either.

"I am not going to sit on my duff waiting until you get here. I promise to be careful. I will be waiting at the bottom of the rope when you get here. I have made some coffee and have it in a thermos with me. We will hike a bit, then sit and have a coffee before we scale the cliff again," Ted said firmly.

"Okay, buddy, but you better be there when I arrive, you hear?"

"Yes, brother, I hear you." Ted chuckled and hung up the phone.

He headed for the door, grabbing his backpack off the chair. He had extra clothes this time although he shouldn't get wet as he didn't intend to cross the river.

Chapter Seventeen

Emma was sitting talking on the phone. She was wiping the tears from her eyes as she listened to Beth crying on the other end. "Beth, we will find him. We have to. I couldn't survive if he didn't come home." She swiped her hand across her cheek, where the tears were running down in rivulets. She wished she had a box of tissue close by, but she didn't want to hang up when Beth was crying so hard.

Then Beth said, "Emma, do you think I could come over?"

"Of course. Beth, you know you are always welcome."

"Emma, do you think he has run away to get clear of me? I thought we were getting on fine, but this thought ran through my head several times during the night. I don't know why?"

"Beth no, he loves you. He was looking forward to your dinner date when he left yesterday morning." Beth could be heard crying more deeply.

"Beth, you had better not attempt to drive, you are too upset. I will send Roger over to get you. Wait for him, okay?"

Beth's reply came out muffled in sobs. "Yes." Then the phone went dead.

Emma passed the information to Roger. Going into the kitchen, she told Matilda there would be two for lunch as Beth was coming. Matilda was glad Emma would have someone with her to help pass the day.

Emma went back into the study to get the disk that Jimmy had brought home and put it into the computer. She took the list from Jimmy's open briefcase. The list had the names marked with asterisks. Then she paged down on the info on the screen. She scanned the accounts for shipping information for these bogus accounts. A pattern was forming. They were all carried by the Belle Star. Then she called up the third bogus company. Sure enough, the carrier was the Belle Star. Was this the link they were hoping to find? Perhaps this was what Jimmy had discovered? He said he felt he was getting close to an answer. Could this be what we are searching for, and the Belle Star is involved?

Emma picked up the phone and dialed the shipping office. Alan lifted the phone after greetings passed between them, she asked for her father.

Alan said, "he is out on the docks somewhere. Do you want me to have him call you when he comes in?"

"Yes, please do that." Why had Alan not mentioned Jimmy? He must know that he is missing. Did he have something to do with his disappearance?

"Alan, when did you last see Jimmy?"

"Emma, like I told your father. I haven't seen him since Thursday although I saw his car in the parking lot yesterday," Alan said with a strained voice. He was disturbed for her, knowing how upset she was, and he felt guilty for lying.

"Thank you, Alan. I'll wait by the phone for Daddy's call."

"I will tell him as soon as I see him. I could go out and see if I can find him. I see Cliff but not your father." Alan put down the phone. Upon opening the door, he called, "Cliff, do you know where Malvin is?" Cliff pointed down in the direction of the Belle Star, but Alan couldn't see him.

"Cliff, can you tell him Emma wants him to call her." Alan went back into the office and sat down. There was a definite slump to his shoulders. When he got into this situation, he never realized it would come to the disappearance of Jimmy. He was sure Jimmy had found out something by the way he had been acting Thursday. Other than to say good morning, he hadn't talked to him on Friday. Why did I deny seeing him to both Emma and her father?

The only reason he got involved was Lucy's medications were costing a fortune. He had no other way to provide them. What should I do now? Should I confess? Does anyone know that I am involved? No one has said anything to me. Surely if they suspected me, they would have said something.

He picked up the phone and called home. Lucy answered cheerfully, knowing it would be Alan. The drugs were helping, but not fast enough, she was still quite ill. They talked, then he said he would be home as soon as possible. He put his face in his hands. A shudder racked his body. He couldn't say anything about his involvement. Lucy was too vital to him. She would stop taking the drugs if she ever found out what he had done. Besides, who would take care of her if he went to jail. He straightened up just before the door opened, and Malvin came in. Alan looked at him expectantly.

"Did Emma want me to call right back?" Malvin asked.

"Yes, she said she would sit right by the phone, awaiting your call."

Malvin could see Alan was upset about something, but Alan didn't let on what was bothering him. He knew Alan was involved, hoping he would do the decent thing and come forward to help. Alan picked up a pen, starting to write. No help was forthcoming. A disappointed Malvin headed into his office and shut the door.

"Emma, did you need me? Is everything okay?"

"Daddy, I was going over the disk that Jimmy brought home and the list from Jimmy's briefcase. I came up with some information I thought you might like to know."

"What is that?" implored Malvin.

"Well, those two bogus companies from the list, I asked the computer whom the carrier of the shipments was, and the answer came up the Belle Star for both of them. Then I checked the third bogus company. The carrier was the Belle Star too. Do you think the Belle Star and Jimmy's disappearance are linked? That ship has been in dock since Thursday, hasn't it?"

"Yes, Emma. It does sound strange. That must have been what Jimmy discovered before his disappearance. Can you print off the invoices, dates of shipping, and the carriers? I will need them for evidence to obtain a search warrant for the Belle Star. It is time to get the police involved. Thanks, you did well."

"I have been questioning the stevedores, but I haven't come up with anything except that Jimmy did go on the Belle Star yesterday, but they saw him get off again. Nobody could recall where he went after that." Malvin's voice was trying to be hearty, but he certainly didn't feel that way. "Emma, I have to go now. I have some more men I want to question."

"Daddy, I love you." Emma put in quickly as her father hung up.

* * *

Ted's trip down the jagged cliff face was speedy and without incident. He got started on the trek to where he had left the pouch. He felt sure he could spot it easily enough with a white hanky in the crevice. He knew all the rocks looked the same, just different sizes and shapes. This valley had a lot of them.

After he managed to locate the rock formation, he could easily see the white hanky. He was relieved that he had made the decision not to wait. He sat down on the rock and opened his backpack and took out the thermos. He poured a cup of coffee. The steam rose in the air. He took a drink and put his head back as if he was enjoying the sun on his face between sips.

He was checking out the clifftop. No one was in sight. Then he looked over the rim of the cup as he'd changed his position on the rock as if it was bothering him. He took another drink and again looked over the rim. Still, no one in sight, so he put his backpack on the ground by the crevice. Flicking out the coffee dregs returned the lid to the thermos. Holding the flap up, with his other hand, he reached into the crevice for the hanky and the pouch. He slid them into the knapsack at the same time as he pushed the thermos inside.

He reached in as though rearranging the bottle and pushed the pouch inside the blue nylon bag burying it inside the clothes. Then he pulled the string closure. Then he looked at his watch and realized he had to get back for Tommy.

He stood up and shouldered the backpack feeling a twinge as his back was still tender. He started to walk towards the waterfall.

Looking up, he saw Tommy waving at him. He launched into a half trot as that was all the terrain would allow.

Tommy was checking the rope to make sure it was still appropriately lodged. He stood looking down. He was not as experienced as his brother. But he did enjoy it. Ted had made good time. He was almost back to the rope. He stood there watching Tommy repelling down. "Ted, what took you so long? You are out of shape." Tommy yelled with laughter.

Ted yelled back. "What's the matter afraid to come down without me to catch you?" He was only bantering with his brother because he knew he was quite capable of getting down. It was the going up that was Tommy's difficulty.

"Well, brother, are you still good for a hike," asked Tommy.

"I'll outdo you anytime. I'm not that decrepit yet. Not even my back will slow me down." He turned to stride out, leaving Tommy to catch up. They were both healthy specimens, Ted as stevedore and Tommy, a construction worker.

"Are you going back to work tomorrow?"

"My back feels pretty good, just the odd twinge to let me know it is tender. That is why I have been climbing these last two days trying to get my strength back."

The two brothers were striding out at a good pace, something they had both done many times over the years since Ted bought the place. After they had been walking for a while, they heard voices up ahead. They looked for the individuals to go with the voices. Eventually, they could see three boys skipping stones on the far shore some ways down the river.

"Tommy, my raft is down there, almost in line with the boys. I want to retrieve it. I left it there yesterday when I got carried downstream in the fast current. I got soaked when I had to swim ashore to get the raft out of the current. So naturally, I got wet, all I could think about was getting back, and get my wet clothes off. I didn't have any spare dry clothes in my backpack."

"I take it now you have dry clothes in there now." He patted Ted's pack.

"Yes, after the fact."

When they recovered the raft and pole, the boys were yelling at them. "Can we borrow your raft?"

"Afraid not. The current is too fast, and it would only carry you down the river. You boys, be careful, don't go into the water," Ted yelled.

"Okay, my dad warned me of the same thing," said the blond boy in reply.

Ted put the raft into the water with Tommy's help. They both took the rope and started pulling it along the shore. Tommy was doing most of the pulling. Ted was mostly guiding it to keep it close to shore. But the speedy current was dragging against their efforts, so it was harder to maneuver than it appeared. After a while, Ted pulled it up on the bank with Tommy's help.

They sat down on the ground. Tommy took off his backpack and pulled out a bottle of water. Ted took his off and removed the coffee. Tommy handed the water to Ted. He took a swig and gave it back. Ted, in return, gave him a coffee.

Tommy set down his coffee and dipped his hand in the water and sluiced it up over his face and neck. "Hey, that's refreshing. You should try it."

Ted reached down and did the same thing. Then he flicked a handful at Tommy.

Tommy laughed. "Do you ever think about Emma?"

"Yes, I do. Too much, I guess, as I haven't heard from Emma since I had the second operation."

"Do you intend to see her?"

"Yes, I intend on seeing her, but I don't know when at the moment."

"I doubt they will let you in the gate at her place after the way they treated Sally and me. They have it closed up like Fort Knox."

"I have her purse. There is a card mentioning she has an appointment with the dentist on Tuesday. I am thinking of meeting her there," Ted said forcefully.

"How can you if you are going back to work?"

"I will take time off if necessary. I have to see Emma." Ted flipped the excess coffee out of his cup before he returned it to his backpack.

"Time to go."

Once again, they put the raft in the water and continued upstream, dragging the raft along with them. Finally, they reached the place where Ted secured the raft. They lifted it effortlessly onto the shore and tied it to its anchoring bolt.

Then the two men headed for the dangling rope. Ted took the easy way, which wasn't like him, as he was like a spider scaling the cliff usually. He climbed it with ease, and then he aided Tommy in his ascent, pulling up the rope as Tommy walked the cliff face.

Ted wound up the rope and hook and headed for the house. The phone was ringing. Ted sprang across the yard in haste, leaping on the veranda and sped inside, grabbing the phone.

"Hello."

"Hello, is this, Ted Maxwell?"

"Yes."

"This is Emma."

"Emma?" Ted froze in place. She sounded either shy or scared. He couldn't quite figure it out. "Hi, Emma, how are you?"

"Ted, I have not been well," she said in a faint voice.

"I am sorry to hear that." Ted waited.

"Ted... Jimmy..." He could hear her start to cry. She was having difficulties talking.

"What is the matter, Emma?" Ted asked soothingly.

"Ted, Jimmy is missing." Emma was crying in earnest now

"Emma, what are you saying? Try to stop crying. I thought you said Jimmy is missing."

"Ted, oh... I... don't know what to do."

Ted didn't know how to handle this sobbing girl. What to say now?

He finally heard her taking deep breaths as though she was trying to control her crying. "Ted, he went missing Friday. He was looking into the embezzlement problem. I was last talking to him on Friday morning. He said he almost had it figured out." Her voice was still meek but stronger.

"Emma, what did he figure out, did he say?"

'No, Jimmy was quite secretive. He wouldn't let me tell Daddy either. Now we don't know where he is. I don't know what to do anymore. I called everyone I could think of, and nobody has seen him."

"You know Emma, he might have gone off somewhere without mentioning it," Ted said helpfully.

"No, Ted. He had a dinner date with Beth, his girlfriend, and another couple on Friday night. He wouldn't miss that without letting someone know." Emma's voice was getting stronger, thank goodness.

"Emma, do you want me to come over?" asked Ted casually.

"Ted, I would like you to come. Beth is coming. We will be useless together with the way she has been crying on the phone. I don't want to sit here and cry anymore. Please come."

"All right, Emma. I will be there after I shower. I have been rock climbing," Ted replied.

"Hurry, Ted. I live at..." He heard her talking to someone in the background Beth must have arrived.

"Emma, I will have a quick shower and be right over. Tommy's here. He knows the address. You look after Beth. I will be there as soon as possible."

"Ted, thanks, I'll be waiting for you."

He broke the connection and turned to Tommy.

"I guess you heard that was Emma. She is pretty upset. Jimmy was investigating the embezzlement. Now he has disappeared."

Tommy looked at Ted. He could see his deep concern. "Embezzlement? So that is what this is all about. What can I do?"

"Just write down the address and how to get there." He called over his shoulder, heading for the bathroom while undressing on the way. He entered the shower quickly soaped and rinsed himself so fast some of the suds were still clinging to his body. He grabbed a towel, speedily dried himself. He entered the bedroom. He threw the wet towel on the chair, sloppily discarded. Ted grabbed clothes to wear in his haste. He walked back into the kitchen, buttoning his shirt.

"Thanks for going with me today, Tommy." Ted tucked his shirt into his jeans. "Do you have that address for me? You can stay and have a shower if you want, but I am leaving. Just lock up when you finish." Ted grabbed the piece of paper with the directions, heading for the door.

Ted remembered the backpack. He reversed direction and grabbed it, and went into the spare bedroom, putting it in a lockbox against the bottom of the bed. He piled additional bedding on top of it. Turning the key and placing the key under the mattress in his hurry.

Tommy was looking at him strangely when he came back into the kitchen. "What was that all about? I thought you were in a hurry?"

"I had some wet clothes in there. I thought I had better take them out of the backpack before they got smelly." Ted didn't look at his brother as he lied to him. Then he raced out of the house and lopped to the car and quickly sped away.

Tommy headed for the shower. He was pulling off his clothes when he entered the bathroom. He glanced around but didn't see the knapsack or the wet clothes. That was odd. Then he thought maybe he had hung them over a chair in the bedroom and thought nothing more about them as he turned on the shower.

Chapter Eighteen

Ted arrived at Emma's in good time. He pressed the buzzer on the gate. A male voice asked who he was. "Ted Maxwell for Emma. She invited me." The gate swung open as it was a well-maintained electronic device.

He drove up to the house. Emma must have been watching out the window. By the time he got out of his car and walked the stairs, Emma was standing in the open doorway. Her cheeks held tears. Emma stood there, looking at him. He was taller and more muscular than she remembered.

"Hello, Emma."

"Hello, Ted. Oh uh... please come in." Emma was overwhelmed by his height. She felt petite as she craned her head to look up at him. "Why are we standing here? I should be inviting you into the living room. Oh no... we should go into the study where Beth is." Emma didn't know why she was acting this way. She usually was very decisive.

"Do you want something to drink, Ted?" she asked as they cleared the door into the study.

"No, Emma, not right now." Ted walked over to the sofa where another girl was sitting. She had red-rimmed eyes.

"I take it you are Beth. I am Ted. Ted Maxwell," he said as he held out his hand. She placed her hand in his.

Emma came over and stood beside him. "Beth, would you like some tea or coffee?"

Beth looked up at Emma. "Yes, please, tea would be nice."

When Emma re-entered the room, Ted was standing talking to Beth getting to know her. Emma came over and sat beside Beth. Ted sat in a chair across from them.

"Emma, now tell me everything you know," he suggested gently.

Emma's eyes filled with tears, but she swallowed hard and held them back.

"After I came home from Tommy's, I told Jimmy what I suspected. He was horrified that I could think he was capable of such a thing. Then he said the same as you did that even if I had succeeded, there would have been an audit. I would have died, needlessly." Emma's voice was getting sturdier.

"Go on, Emma, what then?"

"Well, he said he wanted to look into the situation himself, not letting Daddy know. The fact that I was laid up with my ankle..." Emma paused, looking guiltily at Ted then rushed on. "It was a good opportunity for him to be in my office accessing my computer. He discovered the same thing I had and copied the information to a disk and brought it home for us to study more."

She paused. She knew she would eventually have to acknowledge her foolish escapade. Her messages to him, 'I hate you! I hate you!' needed an apology.

Ted sat, watching Emma realizing she was under some discomfort with him being there. He decided it was time to ease her mind by discussing the situation.

"Emma, I know you are feeling guilty about what happened, but it would be best if we put that behind us and concentrate on Jimmy and his problem."

Emma sighed with relief. "Ted, I feel terrible about how I treated you after you saved me. Hitting you and yelling, 'I hate you.' I know now how foolish I was. You saved me. I wasn't even grateful. I am sorry. I am glad now that you saved me," Emma said as if she didn't think he would forgive her.

"Listen, Emma. You didn't know what you were doing. You were in shock. I want you to forget that. We need to concentrate on Jimmy. I have put that all behind me. I think you should too, okay?"

She looked as though a significant weight was removed from her shoulders.

"Emma, when your Dad comes, do you think he will object to my being here? He didn't seem too happy about me when I saw him last."

"That's because I said that I didn't want to have anything to do with you. He wants to protect me and consider my wishes. He doesn't know all the details of the situation," Emma stated.

"Emmy, back to Jimmy."

"We were viewing the accounts and found a pattern. On Friday, Jimmy went into the office after telling me at breakfast that he was sure he had a lead but wanted to check one more thing. I begged him to tell Daddy, but he refused. He went into the office, and no one has seen him after that except for a couple of stevedores. They said they saw him board the Belle Star but that he left the ship half an hour later."

"Then nobody seemed to recall seeing him after that, but his car was still there at the end of the day. He had just disappeared." Emma's voice trailed off just as Matilda arrived with the tea cart. Matilda picked one already poured tea, taking it over to Beth. "Sweetie, I fixed this special for you." Beth murmured her thanks and started sipping the tea thankfully.

Ted asked, "where is your father? Does he know what is going on now?"

"Yes, I told Daddy when Jimmy went missing on Friday. He is down at the docks questioning the dock workers."

"Have you any inkling who else is involved?"

"Yes, Alan, one of our employees. Jimmy and Daddy hesitate to question him because they think he is probably an accomplice in a minor way. They feel if they question him, it will get back to whoever is doing this, and they will disappear." Emma finished lamely.

"Is there anything else?"

"Daddy wants to have the police issue a search warrant to board the Belle Star, which seems to be involved. But he doesn't have enough evidence to have the police issuing one. Also, Jimmy isn't considered missing for 24 hours, which is after 5:00 today."

"I have been recording dates, invoices, shipments, and time of arrival of the ship Belle Star from the bills of lading, over the period these two bogus companies have been active."

Ted was contemplating phoning the shipping office to talk to her father but thought better of it. What would be the best way to handle this? Maybe Colin would help him out. The two of them were seen on the dock daily. He felt the Belle Star was the likely place to find Jimmy also but how to get aboard without tipping their hand.

He didn't know how strict the Captain was with his crew. Sometimes the men were allowed to have poker games rather than getting drunk and disorderly in town. He and Colin could easily pull that off, having attended poker games on other ships these past years but never on the Belle Star.

"Emma, I think I will go down to the docks. But first I'm going to call my friend Colin. I don't know if he is working or not today. Can I use your phone?"

"Sure, it is over on the desk in the corner. Help yourself." Emma was acting much better towards him. He was glad they had cleared the air between them. He got up and walked over to the desk and picked up the phone.

A voice answered after two rings, he asked for Colin. They replied, "he is working today." Ted was happy about that because now he would enlist Colin's help.

"Emma, I'm going to leave now. If your father phones let him know I am going to look for him to discuss Jimmy. Are you and Beth going to be okay?" Beth now sat quietly. The tea must have done some good because she was looking better.

"Yes, we will be okay, won't we Beth?" She looked over at her for confirmation.

Beth nodded her head. Emma stood up and followed him to the door.

"Ted, I want to thank you for helping me. Daddy hasn't called since mid-morning, so I don't think he has found Jimmy. I hope you find him."

"If he is down at the docks, I will find him. I will meet up with Colin there. It is more natural for us to be on the docks than your father." He reassured her. "We'll find Jimmy."

Emma stood in the doorway, watching him leave. She felt better already. After the car disappeared through the gate, she closed the door and went back to Beth. Her steps were lighter. "Beth, would you like some more tea? Now, all we can do is wait."

* * *

Ted knew of a fast route to the docks. He headed into the parking lot, hoping to find a vacant spot now that the day was almost over for some dock workers. Their hours were staggered. The first ones on duty should be leaving soon.

He found a place finally near the dock area. He got out of the car and looked around. The Belle Star wasn't lying low in the water, so either she had been almost unloaded or was awaiting her new cargo for loading.

If the last was right, they should be sailing soon, so they didn't have much time. Ted didn't know whether to find Colin first or Mr. Gibson. It was decided for him when he walked away from the parking lot. Emma's father walked towards him. His head was down as though he was deep in thought. Ted headed for him. Malvin must have heard something because his head came up, and his eyes met Ted's.

"Hello, Mr. Gibson."

"What are you doing here?" He knew it was Ted, the man from the hospital.

"Emma called me. She wants me to help find Jimmy. I hope you don't mind? I am a stevedore. I work in this area of the docks, so it'll be natural for me to be here. I am going to enlist my friend Colin to help me." He paused to see how Gibson was taking it.

"Well, I think I could sure use your help." He stuck out his hand as if to say let bygones be bygones. Ted took his hand, shaking it firmly.

"Emma has filled me in on most of what is going on. What have you found out today, if anything?"

"Not much no one seems to have seen him after he came off the Belle Star yesterday, at least no one is talking. I don't know which," he said in exasperation.

"Will you give me a free hand to do what I think is necessary?" Ted asked.

"Anything I just want my son back," he replied with a heavy heart.

"I know you and Jimmy felt there was no point in questioning Alan. But I think maybe there is. Has he worked for you long?"

"Yes, Alan has worked fifteen years for the company. But I know he is a minor player in this," replied Malvin.

"Still, he might be just scared enough with Jimmy missing to let something out. I think I will strike up a conversation with him when I get a chance."

"Okay if that is what you think. I am just thankful for your help," Malvin said, still doubting having Alan questioned.

"How long has the Belle Star been here?" inquired Ted.

"It has been here since Thursday. It is just about ready for loading and will be sailing on Tuesday." Malvin said. "There are funny goings-on regarding that ship," he added.

"Emma mentioned, the facts seem to point towards that ship. But you said Jimmy was seen going on and getting off again."

"Yes, that was what the men said that were working in the area that day."

"Well, I think I will try to talk to some of the crew," Ted said. "in the hopes of getting on that ship. Maybe get a poker game going or something."

"Well, good luck. I had no success. Captain Jorgensen let me on the ship, but he never left my side. He curtailed my search. I think he is involved in this mess, but I can't prove it."

"I am going to check in on my friend Colin and see if I can recruit his help. Are you going to stick around here?"

"Yes, I'll be in my office, but I don't think you should come there. I will meet you back near the gate in about 2 hours."

"Okay." They both noted the time was 5:30 on their watches.

Malvin kept heading to the shipping office while Ted continued down the dock.

He was not able to make contact with Colin right away. The guy's joking comments were stopping him. "Are you a man of leisure now? Do you plan on working someday? Since when did an itty-bitty sore back require time off." He gradually surmised the scuttlebutt passed around was about a bit of a sore back, but no mention of operations.

When he finally got away from the friendly ribbing, he went

looking once again for Colin. He found him further down the dock talking to one of the Port Authorities. Colin looked up. Ted was walking towards them.

"Hey, buddy, what are you doing here? I didn't think you would be back so soon. Tommy said you were really banged up and would be off until next week sometime."

"Call me Superman. I bounced back sooner than I thought."

"Welcome back, by the way, how are you?"

"Fine. Are you on the late shift or early shift?"

The Port Authority fellow interrupted. "I will leave you now. Welcome back, Ted. I need to see about a problem over on the next dock."

"Is there something the matter over there?" Ted asked in all innocence.

"It seems some activities are calling attention to the Belle Star. They want me to give her the once over. Nothing for sure reported," the man stated. "See you guys." He lifted his hand in a wave as he walked away.

Turning back to Colin. "Well, are you on the early shift?"

"Yes, I am leaving now, but I have to punch out first. Are you down here for a reason?"

"Yes, I need to talk to you, but in the meantime, I'll wander around until you get off shift."

"Are we going for a beer?"

"No, we will hang around here for a while. You will understand when I explain. I will meet you back here."

Colin said okay as he walked away. His friend sounded secretive.

Ted kept on towards where the ship Clancy II was docked. There was lots of activity going on there as if it had just arrived in port. Nearing the ship, he started getting comments of 'there is the shirker now.'

"Hi, Ted. How is the man of leisure, goofing off as usual?"

Laughing good-naturedly, Ted responded. "Hi, guys just a man of leisure that is for sure. Just thought I would come down and watch you work." He stood in a relaxed stance, watching them. When the men's attention went back to unloading, Ted eased over to Larry and asked him, "is there any news going around here, any rumors? I just want to get caught up on the scuttlebutt. I miss the group down here. You know how it is," Ted said as if he hadn't a care in the world.

"Well, it appears to be rumors are about the Belle Star. Something about some men on it that shouldn't be there or something. The crew isn't talking. I met up with a couple of them at the bar over on Craig St, and they clamped up when I queried it. Other than that, just the same old stuff load, unload, load, unload," he said laughingly. "Oh yeah. I also got wind of some executive that was missing. They say he ran off with some blond bimbo and must have tied one on because he hasn't shown up yet. But I don't know anything other than that. The executive probably is shacked up for a while, and his old lady is looking for him." Larry was the kind of guy who'd like to embellish stories.

Ted tried not to look too interested. He wanted to let on that he was missing the job and only passing the time of day.

The news about Jimmy running off, Ted wondered who started that one. He walked over to another man who appeared to be new.

"Hi, I'm Ted. I haven't seen you around here before."

"I'm Cal. No, I just started last week. I haven't seen you either," he replied friendly-like.

"Do you know anyone else that has just started new?" Ted was curious why this man was here because he didn't look like he belonged.

"Not that I know. The Union Office sent me over. I usually work on construction jobs, but they switched me from my local to the Union for stevedores and other dock workers. Probably a mix up in paperwork by some office flunky," he added. Then walked away to help move some crates that had been piled haphazardly on the skid after removal from the ship's netting.

Ted stood, watching him wondering who he was, definitely not a construction worker either. He smelled a rat and figured he must be an undercover cop or something. Why would an undercover cop be assigned here right now? Ted was getting bad vibes. Maybe this was bigger than he ever imagined. He hoped he was able to find Jimmy before things got out of hand. He headed over to where he had arranged to meet Colin.

Colin was standing there with his arms crossed.

"What's up? Why all the secrecy?"

"You know when I asked you to check up on the Gibson's as to where they lived?"

"Yeah."

"Well, the son Jimmy has disappeared. I want you to help me find him," Ted said.

"I heard he ran off with a bimbo."

"Well, that's not true. I don't know who started that rumor, but they are wrong," Ted said firmly.

"What do you want me to do? How are we going to find him? I don't mind helping but fill me in first."

"I got a call from his family asking me to help locate him because I know my way around the docks. By the way, I noticed a new guy helping unload by the Clancy II. Do you know anything about him?"

"Not really, he just appeared one day. He does more observing then working, from what I have seen," Colin said.

"He doesn't seem to fit in as a dockworker, in my opinion. I think I will keep an eye on him." Ted then filled Colin in on some of the events briefly with little detail, but enough to let on the Belle Star was suspect in Jimmy's disappearance. "Do you know any of the crew of the Belle Star? Have you run into any crew on the docks or in the bars around here?"

"Not really. I did work over there unloading, but the crew seemed to be keeping to themselves pretty much. Although I hear some of them are frequenting the bar over on Craig Street. When are you coming back to work? I didn't see your name on the roster yet." Colin poked him on the shoulder.

"I was going to check in when I got here, but I haven't made it over there yet. I will before I leave. I need to be back on the roster so that I can move freely about unnoticed." Ted continued. "Do you have any idea how we can get to the Belle Star crew? We need to get chummy somehow. I want on that ship before it sails Tuesday."

"What about a card game that usually works?"

"Yeah, that's what I thought too. We have to run into them accidentally first. We want the game on the Belle Star," Ted stated.

"Any ideas? Maybe we should drop into Craig Street bar tonight," Colin said.

"Look, we don't want this too obvious, so you go over there, and I'll give you an hour. Then I'll show up to let you know I am back working. How does that sound?"

"Good idea. Maybe I can strike up a conversation before you get there. "Anything else you want me to do?"

"Yes, start asking questions on the QT about the Belle Star's activities. We need to know anything, even if it is a minor detail. It may be a clue of some kind. Okay?"

"Sure, I am finished now. I am heading for home."

Ted thanked his friend. "I need to make a few phone calls if I am heading to that bar later. So, say you get there about eight before the bar gets too busy. A few of the Belle Star crew should be there by then. If it's too busy, you won't be able to strike up a conversation very easily. I'll try to get there closer to nine."

"I'll be there at eight or shortly after."

"Well, I'm heading for the office to book back onto the job. Then I will sniff around for a while. So, see you at nine." He slapped Colin lightly on the back. "Thanks, buddy, I appreciate your helping me out."

"No problem. Glad to have your back." Colin walked away. Ted turned towards the office.

Chapter Nineteen

Emma was waiting on tenterhooks. Why didn't Daddy or Ted call? Was this the way it was going to be forever? No information, but sit and wait. The phone rang, she jumped up to answer it, not waiting for Matilda. "Yes." as if expecting her Dad or Ted.

"This is your service representative I take it you are Emma Gibson?"

"Yes?" The yes had a definite question to it. This voice was not the one she wanted to hear. "What service representative?" she asked.

"Your car. It is time for you to come in for your six months car checkup and have it serviced. Can I schedule a date and time for you?"

"No, I don't want it serviced right now. Our chauffeur looks after that," she added rather than say she demolished the car.

"Can I speak with your chauffeur? I want to tell him about the special we are featuring this month."

"He is not here right now. He is out on some errands for me." Emma said goodbye. The voice at the other end gave off some foul words, which would cause quite a red face had Emma heard them.

She thought that is strange as she knew no service representative had ever called her before. They must be slow if it is necessary to drum up business in this manner. She went back and sat beside Beth, who was looking at her anxiously.

"Do you know that phone call was bizarre. I have never had my car serviced at any time since I have owned it. Roger does that. He loves to putter around cars and takes pride in servicing them himself.

Oh well, he must have meant to call someone else. Although, he did ask for me by name. I wish Ted or Daddy would phone." She relegated the service call to the back of her mind.

* * *

Ted had exhausted his questions for the dock workers after signing in for the duty roster. He had tried to make it sound like he was missing the job so much he wanted any dock news from the ship's crew and their stories. He hoped that they might not realize he was looking into Jimmy's disappearance. He was careful not to bring Jimmy's name into any of his conversations.

He went searching for Mr. Gibson before he headed to the bar to find Colin. He made sure no one was around. There was a light in one of the side offices. Ted rapped on the door. A figure silhouetted the door whom he recognized as Emma's father. When the man from within opened the door, Ted walked inside. Other than a worried look on his face, he was still a powerful-looking man.

"Mr. Gibson, I know you preferred to meet me elsewhere, but I didn't want to wait that long. I was careful. No one saw me. I am sorry to say I haven't found out anything positive."

"Ted, I want you to call me Malvin. I am sorry to hear you haven't found out any more than I did."

"My friend Colin will go to the Craig Street bar tonight to strike up a conversation with some of the Belle Star crew that have been frequenting that place. He is going early, before the place gets too crowded, for easier contact. I am meeting him at nine to tell him that I am back on the roster for work. We are hoping while there to start a conversation about poker with the crew. We hope that if all goes well, they will invite us on board for a poker game. Colin and I have done this in the past on other ships. It may be harder this time as the crew seems to have an unfriendly attitude since their arrival. I don't know whether this is normal or if this is on the Captain's instructions for their time in dock." Ted paused to let Malvin state his views.

"Well, I have had contact with Captain Jorgensen before. He has never been amicable, but he is even less this time for some reason. I doubt you will be successful with that proposed poker game. But I hope you are. I know the Belle Star is the clue to Jimmy's disappearance, but several said he came off the ship."

"You know there is a possibility that they took him back on board, and no one happened to be watching at the time. Everyone has their duties, with the swinging cargo overhead, it isn't wise to be gawking about."

"That's true," Malvin agreed.

"When I go in for work Monday, I want to talk with Alan if I don't find out anything from the Belle Star crew. I know you and Jimmy didn't want that, but perhaps he is feeling bad about being involved now that Jimmy is missing. We have to try everything because that ship will pull out on Tuesday, and our opportunity may be gone. Emma mentioned you wanted to get a search warrant."

"Yes, but I am not sure I have just cause or enough evidence to justify the warrant. Emma has been compiling information about the bogus companies trying to link them with the Belle Star. I am also going to contact the police and report Jimmy missing as it is now over 24 hours. We will need them for the search warrant," Malvin alleged.

Ted replied, "I would like you to hold off until Monday at least because we don't want the docks crawling with cops. That might cause the Belle Star crew to go underground for sure. I hope you don't mind me making that suggestion."

"Okay, I'll wait till Monday but early Monday if you don't find out something in the meantime. We can't let that ship leave until we are sure Jimmy isn't on it. Can I offer you a drink before you go?" Malvin started to turn towards his office.

Ted stopped him saying, "no, I had better get going Colin will be waiting for me. He may be running out of the small talk with the Belle Star crew, although he is quite the gabber when required."

Malvin turned and held out his hand. "Thank you, Ted. I appreciate your helping us. I haven't called Emma. I have been putting it off until we met up. Now I will call her to let her know that I approve of your plans. Maybe it will put her mind at rest."

"Say hi to Emma for me and tell her I will do my best to find Jimmy for her."

"Thanks, I know she will appreciate that. I know she has expected more of me, and I haven't delivered." Malvin's voice was berating himself.

"Don't ride yourself like that it is harder when it is a loved one involved. Stay focused on the end result, which takes patience and time when you are dealing with the scum of this world. Well, I had better be going." Ted turned and opened the door and faded into the night.

* * *

Ted stood on the curb, looking back and forth, noting the emptiness of the street. He headed across the sidewalk and entered the bar. He stood there, letting his eyes adjust to the dim lighting. He saw Colin in a booth against the far wall. Two men were sitting with him. He felt sure they must be Belle Star's crew. Colin didn't look his way. Ted walked over to the bar and ordered a drink. He stood talking to the bartender before surveying the room. This time Colin looked up, seeing Ted. Then he said something to the two men before he waved Ted over.

Ted ordered another round for the table before sauntering over to greet Colin.

"How's it going, buddy? How have you been? We missed you down at the docks." Colin turned to the two men to explain Ted had been off work due to an injury. Then he proceeded to introduce him to the two men who filled in their names as Anton and Luigi.

Ted sat down. "I hope you don't mind, but I ordered you another round of drinks." He then turned to Colin. "I wondered if I would find you here. I dropped into the office and put my name back on the duty roster. I am officially back to work as of tomorrow. I dropped in here, knowing this is your favorite drinking hole close to the docks."

"Yeah, I dropped in just in case some of the guys would be here. I was hoping to strike up a game for tonight, but they must have gone elsewhere. I stuck around, hoping they might show up."

Colin had turned to the two crew members. "Hey, would you like a poker game?" They looked at each other than said sure.

Ted replied, "I'm in. Do you think anyone else here would like to join us?"

"No, don't ask, let's go back to our ship. We can find more guys there," said Anton looking at Luigi to see if he thought it was a good idea.

Luigi said, "sure, we can get a game going easy." The drinks arrived. They consumed them with the sailors imparting some of their experiences." Ted and Colin were relatively quiet with only a word here and there to keep them talking. It was working out better than they had imagined. The drinks finished, they headed back to the docks in Colin's car. They would come back and pick up Ted's car later.

When they got back to the dock, the Belle Star was in semi-darkness, so activity was at a minimum. A voice halted the men climbing the ramp. Anton said, "we want to get a game going. We want to bring on board two dock workers, we met in the bar."

"Okay, I know a few will join you as not many went on shore tonight." He stepped back, letting the men on board. Ted was looking around while following the men to the stairwell leading below.

"We go to the cabin nearest the galley. It is the largest. The First Officer likes a game in his cabin." The two men were leading the way quickly, not giving them much time to look around. Then they did an odd thing. They trekked a long way around to get to the cabin, entering several corridors as though they were circling the ship. Ted had been on many ships over the years. There seemed to be no explanation for the route to arrive at their destination.

At first, he thought it was because they wanted to round up more players. But they saw no one in their travels until they passed the galley. They could see two men sitting having coffee. The men looked up as they passed without pausing. Anton opened the door after he knocked. The First officer eased off the bunk as Anton said, "I brought someone to make up a poker game, are you up for it?"

"Sure, you know I am always ready to take your money," he said with gusto and backed up to let them in. There was a table folded up against the wall, which the First Officer opened with a flourish and placed it next to the bunk. There were several wooden-legged canvas stools that he dragged out from under the bunk.

When the men sat down, the First Officer told Anton to call Giovanni. He should be in the galley. Anton reversed his steps and stuck his head out in the hallway. He yelled to Giovanni.

A man entered. The first officer sat on the bed, pulling the table towards him. A couple of decks of cards appeared, and some poker chips from a pouch-like contraption hanging from the end of the bunk.

The men were pulling money from their pockets. Thankfully Ted had extra cash on him. Chips replaced the money. The First Officer was in complete control now.

Ted looked at Colin. He had a feeling that he was going to be leaving here with empty pockets. This guy acted like a professional. Oh well, if they got the desired results, it would be worth it.

The other man from the galley appeared with some beers and stood watching, as though he had lost too many times to join in. The beers were given around. Dealing started, then they called out the number of cards they needed as play went around the table. The First officer raised, the chips piled up quickly until it was down to Ted and the First Officer, whom the others referred to as the 'First.'

Ted had an inside straight, and the First put down a Royal Flush. Ted was not surprised somehow. The game went on without much in the way of table talk, but the beer was steadily flowing although Ted had stopped two rounds back. His pockets were almost empty, but Colin had picked up a few pots and was still going. Ted asked to use the head.

"Sure, down the corridor, we came up. It is the fourth door down," said Anton.

Ted headed out the door, then stood there watching, but no one seemed to be paying attention. So, he went the other way, wondering why the long route to the First Officer's cabin? Was there something they were not supposed to see? Ted was approaching another corridor when he heard a door open on the passage around the corner from where he was standing. He heard a voice say.

"He is still out. He hasn't moved since I last looked in on him."

Another voice spate out. "Good."

The door clanged. Footsteps receded in the other direction away from where Ted had stopped. He felt sure Jimmy was detained here.

He reversed direction and headed back when he got to the First Officer's quarters, he slowed down, but everyone was still intent on the game. Now it was Colin and the First left bidding. Ted headed quietly pass and reached the door that Anton had mentioned. He opened the door and went inside. All the while thinking, how could he save Jimmy? He couldn't walk by the sounds of it. They were keeping him drugged. Finished, Ted headed back just as Anton came looking for him.

"I thought you had got lost."

"No, just taking care of business." Ted left it at that.

Anton let him pass and continued down to the head. Ted re-entered the First Officer's cabin. Colin must have won the pot because he had a pile of chips in front of him. The First was wearing a scowl.

Ted said, "we better call it a night, or do you want to stay longer, Colin?"

"No. I better come with you." Colin pushed the chips toward First, who was wearing a deeper scowl now as he counted out some bills that became quite a pile for Colin. "I have to take you back to pick up your car. Thank you, gentlemen. It was a good game."

Anton was back. First said, "Escort these men off the ship." His glare held a meaningful look.

Anton stated, "follow me again." Leading the way. Ted and Colin followed, wanting to get out of there as fast as possible.

The crewman was silent. Perhaps in hopes of dissuading them from questions or interest in the ship. When they got topside, they breathed in the night air as a relief or release from the stuffy cabin below. There were strange noises to their left, but they couldn't see anything in the darkness.

They headed directly to the ramp, the watch didn't stop them, but Anton mentioned. "I am down almost $20.00, but this guy here is much richer."

Colin said helpfully, "do you want a return match tomorrow night? I'm game. Are you in, Ted?"

Ted replied, "I'll have to come up with some money I lost quite a bit tonight."

The watch shuffled his feet meaningfully. Anton quickly said, "I'll let you know, but I'm not sure right now. If we can, I'll meet you in the Craig Street bar."

"Okay," said Colin. "Let's go, Ted."

The night duty crewman stepped forward, encouraging them to leave the ship.

Colin and Ted were trying to be nonchalant. It was never wise to win big on a foreign vessel. However, the crew didn't seem to be deterring them at all. They kept walking down the ramp.

They waved to Anton, and the watch then strolled down the dock towards Colin's car parked on the street. Ted noted there were no lights in Gibson's shipping office, but there was a light in the night watchman's hut.

They had gone another ten feet when they came across Charlie, shining a flashlight around checking out the vacant buildings. The flashlight flicked onto the two men and then away.

"Well, what are you two doing here this late?" A little fear in his voice as Ted and Colin were both big men.

"It's OK we were just on the Belle Star for a poker game. We thought it was about time to call it a night. Goodnight." They quickly walked away.

"Not so fast," said Charlie. "Who are you?"

"It's okay. We are just a couple of dock workers who were looking for a game," Ted replied, his voice non-threatening.

"What are your names?" Charlie was persistent.

"Ted Maxwell and Colin Brant," replied Ted. "We were on the Belle Star for a poker game and no other reason. I get the impression that you are nervous about the Belle Star?"

"My boss told me to keep an eye on it. There have been some strange goings-on there for a couple of nights."

"Well, we assure you we are not involved. You will have to take our word for it. We will say goodnight and be on our way." Trying to put Charlie at ease. A night watchman is a lonely thankless job that wasn't for Ted, but it had to be done by someone.

Charlie's wary look was starting to disappear when he finally shrugged his shoulders and told them to be on their way. Ted and Colin vanished into the black night.

When they were out of Charlie's hearing, Ted said, "they are holding Jimmy in one of the cabins on the Belle Star. When I went to the head, I took the other direction to see if I could figure out why the long way around to the First Officer's cabin was necessary, when they brought us on board. When I was nearing the next corridor, I heard two men talking around the corner. They said he was still out and hadn't moved. I am assuming they have drugged Jimmy. The two men closed the door and walked the other way. I was all ready to put on a drunk act if they had come my way."

"I thought you had found something as your stance indicated, but you played it quite well. It's just, I can read you so well. What are we going to do about it?"

"Well, first I want to go see Mr. Gibson and tell him. On the way, we will think seriously about how to approach this as we don't want them killing Jimmy with an overdose or anything," Ted said in a worried voice. "It's pretty hard to rush a ship that size. We may need to get the police and Port Authorities involved to detain the ship. I can't think of any other way. What about you?" Ted asked.

"No, it might turn bad if we try anything."

Chapter Twenty

By now, they had reached Craig Street and Ted's car. The bar was still open, loud voices issued from it as though an argument was in progress. Ted said a quick goodnight. "I will keep in touch." Then he got out and headed for his car before something erupted besides an argument. Colin watched him get in his car before leaving. Ted gave him a high sign of thanks. They both knew things could get ugly where drinking was concerned.

Driving to the Gibson's, he could see the lights were out in the front of the house, but he hoped Malvin would still be up. He pulled up to the gate, pressing the button. It was a while before a sleepy voice said. "Yes."

"Sorry to come so late. I am Ted Maxwell. Mr. Gibson is waiting to hear from me." The gate swung open, and he drove inside.

Roger must have buzzed the house as a light appeared in one of the rooms in the front of the house. Then over the front door as he pulled up. The door was thrown open. A fully dressed, very tired Malvin stood there. Jimmy's disappearance was taking a toll on this otherwise robust man.

Ted alighted from the car. Malvin's face brightened, hoping with Ted's late arrival for positive news. He wanted to think the best scenario.

"Come in. What did you find out?" Malvin asked as he shook his hand, letting that be his greeting. "Come into the study. I need a drink. Would you like one?" Delaying Ted's report dreading that it wasn't good news after all.

"No, Malvin, I have had enough drinking for tonight," Ted replied. Malvin headed to the bar.

"What did you find out?" he asked, fear-laced his voice.

"I have found Jimmy."

Malvin swung around. "What?"

"Yes, I have found Jimmy. He is on the Belle Star as you surmised."

"How did you find that out?" Relief in his voice.

"Colin and I managed to get on the Belle Star for a poker game. When I took the wrong direction to the head, I overheard two men talking. They said some man was still out cold. I am assuming they were talking about Jimmy. They are drugging him. I didn't get the feeling they were talking about a fellow crew member."

"Good." Malvin took a generous drink of scotch.

"Now the problem is how best to get him off there safely. I have been racking my brain ever since I found out. I very much doubt we can rush on board and retrieve Jimmy before they kill him." He paused to think.

"Another game on board won't work because at any sign of trouble. The Belle Star crew will easily overpower us. So, I think our best bet is to get the Port Authorities involved and if necessary, the police. The problem is that it may get tied up in red tape, and with the ship sailing Tuesday doesn't give us much time."

"Yes, we want Jimmy off there quickly and safely before the Belle Star sails."

The two men stood looking at each other, Malvin with hope in his eyes and Ted in doubt for Jimmy's easy rescue. The two men were trying to come up with an alternate plan for Jimmy's safe and speedy recovery.

The doorway held a vision of loveliness that caused Ted to stare. Emma came forward with concern. "What happened? Did you find Jimmy?" Emma was utterly unaware of her stunning beauty in the nylon peignoir set. In her concern for Jimmy, her attire had not entered her mind.

Ted could barely speak. "We know where he is, but we can't rescue him until we come up with a positive plan so Jimmy will not get hurt."

Malvin came over to his daughter and took her hands. "Jimmy is alive. We believe he is on the Belle Star. The difficulty is that Jimmy is drugged. So, whoever rescues him will have to carry him off so they won't be able to escape fast. Also, there are too many crew members on the ship for only one or two to carry out such a daring plan. Anymore would never be able to get on the ship without something happening to Jimmy. The element of surprise is what we need."

Ted was ready to scale the ship right now if this vision of loveliness would be his for doing it. He shook his head, realizing how impractical his thinking was getting. "Yes, we have to be careful, any wrong move that tips our hand could be fatal to Jimmy," Ted reiterated.

"Emma, now that you know where Jimmy is and that he is still alive, I want you to go back to bed and try to get some rest. Hopefully, we will come up with a workable plan before morning. Leave Ted and I, to mull over the problem even if it takes all night."

Emma thought it was best to leave as she would only slow things down with her questions. She turned to Ted. "Thank you, Ted, for locating Jimmy. Thank you for the peace of mind you have given me." Emma left the room without a backward glance.

Ted was nearly salivating.

Malvin invited Ted to sit down so they could consider how best to handle the situation.

"Nobody can enter that ship without the watch seeing unless they use scuba gear and climb on the ship from the waterside." Ideas were flowing around in Ted's mind. "We will need at least four men to be effective. The time element is important. We will need two men to control the corridor while the other two men gear Jimmy up in a wet suit, which will take time. Then he will have to be carried topside. The problem will be to contain the crew if we are spotted." Ted paused. "I know where to get the men. I belong to a scuba diving club. We go out regularly in our free time. That's not the problem. It is evading the crew. It is next to impossible for four men to get on a ship, grab Jimmy, and get off again without detection."

Malvin was trying to think of something to help, but he was out of his element here with a problem like this. Ted's mind was whirling. The one stumbling block was how many men were on guard at night while the other crew members were sleeping. Ted felt they could get on the ship unseen with a diversion. "Malvin, with the shady activities on board at night lately, we may need a diversion while we get on and off. The diversion is only necessary if things continue with night activity. We can't take the chance everyone will be sleeping but the night watch." Ted was frowning. He was deeply concerned about Jimmy losing his life if that ship sailed with him on board.

"You know Cliff, and I could call Captain Jorgensen onto the dock, would that help?"

"No, we don't want to arouse his interest. He may be below in his cabin. I happen to notice unknown movement tonight as well. We can't be sure the night activities will stop. We haven't got a lot of days left for observation. So, we will have to put a diversion plan in place."

"How do you propose getting into the water without being seen?" Malvin asked.

"That won't be a problem as we will be entering the water from another dock."

Ted was trying to devise a diversionary tactic. "Would it be possible to set a shed or garbage container on fire on the pier? I know you won't want to lose a shed, but if Jimmy is coming off that ship alive. You must be willing to forfeit something."

"I would be only too glad to light the whole dock on fire if it would help."

"The most realistic would be the watchman's hut. Which is very visible to the Belle Star and is close enough to the other buildings to be a threat that the whole dock may go up in flames. Now we don't want to get carried away here. But we want to have the fire big enough to attract the attention of the crew awake on that ship. We want to give them a front-row seat to the flames on the dock. We need a diversion to last for at least 3/4 of an hour or more."

"Charlie is a good man. He will do a good job of it and make it very realistic. But I don't want to be anywhere near the fire. My presence might tip your hand."

"Fine, this has to go off like clockwork. We will have to set up a time frame with Charlie, giving him time to have a sizeable fire evident before we reach the ship. Hopefully, the fire department on the way.

We don't want to be so realistic that he burns the whole dock after all it is my livelihood down there," Ted said with a grin.

Malvin was aware Ted worked as a stevedore when he went to see him in the hospital. He made a point of finding out about this young man. The plan he came up with would be risky for him and his buddies as well as for Jimmy.

"When do you plan to execute this feat?" Malvin asked, knowing Tuesday wasn't that far away.

"We have Sunday or Monday night to get this in place. It depends on getting enough of the guys to come forward. Some may be out of town on salvage jobs at the moment," Ted informed him.

Malvin picked up his drink and raised it to Ted. "A salute to you and your bravery." He took a drink, comforted for a possible successfully rescue.

Knowing no one was reachable this late at night, Ted got up to go. The discussion concluded until he had the divers in place. He headed for the door. Malvin followed.

"You know Ted. This is beyond anything I expect of you. We could always get the police and Port Authorities involved."

"No, on thinking it over, they are liable to kill him before the Port Authorities can execute a full-blown search. I think this latest plan could work if Charlie is successful with that diversion."

"Charlie will have a glowing shed before you get there." Malvin was looking forward to the pleasure of supplying the fuel to feed the fire.

Ted said goodnight and headed over to his car. Malvin closed the door with a lighter heart then he had had for days.

Ted was ready to get into the car when a ghostly white figure came out of the night. He recognized Emma emanating into the spotlights spread out amongst the shrubs.

"Emma, what are you doing out here?" Ted asked with concern.

"Daddy would have a fit if he knew. I had to find out what was going on. I couldn't sleep until I did." She came up closer to him. He was looking down into her sweet, trusting face. He felt good inside.

"Emma, it is sufficient that you know that a plausible plan has been worked out. If I can get the help, I need to pull it off."

"When will it happen? At least, let me know that?" Emma pleaded.

"Sorry, Emma, that hasn't been decided yet. I will let you know in due course. But the fewer who know, the better."

"I wouldn't tell anyone," Emma said in horror, afraid that he might not trust her.

"But Emma, it's not you, it is just an outline at the moment. The plan isn't complete yet." Ted wanted to pull this vision of loveliness into his arms.

"Emma, go back into the house and try to get some sleep."

"Ted, I want to thank you for helping Daddy and me." She paused. "You know I haven't thanked you for saving my life yet." She stood up on tiptoes and placed a light kiss on his lips. Then turned and ran towards the side of the house. The night swallowing her in its darkness.

Ted got into the car. After that kiss, the ride home didn't seem quite so long.

* * *

It was after midnight; the night was bleak, and that went along with Captain Jorgensen's mood. He was aware that his companion still hadn't located the car or the diamonds. He was losing his patience quickly. He had already been snippy with his First Officer for no reason.

He gazed at the man before him. He was feeling it was risky being involved with him anymore. Maybe he should throw him in with Jimmy and get rid of them both at sea. But that would not help find the diamonds.

"What have you done to recover them?" asked Captain Jorgensen angrily.

"I'd tried to find out if I could get the girl to bring her car in for servicing at a friend's garage. It appears that the chauffer likes to be a mechanic in his spare time. He services all the cars. I tried to get access to the garage area, but it was difficult as the chauffeur has living quarters above the garage. Every time I tried to get near his dog barked and he came out nosing around. I couldn't take the chance of getting caught as the family knows me."

"Well, use your friendship to be there for some reason if the family knows you. You can think of something surely."

"But the chauffeur is always about during the day," he said plaintively.

"Surely, the chauffeur does drive Mr. Gibson around or the daughter?"

"Yes, but how will I know when that is?"

Captain Jorgensen was losing his cool. He was sorry, he was involved with this young man. He had seemed more assertive in their earlier dealings, but now that things were going wrong, he wasn't handling it well.

"You are to post yourself outside that gate until the chauffeur leaves, even if it is from now until doomsday. Get those diamonds, do you hear me and I don't want any more excuses. Get out of my sight. And when I see you again, it better be with the diamonds in your hot little hands, or I will cut them off. That is a promise. The watch will get you off without anyone seeing you. Now go."

The crew member waiting outside the Captain's quarters turned and headed topside with the young man following. He wasn't walking too sprightly. He wished now the diamonds didn't involve him. The embezzlement was one thing he could handle. Then he realized that he had been set up with the theft guilt, forcing him to move the diamonds from the 'Fence' to the ship. He should have waited rather than storing them in Emma's car wheel three weeks ago. Things had gone wrong when Jimmy's sister quit coming to work each day. Jimmy had told him she was under doctor's care and would be off work indefinitely. How could he possibly have known? She had always shown up like clockwork each day in the past.

The night was cloudy, so it was easier for Coulter to slink off the ship. The next step would be to stake out Jimmy's place. This was not the way it was supposed to be. He needed some quick money to cover his gambling debts, not to get involved in diamonds. Why had it gone on for so long, they kept telling him it would be over in no time. Now months later, and no closer to being over, especially since the hidden diamonds were in Emma's unavailable car. Coulter needed this to end. He just wanted to walk away from the whole mess. He doubted that Captain Jorgensen would look at it that way.

Why did the Captain have to be there that night when the loan shark had called in his tab? Somehow the Captain had every little detail of Coulter's past, which hadn't been exactly stellar, being a relentless gambler. Captain Jorgensen offered to pay the debt provided he followed through on a job he would specify. He was horrified when it turned out to involve Jimmy, his best friend. They had needed someone with a knowledge of bookkeeping and the system in the shipping office. As he had Emma's job before she started, he was perfect for the job, setting up the bogus accounts. It was only later much to his detriment that the 'Diamonds' entered the picture, blackmailing him for setting up the fake accounts and monies received to pay his debt.

Previously, he had conned his aunt into repayment of his gambling debts, with a lie by saying he was investing her money into a sure deal that would multiply her money in no time. The last time, he had tried to get money. She had already invested in a building project for the elderly.

In desperation, he got involved in altering the books of Gibson Shipping. Now he had to find the missing diamonds. He wasn't a thief. He just had a bad gambling habit.

Coulter didn't feel comfortable slinking around in the night shadows. Therefore, the suggestion of hiding the diamonds in a car wheel on the dock ran against his nature. Why didn't he hide the diamonds at home or his place of employment? No one would have found them. No, the Captain had insisted on a safe car on the dock. The only one he could think of, that was there steady as clockwork, was Emma's car. At the time, he felt it was foolproof to hide them there. Besides, she had put him out of his job.

He had observed, the car had been there daily until a week or so ago. Then Emma got sick. When he had asked Jimmy about her illness, he said she wouldn't be in for a while but gave no details. He only knew that she never missed a day of work in the past three years, according to a dropped comment by Jimmy. So, it must be pretty serious whatever she had wrong with her. Now he had to find her car, no easy feat. The car was behind a wall and protected by a guard, the overzealous chauffeur, and his dog. He had quite a few scrapes and bruises after the night he had scaled the wall the last time with the dog chasing him. He was never a climber in his youth nor very athletic.

After stopping at a bar for a few drinks, Coulter arrived at Jimmy's place. The lights were out in the house. It was nearly dawn. He thought there was no point going home as he would never sleep, and his black attire would be suspect by his family as he wore a suit for his office job. He had been off work more and more lately. Now he was going to miss Monday also if he didn't get in there and find that car. He wanted no part of that wretched car.

His brain was not working suitably anymore. Today was Sunday. He would be expected to be home for the usual Sunday trip to the church. His mother was rigid on that, while he still resided at home. He had been going to move out a few times, but his gambling was taking his money.

Why did he not get rid of his gambling habit? He knew it cost him a fortune. He had been so lucky in the beginning, but lady-luck had abandoned him for the past three years. He was so hooked it was like a fever he couldn't break. When he was ready to give up, he would have a run of a week or so of winning. Then he would start going more often. The winning would stop, causing his debt to be deeper than ever. Oh well, no use crying over spilled milk, he had other things to worry about now. Like a car that he couldn't get access to that held the diamonds that would release him from bondage.

He jerked awake with a start. The gates were opening. A car was arriving. It was daylight. He could easily see the entrance from his parked car down the street. They were gates that moved silently but clanged when the lock was engaging. He looked at his watch. It was nine in the morning. He had slept for 3 hours before the car arrived. He didn't see who it was, nor did he recognize the car. He rubbed his face. He needed a wash and shave. Why had he not gone home? He decided that there was no hope of the chauffer leaving now they had company. He would chance going home for a while. His mother would be at church. Coulter started the car and headed to an area a couple of blocks away. His family had been residing in the house for over 100 years, passed down through his father's family.

Chapter Twenty-One

Ted was let in the house by Matilda this time. She gave him a big smile, and thanks for finding Jimmy. She showed him into the breakfast room where Emma and Malvin were both sitting having coffee.

"Good morning, Ted, will you join us?" Shaking hands. "We both seemed to have risen late this morning. The optimism of this plan made us able to relax longer." Malvin looked at his daughter. She was staring at Ted with flushed cheeks. He wondered what that was all about. Did it have something to do with the way she refused to see him after her rescue?

Ted smiled at Emma as he sat down. "Good morning, Emma. Good morning, Malvin." His eyes still looking at Emma as if awaiting her response.

"Hello, Ted," Emma said softly. She is embarrassed about something, Malvin thought.

"Well, Ted, how did you make out?" Drawing his attention away from his daughter.

"I did manage to get three other guys, but the two I particularly wanted are away on a salvage job. However, the three I have lined up will get the job done as well."

Ted thanked Matilda for the coffee along with a piece of homemade coffee cake. He didn't usually eat sweets in the morning, but he thought it best not to offend her.

"You know the biggest problem we will have is that Jimmy is

drugged. He will not be any help to us getting him suited up. That is going to be the biggest delay. That fire better be a good one. It would help if Jimmy is due for another drug fix and be semi-aware of us. The longer we take, the more powerful the fire must be. The more damage for you to bear."

"You let me think about damage control. I will have Charlie call Cliff at the same time he calls 911. Cliff will come to help Charlie do what is necessary."

Ted was relieved at the assurance. He didn't like the idea of a fire, but they had no other choice as Jimmy's life may depend on it.

"Well, it is set for tonight. We can't take the chance of waiting as the crew may be awake Monday night, getting ready for the early Tuesday sailing. The more crew that are asleep, the better chance we have of pulling this off safely. Hopefully, the siren noise will not penetrate their sleep being encased below in their quarters. The element of surprise is important. They won't be expecting a rescue, I hope. At least the ones that are awake will be on the opposite side of the ship from the rescue."

Emma piped up. "What time tonight?"

Ted glanced at Emma, wanting to shield her from any unsavory events. The rescue could get bloody if they get discovered before they managed to vacate the ship. There was no doubt in his mind that the crew members were able to obtain guns if necessary.

Emma addressed her father. "Daddy, what time is this taking place?"

Malvin looked at Ted. "We aren't sure it depends on everything being in place."

"Emma, it is important we keep this a secret as we don't know who is involved other than it is someone close to the family. I'm asking you to tell no one, not even Beth. In case it reaches the wrong ears," asked Ted.

Emma looked disappointed that her silence wasn't to be trusted. "All right."

"Emma, would you like to go for a drive?" Ted threw in.

"Yes, a drive would be nice. I will go and get ready." Emma left the room quickly. Malvin and Ted shook hands again in relief that the rescue they were planning might indeed work. The next hurdle would be to keep the details from reaching others.

Ted queried. "How much do you trust Cliff? It has to be someone close to the family, and money is the big factor here. I am getting the feeling that there is more than embezzlement involved to warrant Jimmy's abduction."

"Cliff has been with me for a long time. I would stake my life on him. I know it is a risk, but we never can believe someone close could do such a thing. But there are always extenuating circumstances, and that may be the case here. You will have to trust my feelings on this, as we need him to work the fire to keep it going but controlled. Charlie can't do it alone, that is for sure. I don't see we have any other choice, do you?"

Ted studied Malvin hard. He was putting the lives of three other men in possible danger. That was a big responsibility. But he didn't have much choice.

Emma arrived back breathlessly as if she had run a marathon. "Ted, can we drive Beth over to Coulter's place she left her purse there the other night?" Ted was not happy. He wanted Emma alone.

"Okay," he said in a resigned voice. "Tell her the bus leaves in 10 minutes." He joked. "Remember Emma, small talk only in the car."

Emma knew that Ted was only cautious.

"Okay." She quickly turned and went to get Beth, who had stayed overnight. Beth, who had slept in, was dressed. She had skipped breakfast and was now anxious to leave.

The three headed for Ted's car and the day ahead.

* * *

When they arrived at Coulter's place, they were surprised when he opened the door. Emma knew that Coulter's family always went to church on Sunday. Jimmy had chided him about it one time in front of her. "Coulter, what are you doing here? I expected the butler."

"I live here," he said, trying to be funny, concerned that these three had arrived on his doorstep unannounced.

"No, I mean, how come you're not at church?"

"I tied one on last night and didn't get myself together in time to be included in the family church trip." He was trying to keep it light, but he wasn't feeling comfortable inside.

"Emma, what do you want, and did you drive your car?" He had been thinking of how to get to her car before they arrived, that comment slipped out.

"Beth left her purse here. She wants to pick it up." Emma ignored the irrelevant question about her driving.

"Oh yes, my mother said your purse was here, Beth. I will get it for you. I am sure it will still be in the living room somewhere. Why don't you come in and show me?"

Turning to Ted, he said. "Why don't you two go on and I will drive Beth home. I was heading that way anyway. Beth wait a minute while I walk these two to their car. I'll be right back." When they arrived at the car, he was relieved to see that it wasn't Emma's car. He was going over to Emma's after he dropped Beth off.

"Are you two going for a spin somewhere?" He pretended to not care about the answer as though he was just polite.

Ted said, "yes, we are going for a drive to my place. We will probably be gone all day." Ted felt that this man was more interested in his answer, then he was showing.

"Right, you two have a good day. Oh, Emma, don't worry about Beth. I will take her home. I'm heading over to Diane's place to wait for her return from church. She will need an apology. I rather embarrassed her at the Country Club last night." He stepped back and gave them a wave. Coulter was anxious to get back to Beth, eager to question her about Emma's illness. She certainly didn't look sick now.

* * *

Ted looked over at Emma. She still looked uncomfortable in his presence. He was hoping to change that today. He wasn't sure going to his place was a good idea. But he had to find out how she would react to the scene of the incident. Would she freak out or would she take it in stride? Their destination loomed ahead.

Emma was getting jittery. How would she act when she saw the waterfall and the cliff again? Would the memories of the near-miss affect her? Added to that, Ted was creeping into her mind since he had responded to Jimmy's being missing.

"Do we have to go to the waterfall?" Looking troubled and agitated.

"No, we can just go into the house and have a drink."

"Good," Emma said with gusto, relief in her expression. Ted reached over and took her hand, squeezing it then let it go. He didn't want to come on too strong and frighten her.

The car stopped when it reached its destination. Ted quickly got out and came around to help Emma. He took her hand. Her body language was indicating a big ordeal ahead for her.

He headed up the stairs onto the veranda. They stepped inside. "What would you like to drink? Water, soda, beer, or brandy? I'm afraid that is all I have," he said lamely.

"No tea or coffee?"

"Yes, coffee sorry no tea, but I'll get some the next time I am in town if that's what it takes to get you here," he said hopefully.

"Coffee is fine." Emma had still not let go of his hand, clutching it tightly.

Ted was leading her along towards the kitchen as though it was perfectly natural for them to be fused together. They reached the kitchen. "Emma, do you think you could let go of my hand long enough for me to make the coffee?"

Emma dropped his hand like it was a hot poker. "I'm sorry," Emma said weakly. Why was she acting this way? She certainly wasn't a shrinking violet. She firmly walked over to the table and sat down, avoiding looking out of the window in case she would see the waterfall. "Do you think things will go well tonight?"

"I am hoping so. I will drop you off early so I can meet with the guys for a briefing."

He set a cup of coffee in front of her, which she drank, although it was the last thing she wanted. She just knew she had to keep doing something. She was avoiding Ted's eyes as she looked around the room. No dirty dishes were evident and no unnecessary clutter. She was guessing this man had probably lived alone for a long time.

Ted was patiently waiting for her to stop perusing the room. Her eyes would eventually have to light on him. He sat, studying her face. The serene way she was sitting and observing.

Finally, her eyes met his in a beguiling way. Emma blushed. This man was everything she had ever imagined in a man and more, far more. She felt fragile as though he wanted to protect her from everything immoral in this world. Still, he didn't speak, just studied her face watching the blush fade and curiosity take over.

"What are we going to do now that we have finished our coffee?" Ted asked.

The coffee had disappeared as though there was a hole in the cup. "Ted, we're not going to go yet, are we?"

"No, Emma, but when you are ready, we are going for a walk."

"I can't," Emma said quickly with dread. She knew where he wanted to walk. She trembled at the very thought of that.

"You know Emma. I am your friend. I wouldn't let anything happen to you. You know that, but I also want you to come here occasionally. I want to take you down into the valley someday."

She was frantically shaking her head in a 'no way' manner. She was doing it so vigorously her whole body was rocking.

"Emma, you will be okay. We will do this together," Ted said ever so gently.

She did not want to see the waterfall or cliff. The memory of the near demise was still too real, mainly when she went to sleep at night. Her screams of panic when the car jolted to a stop. The slipping of the wedged vehicle from the rock.

"Emma, you are never going to get over this unless you face your fear. That is why I brought you here today. Your father told me about your nightmares. He feels that it has to do with the cliff incident, not Jimmy."

She was holding his hand again like it was a lifeline.

"Emma, we are just going to walk over to the waterfall. You don't have to stand on the cliff edge. We will observe the waterfall, okay?" Ted got up, reaching out his arm, moving around the table to her side, as she wasn't letting go. She looked up at Ted pleadingly. Her near-miss with death was not something she wanted to recall.

"Waterfalls are beautiful with the sun reflecting a mass of rainbows. The cliff goes into a beautiful valley. It is a flourish of beauty as far as the eye can see. I know you aren't ready today for all that, but at least try looking at the waterfall." He was gradually pulling her up in front of him. When she was fully standing, he tucked her into his side. His arm was around her waist — their linked hands in front of them as he headed for the back door.

All the while, he was murmuring words of encouragement. Emma finally started to relax. Ted knew they couldn't both get out the door at once. He grabbed for their jackets, which brought his body away from her. Their hands never broke contact. Emma was still hesitant about this walk. She was lagging.

"Today is the perfect day, no clouds in the sky. Let's make our way towards the waterfall. Isn't that a pleasing sound the cascading water echoing into the valley below?"

Emma was mesmerized by the height of the waterfall and the cascading rivulets lit by sunbeams. She made herself concentrate on the beauty of the waterfall. The arcs of color as the water danced in the sunlight.

Ted was efficiently controlling Emma's body as she admired the falls in deep concentration. He was guiding her steps around the protruding rock formations. Before Emma even noticed Ted had her close to the edge of the cliff. She was clinging to his body like glue. Then he put his hand under her chin and raised it so he could look into her eyes.

He bent forward, dropping a kiss lightly on her lips then more profoundly. Emma was responding. He slowly maneuvered her body around until she was facing out. Stepping sideways, so when she opened her eyes, the valley was there. She caught her breath in fear, but the beauty that she could see altered her anxiety.

"Oh Ted, no wonder you love this place so much," Emma said in wonder.

"Emma, do you realize you are standing on the cliff edge?" He whispered ever so quietly.

Emma looked down quickly. She was still euphoric from the beauty of the valley and their kisses. He turned her and raised her face once more and rejoined those lovely lips with his.

Ted held her close, savoring their kiss. His mind leaped to wanting her as his soul mate. Convincing her would be crucial. He knew she wasn't ready for that knowledge yet, releasing her, noticing a dazed glow on her face. His heart leaped with the wonder of her loveliness.

Chapter Twenty-Two

Ted was standing with his arm around her waist. Both were facing the beauty of the valley again.

"Emma, I want you to look down and observe where the car eventually landed. You can see it by the burnt shrubbery. Can you do that for me?" He whispered his mouth close to her ear.

"I think so," Emma said quietly.

"I have you close against me, so you are safe. I know you can do this."

He eased their bodies forward in unison. Emma looked down. She concentrated on the burnt shrubbery rather than the height. There was less than she had imagined considering the ball of flames that had shot up in the air when the car exploded. Her body was relaxing in her continual concentration of the area.

Ted was so pleased with her. He put his fingers under her chin and planted another light kiss on her full lips. "That's my girl, you've done it. I am so proud of you." Another light kiss until she stood up on tiptoe and circled his neck with her arms forgetting how close to the edge they were. Their lips were now united together at Emma's provocation. His heart expanded with this unexpected development. She was light as a feather with her arms locked so firmly around his neck. He moved away from the edge.

Finally, their lips parted. Ted slowly broke the body contact, thrilled with her loving kiss.

He steered her to a big spacious rock to sit and enjoy the view of the waterfall and valley getting to know each other. It was natural to drift into kissing. His tender kisses were melding their pliant bodies together. Gradually Ted knew he had to control these steamy kisses. A conversation was needed here.

"Emma, I am so proud of you. How do you feel?"

Her eyes still closed while savoring the kisses. "I don't know how I feel," Emma said honestly. "I guess the best word to describe it is euphoric." Ted chuckled, feeling reassurance that she responded better than he could have hoped.

"Emma, it is time to go home. We will enjoy the valley another day and the kisses, of course." Ted added with a twinkle in his eyes. Ted guided their steps back to the house. He led Emma into the living room and gave her the remote for the TV.

"Emma, I want to get changed for tonight. We will have to leave soon. Will you be comfortable here?" Ted asked, anxious to please her.

"Ted, I will be fine, go get dressed. I will nose around, do you mind?"

"Not at all, my place is your place. I want you to feel that way too." He gave her a pleased look as she had wandered over to the shelf of family pictures at different stages in his life.

Ted went down the hall with a happy heart, not thinking about the job ahead of him. After he dropped off Emma would be soon enough for that.

He whistled the wedding march as he pulled on his clothes. There was no stopping his mind after those kisses, on the cliff edge. Emma's fear seems to have disappeared under the rapture of his kisses. Let's hope it stays that way when she goes to bed tonight.

Emma meanwhile was thinking Ted was pretty wonderful. He seemed to care for her like she was special. It had been a long time since she had dared to think of herself. It had been all about Jimmy ever since she had discovered the transgression. Now she hoped that Jimmy found the evidence to clear himself. Who could have done this to us? Someone close to them, but who?

Tonight, Ted will bring Jimmy home. Her heart was daring to hope. She felt so lost without him. Ted reappeared into the room, startling her from her thoughts of Jimmy.

Ted was watching her. She was holding a picture in her hands of him when he was about thirteen, an eager, happy boy. She was studying the picture.

"Emma, we have to go now," he said quietly so as not to scare her. She turned around, looking at him then down at the picture.

"Ted, you looked so happy here, but that same happiness is missing from your later pictures," she said sadly.

"My mother was taking that picture. It was the last thing we did together." The sadness in his voice was very noticeable.

"Life can be hard sometimes," she said, thinking of the loss of her mother.

Ted didn't want to disturb her, but he knew they had to leave.

"Emma, the time is passing." He held out his hand. She took it willingly, noting his physique. His dark wavy hair was longish. The envy of many a female. His eyes of deep brown and his black-clad body which gave him a look of both sinister and alluring. A rugged stature of a man with muscles bulging through the tight top. A man who could end the turmoil in her life.

Ted thought she looked so sweet and trusting. He bent forward, kissing her. She put her hands on his chest. He could feel their warmth against his heart.

The spell broke when there was a noise outside. Ted stepped to the front door. Tommy was sliding from his truck.

"Hi, Tommy, what brought you here?"

"I came to tell you someone is at my place, looking for you. She is a girl you use to know. Her name is Diane. She found Maxwell in the phone book, thinking it was you. She is fearful for her boyfriend and wants your advice. Are you coming?"

"I can't, Tommy, I have to be somewhere else, so can you stall her until tomorrow?"

"I think not, can't you come for even a few minutes? She is pretty distraught about something."

"Okay, Emma, and I will follow in my car."

"Emma is here? Things have changed evidently." Tommy observed Ted's impatient look. "Okay." He got back into his truck and took off for home.

Emma was standing at the door as if waiting for permission to leave.

Ted pulled her out of the house, then let her go as he put the key in the lock.

When they were in the car, Emma said, "I hope Beth is alright and got home okay. I worry about her. She is deeply distressed. You know I think it is rather odd the way Coulter was so insistent about taking Beth home. I wonder why I felt that way?"

"Another thing that bothers me, why would he ask about my car? That is strange. He was acting weird. I don't think it was being hungover either. He has a fiancée Diane. Do you think that is who your brother is talking about?"

Ted replied, "I don't know Coulter at all. You would be the best judge of his behavior. The car bit was peculiar."

"And do you know what else is doubly odd, Ted? A man called to service my car on a special offer. I never get my car serviced. The chauffeur looks after all the maintenance on the vehicles."

"Yes, that is rather odd," Ted said but with no doubt in his voice. He knew why the man on the phone was calling. The guy needed her car back to recover the diamonds. Ted's finding them had slipped out of his mind until this moment. Was it only a little over two weeks since he heard Emma's first screams for help? Was there any connection between the voice on the phone and Coulter's quizzing Emma about her car?

Ted was concerned about going to Tommy's because he wondered how Emma would feel facing this girl if it was Coulter's girlfriend.

"Emma, how well do you know Coulter's fiancée?"

"Not well, but she has been to a few parties at our place that Jimmy has had. She seems to cling to Coulter, but he doesn't seem to mind. So, we never really talked much. How well did you know her?" she asked with speculation in her voice.

"Not well, either. I met her one time at a bar in town with another girl. I got the impression they were slumming. So, I struck up a conversation with them, to say hands off to the raunchier of the crowd. We talked for quite a while. I eventually took them both home as they had been drinking considerably. Diane was last out of the car because she lived further away. She tried to come onto me. So, to get her out of the car, I asked her on a date. I took her for dinner a couple of nights later, not asking her out again."

Ted wanted Emma to have a clear picture of Diane due to Tommy's insinuation. He didn't want her thinking there was ever a close relationship between them.

They arrived at Tommy's place. He was waiting in the driveway for them. "I didn't know what else to do for her, so I left her with Sally. I headed out to your place. I could have phoned, but I wasn't sure you might be out hiking."

"That's alright, Tommy. Let's go in and get this over with as I have to be on my way." He followed Tommy. Emma lagging brought up the rear.

"Oh, Ted." The blond girl went flying into Ted's arms. She was stuck to him like Velcro. "Ted, I didn't know where else to turn. You were such a caring person when I first met you. I need help." She was still plastered to his body when she looked over Ted's shoulder into Emma's eyes. She stepped back guiltily. "Emma, I didn't know you knew Ted," she said, dragging her words out.

"Hello, Diane. Yes, I know Tommy, Sally, and Ted. Hello Sally. Nice to see you again, you are looking good and pregnant now, I see."

Sally patted her stomach. "Yes, it is getting hard to hide."

Ted, anxious to be on his way, asked Diane why she was here.

"Ted, I don't know what to do anymore. My boyfriend is in trouble. I am beside myself with worry. You were the only one I could think of to help me," Diane said.

"What do you mean he is in trouble?"

"He keeps disappearing at night. When he does turn up, his actions are irritable, and yes, even frightening. He is by nature, a very easy-going person, who I have more or less known all my life. Our parents are close friends. I was so happy when he asked me to marry him. It is a two-year engagement now. As the time to start the wedding arrangements gets closer, the more agitated he gets. In the past few days, he has pulled a disappearing act like Jimmy. Do you think whoever took Jimmy took Coulter too?"

"No, I don't, Diane. We saw Coulter this morning. He was fine. He said he was going to your place after he dropped off Beth, who we took to his place to recover her purse. Coulter offered to drive Beth home." Ted finished reassuringly.

"Well, he never came. He has been doing that a lot lately," Diane said worriedly. "What am I going to do? How can I find out why he is acting this way?"

"Diane, I don't have a suggestion right now for you, but I will look into it for you tomorrow. Maybe talk with Coulter. Will that help?"

"Yes, I guess so if that is what you think is best. Maybe he will show up tonight. We could have a serious conversation for a change. But I would appreciate you talking with him too," she finished lamely.

"I have to take Emma home now, so talking to Coulter will have to wait until tomorrow."

He went over to Emma, who was looking on with interest. Taking her arm. "Are you ready to go?" Not giving her a chance to reply, he turned to Tommy and Sally saying goodnight. Ted started for the door without a word of consent from Emma.

When they were in the car, she turned to Ted. What came out was a comment about Diane.

"She was rather clingy for a casual acquaintance, wasn't she?" Letting him squirm a bit. She was aware Diane was a clingy type of girl.

Ted looked at her intently, detecting a twinkle in her eyes, knowing that she wasn't angry over the situation. With a chuckle, he replied, "yeah, she is the clingy type, that's all. Now Coulter is a different matter. He seems to be involved in something. I wonder what?"

"Ted, he used to do the books for my father before I came into the company. Could he be involved in the appearance of the bogus companies? No, he can't be; he never shows any interest in the company, according to Jimmy. To me, he was always just Jimmy's friend. So, I have never thought about it. I must have been subconsciously uncomfortable with him as I took his job."

"Yes, that is a new piece of information to take into consideration. Now, if we could find the link between him and the Belle Star, we would be in business."

"Do you think that is where he keeps disappearing? Do you think he had a part in Jimmy's disappearance? But he was concerned when Daddy phoned him about Jimmy's vanishing."

"We can't jump to any conclusions until I get a chance to talk to him. Now the time must be spent getting Jimmy's rescue in place. Your father knows what he has to do. So, let me do the rest. I know you are uptight about this, if we use the element of surprise, it has an excellent chance of success. An overabundance of confidence is not wise either. We have to factor in the unknown, which is how well the crew is distracted by the fire. If they aren't, we could be in a great deal of trouble before we get Jimmy off the ship. After all, they have the numbers, over our four. Jimmy will be no help in his drugged state." It wasn't Ted's intention to frighten her. He felt he had to make her aware of the possibility that the rescue might fail. "I wish we didn't need the fire and had the crew all sleeping. Due to their night activities of late, we can't take the chance."

Emma was still looking at Ted, ignoring the negative things he was saying. His strong confidence and strength were something she wanted to draw from to get her through this. She put her hand over his on the steering wheel. His hand turned over to grasp hers tightly.

He wanted her to feel confident that he would succeed not just for Jimmy's sake but for her too. She would be devastated if Jimmy died in the rescue. Ted smiled at her confidently while inside; he was apprehensive. Loving her the way he did, Ted just hoped when this was all over that Emma could learn to love him.

They arrived at the gate, which opened as soon as he said his name. The car spurted forward as Ted gave it extra gas in his excitement of the night ahead. When they arrived at the door, Detective Harding was waiting. Why was he here again?

"Hello," Ted said as he came around the car to open Emma's door. "Are you waiting for someone in particular?"

"Yes, I wanted to ask Emma a few more questions if she is feeling up to it? She must be feeling better if she went out with you. It seems that things have changed between you two since I saw you in the hospital. Things seem different now?" with a big question in his voice.

"Well, you know how it is when a person has time to reflect on events. They can sometimes change things." Ted eased Emma up the stairs past the detective.

"Where is your sidekick?" Ted asked.

Harding replied, "he is not attached to me in any way. I can be a free thinker. May I come in, Emma?" he asked respectfully.

"Yes, I guess so, do I have a choice?" Emma's voice was resigned.

"No, not really." Harding followed both of them into the study where Emma's steps led them.

"Please get this over with as soon as possible I have other things on my schedule right now. Will you take long?" Ted inquired.

"No, not if Emma answers my questions honestly," replied Harding as he sat down on the chair while Ted and Emma dropped down on the sofa.

"What do you want to know?" Emma asked with a calm voice as though she had nothing to hide. When in reality, she was quaking in her boots.

"Emma, when you drove out to Old Canyon Road, did you deliberately have intentions of doing away with yourself?" Harding had taken out a notebook that he was looking at intently rather than at Emma. He knew she was about to lie. He did not want to see the emotions crawling across her face. He liked this beautiful girl. He knew she had been through a lot with her near-death situation. But he still had to ask.

"I had something on my mind that I was trying to think out when I realized I was on Old Canyon Road. A deer jumped out in front of me. I pulled the steering wheel sideways. In my panic, I must have frozen with my foot full down on the gas. It wasn't till I hit the rock that I stopped. Then I became aware of what had happened." She stopped and sat there waiting, to hear him pick her excuse apart.

"Where is your brother Jimmy? I hear he is missing. I didn't see a missing person's report, why not?" He shot her a look directly this time to catch her reaction to his latest question.

"Oh." Emma put her head down and started to cry. Ted put a comforting arm around her.

"Did you have to pull that on her so bluntly? Couldn't you have been a little more tactful? After all, this is her twin you are talking about, and they are very close." Emma was crying into Ted's chest.

"Maybe you could answer the question, Mr. Maxwell? Evidently, you two have become very close." The detective was looking on with interest. He would gladly change places with this young man and have this sweet thing crying on his chest. "I repeat the question. Why was Jimmy's disappearance not being reported to the police?"

"Perhaps the reason is that they were waiting for Jimmy to show up on his own. In the belief that he isn't in any danger or anything. Perhaps he got tied up in a long-running poker game or something like that," Ted said factually.

"Miss Gibson, is it usual for your brother to go off to play poker when he has a date with friends for dinner?" He flipped back a couple of pages. "I interviewed Beth Cranston. She said Jimmy didn't show up for their dinner date. She said he wasn't into poker that much when Mr. Stewart suggested the same."

Ted looked at Emma after she removed her head from his chest. He was angry with the detective for making her cry. Although Ted knew the detective had no choice but to do his job. He wanted to wipe away the evidence of her tears, but he didn't want the detective to realize his true feelings for this girl.

She drew a deep breath then turned towards Detective Harding.

"I am distraught by his disappearance. I don't know anything that could help you." She sniffed as if for effect.

The detective stood up and looked at the young couple on the couch. Realizing these two were closer than he first suspected. They had closed ranks against his probing.

"Well, thank you for seeing me. Don't bother to see me out. I can find the door myself." As if he wanted to get away from there as quickly as possible. He was quite envious of that young man sitting there with that girl half reclining in his arms.

Ted sat and held onto Emma, not wanting to let her go. He also knew he had to meet the guys down on the dock on Harbor Street. It was a place where they had leased a small section of a warehouse for their Scuba Diving Club and their diving gear.

Emma was so quiet he thought she might have dozed off, but when he looked down, her eyes were studying his face.

"Ted, do you think you can pull this off tonight? I am so nervous.

That detective didn't help matters."

"Are you aware that you have beautiful eyes?" Ted asked. "They are so blue like the sky. I could get lost in them."

Emma blinked then opened them wide, a new light in her eyes. This man was getting deeper and deeper inside of her. She hadn't been aware it was happening. She squeezed his arm. "Answer my question. I have to know what you are feeling about tonight's success?"

"Okay, I will give you a rating on a scale of one to ten as a six of success, will that do? A lot depends on the crew's interest in Charlie's fire. Cliff is going to contact the fire department with the belief that the whole dock might go up and requires more apparatus. Their noisy arrival will be loud and long in the usual quiet of the night. There is nothing more panicking in the night than the wail of sirens, police or fire trucks, and believe me when that many fire trucks arrive you can bet there will be police along for sure." Pausing.

"Now taking all that in, I ask you to be patient. As soon as we get back to the warehouse, I will phone you. Now be a brave girl until then." He wanted to tell her he loved her, but he had to do that in silence because she was under such a strain.

He was now standing at the door. Matilda stood there watching this strong young man holding her little girl so gently. Matilda didn't want to break up the moment, but she wanted to give him her words of thanks.

He gently released Emma stepping back after he had placed a loving kiss on her forehead. Then he took her hand and squeezed it.

Matilda fearing, he would be gone before she could interrupt, stepped forward, and placed her hand over theirs. "Thank you for your help in rescuing Jimmy."

Then he broke the hold. Matilda was left holding Emma's hand as he said farewell. Then he gave them both a wink going out the door jovially. Knowing he was coming back to this girl made his steps lighter.

Chapter Twenty-Three

After stopping for a meal, realizing he hadn't eaten much that day, Ted arrived at the warehouse. The guys were all there, including Mannie and Dalton.

"Hey, when did you guys get in?" Ted asked, shaking their hands.

"Jordan called us. When a buddy needs help, we are here for you," Dalton said, punching Ted playfully.

"Look guys I have to be honest with you. This may not be a piece of cake. The person we are going after is drugged, so he is unable to walk, I'm sure."

Mannie said, "that's no problem. I am a firefighter, as you know. I hear the fire department is going to be involved. Jordan told us a bit about the situation as much as he knew that is."

"Well, the plan is that Charlie, the night watchman, is to start a fire at 1:15, the reason given. He has to cause a diversion to get the attention of the Belle Star. He has noticed strange behavioral incidents late at night on the ship, he accepted that. The fire wouldn't be necessary except for these nightly activities."

"We have fifteen minutes to get to the ship. But we will standoff boarding as we want the crew to have front row seats watching the dock and its activities. We have to delay until we hear the whistle on the dock near where we will be hiding. Cliff, who works for Mr. Gibson, will be eyeing the situation. When he feels it is safe to proceed, then he will come and whistle. We had to let him in on it because Mr. Gibson can't be seen at the docks."

"We didn't want any details going out until we knew who all the players are." Ted glanced over the men. "I appreciate you all coming. My plan called for four divers. We now have six. I want you to decide who is going. Mannie, I would like you and Dalton to go as you two have had the most training in rescuing, so that means one more as I want to be there too."

"That's easy Jordan should be the fourth. We are just glad to be here. We will be ready when you get back to help the guys out of the water and make sure there is no one else lurking about," Karl said.

"We won't be carrying firearms, so we have to be cautious. Don't get cocky." Looking straight at Jordan. "Now that isn't to say that the crew hasn't got guns. But we can hope the action on the dock will attract their full attention."

"Cliff is going to call in another 911 saying the fire is very seriously getting out of hand to get more sirens wailing in the night attracting the police as well, no doubt. He is going to make sure the fire warrants it, not Charlie."

"After we climb on the ship, we need to get to the cabin quickly, two of us in the cabin and two in the corridor. I will be one in the cabin as I want to make sure Jimmy is okay. Dalton, how about you and Jordan on the watch? We will use liquid soap, making it easier to put a wet suit on him as time is important. We will hit the water at 1:25." He looked at his watch. "It is 12:10 now. Any questions?"

Jordan asked. "What about the cabin, won't it be locked and a guard outside?"

"They have been keeping him drugged, so I'm hoping they don't feel the need for a guard or to lock the cabin. However, I have a tool if we need to pick the lock. Let's hope it won't be necessary as it will cut into our time. Suiting him up will be the most time consumed, but we have no choice in the matter. The water is too cold without a wet suit."

Jordan asked, "do you think he will survive in the water with all those drugs they have been giving him?"

"Hopefully, Jimmy is about due for another dose when we arrive so that he will be semi-aware of things. That's one of the reasons I wanted Dalton and Mannie along. They have the most rescue experience. Jimmy will have the aid of a full-face diving mask with a small air bottle. Hopefully, we will be able to surface occasional, to help his breathing. I am leaving that part up to Mannie or Dalton. Thank you, guys, for being here to help." He knew he was asking a lot of these men risking their lives for someone they have never met.

Ted tried to release some of his tension by walking around. Jordan came over saying,

"Ted, you can only do your best, and that goes for all of us."

"Thanks. I am sorry about singling you out back there, but I don't want to take any risks. We want it to happen quickly but also safely."

Jordan replied, "Mannie and Dalton will be able to work things out in the water if we can get back off the ship without drawing attention. Now come back and have a drink of coffee, and we'll shoot the breeze until it's time to suit up."

* * *

Emma's mind was racing.

Will Ted and his group pull this off? Will he be able to call right away? She just had to put her faith in him. She wanted to call Coulter as she felt now that he was the guilty culprit, but there was to be no contact until the night was over.

Emma brought her mind to the twinkle of light that came into Ted's eyes. His smile made her feel warm inside, and also the shared kisses on the bluff. She put her fingers to her lips. She could almost feel them tingle with the thought of those kisses. Her imaginings were interrupted when her father laid his hand lovingly on her head.

"Darling, I know the waiting is hard. I have every confidence in that young man. Can I talk you into going and getting some rest? It will be hours before we hear anything."

"No, Daddy, I want to stay here where we last sat together. I feel close to him when I sit here, somehow."

Malvin looked closely at his daughter with a satisfied smile. So, his daughter was mesmerized by Ted. He would be pleased if that were the direction that this was going.

"Emma, do you want some tea or coffee I know Matilda isn't sleeping either. I'm sure she would like to be with us while we wait."

"All right, Daddy, tell Matilda I would like tea and to bring a cup for herself."

"That's my girl." Malvin walked towards the kitchen. This waiting was getting to him. The internet hadn't been a distraction.

* * *

It was finally time to suit up. The scuba divers had been chatting trading banter about past times together. Nothing could compare with what laid ahead of them this night. Ted had never seen active duty. Although he had signed up for the Home-guard. He had some weekend training sessions with them.

Arnie and Karl were helping with the equipment checking the air tanks and giving assistance to the divers suiting up. They headed for the wharf after Arnie checked to see that there was nobody around. The more secret their activities, the better the chance for success.

When they got to the wharf, they stood in a circle. Ted put out his hand, and one after another, they put their hand on top until they were all joined. Ted grinned with white teeth against his blackened face.

The black Mannie assured him, wouldn't come off in the water. Dalton had joked it took weeks to get rid of it. That was the least of Ted's fears at the moment. What was Jimmy's condition going to be? Was he still in the same cabin? What if they had moved him off the ship?

They broke apart. Ted's watch showed 1:25, and the four men headed for the edge of the water and donned their flippers. One by one, they slipped into the water. Then came up and gave the two on the dock the high sign. They submerged again with Dalton and Mannie in the lead. Dalton was the navigator. He had a good sense of direction with all his experience. They were each following the headlight on the diver in front of them. The lights were to be extinguished when they got near the ship. The night and the dark water made visibility tricky otherwise.

They had entered the water well away from their destination, so there would be no visual contact from the Belle Star. They arrived at the agreed rendezvous three minutes ahead of time, which pleased Ted. Most of his experience had been during daylight hours. His plan and his determination to be part of the rescue gave him a position on the team.

They were holding onto the under pilings of a dock next to the nearby Belle Star. Would Cliff be here? They could see a red glow in the night sky, so the fire was burning. They could hear sirens coming closer. They hoped Cliff got here soon to signal. They were anxious to get on the ship to do what was necessary to save Jimmy.

Now the night was a wail of sirens. The fire trucks must have arrived at the dock. They knew Cliff was sticking around to ensure the fire's longevity and to put in that second call to 911. He was also going to keep an eye on the Belle Star for movement on deck.

When Cliff finally arrived, they almost thought something had gone wrong. However, the night sky was a red and orange glow with black smoke.

Cliff whistled. They heard it twice, then he broke into a tune, sauntering back towards the fire again.

The divers dipped below the surface and headed for the Belle Star. Killing the lights as they neared the ship. Checking first for the crew, Dalton used a launcher to send the grappling hook on board, hoping no one would be near when it made noise landing.

Giving Dalton time to do the launch, Mannie surfaced twenty feet away from Dalton. He peered upwards but couldn't see any sign of anyone looking over or hear voices. The rest surfaced nearby. Dalton was pulling the line taut. He tested it with his weight; it was holding. They ducked back under the water again, waiting for a few minutes. When they came up, there were no faces or sounds. The men proceeded to the ship. They pulled themselves up hand over hand. They had another rope they would anchor when they got up there, for the escape trip down to be faster.

They started disappearing onto the ship. The prearranged sign of danger was not necessary for the two left scaling the rope. So, all seemed to be going well for the first part. Dalton quickly tied the spare rope securely for the escape. Ted was last on board. He pointed in the direction they were to go, although he had drawn a map of the layout of the ship in the briefing they had in the warehouse. They had removed their flippers and had them anchored to their belts at the back. They wore their aluminum tanks in case a quick exit was necessary.

They sneaked along the corridors to the cabin where Ted had heard the men talking about Jimmy. The door was unlocked, a faint light penetrated the darkness of the cabin from the open door. Ted motioned Mannie in, while Jordan and Dalton took their positions in the corridor. Jimmy was lying on the bunk face down and in a relaxed, drugged stupor.

Ted had the wet suit and full-face mask in a waterproof duffel bag. Quickly he released the suit. Mannie had Jimmy turned over and sitting with his feet over the side of the bunk. They removed Jimmy's clothes. They soaped him quickly. Ted started maneuvering the wet suit onto his legs. It was sliding on better than they had expected. Mannie was pulling up the right side while Ted was pulling up the left. They had him suited up and the air mask attached.

Jimmy seemed to be aware someone was there but not quite comprehending what was going on.

Mannie was carrying Jimmy on his shoulders. Ted looked out at Jordan. The corridor was still all clear, according to Jordan's hand movements. It would seem like the diversion was working.

The men made it to where the ropes were hanging. They quickly put on their flippers. Jordan and Mannie went over first to be in the water to receive Jimmy. Ted and Dalton tied one of the ropes around Jimmy, lowering him to the waiting divers. Then Ted and Dalton quickly exited the ship. They were nearing the water. Dalton being closer, decided this was too slow, letting go of the rope. He headed for the water with a splash. He went under, hoping he would not go too deep for a quick surfacing.

Ted heard the splash, hesitating, then felt his rope pulled upwards. He looked up, and the First Officer held the rope. First must have heard Dalton hit the water. Ted was going down as fast as the line was going up, but he was still too far above the water. He didn't want to let go until he was sure Dalton and Jimmy were away from the area.

The First Officer was yelling for help. Ted was slowly dragged upwards. He would soon run out of rope. His only hope was to drop down and not land on someone below. He was worried that the First Officer's cries for help would get attention. Then running feet, another head appeared above him, grabbing the rope.

The combination of looking up and the heavy action on the rope by the crew, made him whack his head heavily on the side of the ship. Ted let go. His body plunged downwards. The momentum was such that when he hit the water, he kept going down and down and down. Ted felt disoriented. Was he tumbling? Which way was up? He tried to clear his head to orient himself. He was still feeling groggy from the thump on the head, but he knew he had to go up. He shook his head, trying to get a fix on his body. Was he up or down? He had never experienced this before. Although he had heard of others that had this happen.

Ted had decided he must have tumbled, so he turned his body upwards. He was going to strike out with his feet for momentum when someone grabbed his leg and pulled. Ted knew then he was heading down deeper rather than up. He turned himself over. There was Dalton with a light on his head shinning upwards as the way to go. They went up together.

Dalton stopped him before they reached the surface and motioned to go in the direction of the light. Ted changed course as something hit his arm. Then a bullet hit his back. It threw him sideways. Dalton happened to look back and see Ted flounder. He went back and grabbed him. The two dived deeper and swam away from the area. Dalton, an excellent navigator, made it back to the dock where they had waited for the signal. The others were there waiting. Jimmy was on his back. Mannie was holding him up. Jimmy seemed to be breathing okay, so the cold water must have helped ease his stupor a bit.

When Dalton and Ted appeared, they gave a thumbs up. They all dived back under. Dalton leading looked back, noting Ted's slow movements. Ted needed his help.

Mannie was guiding Jimmy with Jordan's help, surfacing periodically to ease Jimmy's breathing, and hoping not to draw anyone's attention, which made for a lengthy process. Noticing Jimmy wasn't breathing too well, they surfaced. They would have to stay on the surface now. The men kept moving slowly due to a semi-drugged man along with a disabled Ted. What had taken them fifteen minutes on the way over was now past half an hour. They weren't there yet. A boat appeared. It was Arnie.

Arnie pulled up beside them. Dalton helped Ted in first as they reached the boat. Dalton and Mannie eased Jimmy in too. Then Dalton pulled himself up behind Jimmy. Mannie said. "Go, Jordan, and I will keep going in the water."

Arnie asked, "are you okay, Dalton? What happened?" The boat was moving full out towards their dock as Dalton yelled back.

"Yes, I'm okay. It was too slow a descent, so I dropped into the water. One of the crew must have heard me. We would have got away clear, but Ted was being pulled upwards quicker than his ascent until he was so high, he had no choice but to drop. When he went under, he just kept going down and down. He seemed to be disoriented because he was trying to go deeper when I found him. When we were back near the surface, they were shooting. They must've hit Ted in the arm. I hope that's all."

Ted was losing consciousness.

Dalton reached for Ted, giving him the once over. His hand came away with blood on it. He looked over at Arnie steering the boat.

Ahead they heard a yell.

Karl was on his knees, grabbing for the boat. Arnie was scrambling out before it stopped and quickly tied the boat to the dock.

Dalton was passing the semi-drugged Jimmy to Karl. Arnie came back to help with Ted.

"Ted has been shot, we think twice, in the arm and his back." Dalton had removed his tank and Ted's in the boat, making it easier to carry Ted.

"Where are the others?" asked Arnie. "They should be here by now."

Just then, two heads appeared in the water, making their way to the dock.

"All accounted for," said Karl in relief.

"We need to shed these wet suits quickly, then get these two into the cars and to the hospital," said Dalton.

Mannie had changed from his wet suit, only partially dressing in pants and thick socks, carrying a sweatshirt. He loped to the car.

The others went inside, taking off their wet suits and donning their clothes quickly. Jordan ran out the door as Mannie pulled up.

"Do you think we need two cars?"

"We will put Jimmy and Ted in this car. You can get in the back with Ted. We'll head out. The others can follow in the other cars after everything is complete here." Mannie reached over to open the door. Jordan climbed in the back. Dalton was carrying Ted, and Jordon helped Ted in.

Arnie had Jimmy putting him in the front and strapped him in while Mannie held him up. After Arnie closed the door, Mannie leaned Jimmy sideways, so his head was resting against the window. He shoved his sweatshirt under Jimmy's head. Dalton gave the car a whack as he closed the door. Mannie maneuvered the car into the night and headed out onto the road and his destination Mountain Hill Hospital.

Jordan said, "we almost did it, didn't we?" Mannie could hear the adrenalin in Jordan's voice.

"Take it easy. Ted's going to be all right. Once we get him to the hospital, with attention, he'll be fine," Mannie said with hope in his voice.

Ted started mumbling.

Mannie asked, "what's he saying?"

"I don't know I can't make it out."

"Emma, call Emma." Ted passed out again.

Jordan said, "who's Emma? Is that Mr. Gibson's daughter's name?"

Mannie replied, "I think so. We will have to call from the hospital."

The hospital emergency sign on the roadside appeared to be directing them down a roadway before the hospital entrance. They went in behind the hospital. There was the sign in big red letters EMERGENCY.

Mannie pulled up with a squeal of brakes that seemed to get some attention from inside. Because by the time he got around to the other side of the car, a stretcher was at the door proceeding towards them.

Mannie yelled to one of the attendants to help Ted out of the car with Jordan's help while he headed for the door with Jimmy. Jordan was issuing information as to Ted's injuries. Mannie was able to set Jimmy down on a gurney near the nurse's station. A doctor came to his side on the run.

"This man has been drugged for at least three maybe four days. I don't know what drug. The other one was shot twice," Mannie said.

The nurses were looking at Mannie strangely as he paraded around in pants and socks and blackface. In his concern for Jimmy, he had forgotten to grab his sweatshirt from the car.

A nurse came forward to check Ted as another doctor arrived, pushing the nurse aside. "Gun wounds, let's get him up to OR immediately." Neither seemed to acknowledge Ted's strange attire. A doctor was checking out Jimmy as Ted's doctor came over. "What's this guy's problem?"

"He was drugged for three or four days but no information on what drug. His attire indicates being in the water but no explanation so far."

Doctor Hall turned to the nurse. "Call Dr. Adams, a drug specialist." He turned back to the other doctor. "Larry, I want you in OR with me to deal with the gunshot victim. He is shot more than once."

"Okay, I will be right with you after I get this guy settled in a room."

Larry swung the gurney into the nearest room and gave the nurse instructions. "Take his vital signs and stay with him until Dr. Adams arrives. I'll arrange for a blood test on my way to the OR."

Mannie and Jordon were pacing up and down. Mannie ignored the looks of the people whose attention was on his unusual attire.

Dalton, Arnie, and Karl showed up. They walked quickly inside and stopped as they reached the area where Mannie and Jordon were pacing.

"Well?"

"Ted has gone into OR. Jimmy is awaiting a specialist in drugs. That is all we know so far," Mannie said.

Jordan said, "we have to call Emma."

"Who is Emma?" asked Dalton.

"We think it is Mr. Gibson's daughter. Ted was mumbling her name on the way here." Jordan went over to the information desk. The nurse said, "who's going to give us the particulars on these two victims you brought in?"

"I will, but first I need a telephone book. Better still phone information and ask for the phone number for Mr. Gibson. I think his first name starts with M." He remembered Ted saying his first name but couldn't recall it now. The nurse was writing down a number. She hung up the phone and handed it to Jordon along with the number. Jordon dialed.

A male voice anxiously answered. "Yes. Ted?"

"No, Mr. Gibson, it's not Ted. It is his friend Jordan. Ted's hurt, but he asked me to phone Emma and tell her, we saved Jimmy. Only Ted got shot a couple of times."

"How is he?"

"I don't know. Ted is in the OR."

"How is Jimmy?"

"They have called in a specialist to see him. He is still under the influence of drugs."

"We will be right there. It will take about 30 minutes. Emma will want to come too. We want to thank you all in person. Will all of you be there?"

"Yes, no one is leaving until Ted comes out of the OR. We are in the emergency waiting area. You will easily recognize us when you come. We are the ones doing the pacing."

Chapter Twenty-Four

Malvin put down the phone. He held out his arms to Emma, who had been asking him questions ever since he had picked up the phone.

"They have Jimmy. He is at the hospital. They are all there. We are going down to see them right now. The doctor has called in a specialist for Jimmy."

Tears of relief were running down Emma's and Matilda's faces. Malvin's eyes felt watery too. He swallowed hard.

"Daddy, how is Ted? I got the impression it wasn't him that called. He promised to call me Daddy. He promised..." she trailed off in sobs.

"Baby, Ted has been hurt. We will see him when we get to the hospital," he said evasively.

"How bad, Daddy?" The tears were uncontrolled.

"We won't know how bad until we get there. Come on, let's get ready to go. Matilda, you stay here until Cliff phones about conditions of the fire."

"Okay, Mr. Gibson, you and Emma go. I'll hold things together here."

Emma was wiping her eyes with the sleeve of her sweater as she headed for the door. She wanted to get to the hospital quickly. Malvin was hard on her heels. He had called Roger so that the limousine would be at the front door shortly.

Emma grabbed her purse, and a jacket. Malvin was right behind her. They ran out the door which Matilda held open. Her "good luck," was heard as they headed down the steps to the limo. Roger held the door for Emma and Malvin to duck inside.

"Where to Mr. G?"

"The Mountain Hill Hospital Emergency."

Roger dived back into the limo, heading down the drive. The gate automatically opened at their approach. They were zooming through the night faster than the posted speed but not exceeding the capabilities of the driver, which brought the hospital in view in record time.

Malvin recognized the men as soon as he went through the emergency doors. They were systematically pacing back and forth, seeming to have their assigned route. There were two sitting watching the pacing.

He walked over to them with his hand out, ready to shake their hands as they paced in his direction.

"Mr. Gibson?" Dalton asked as he shook Malvin's hand. "Dalton Robertson is my name. This is Mannie Johnson, and that is Jordan White, and the two over there are Arnie and Karl."

Malvin went around, shaking everyone's hands.

"I can't thank you enough for what you men did for my family and me tonight."

Emma stood waiting. "Daddy."

"Oh yes, this is my daughter Emma. How are Ted and Jimmy?" All the men acknowledged her.

"The specialist is working on Jimmy in the third room down. Ted is still in the OR," Dalton said. He was watching Emma's face as he said this. Her reaction was obvious. There was more to this Ted and Emma thing than he realized.

Malvin said, "Emma, you wait here. I'll see about Jimmy. These men will look after you, okay?"

When she turned to follow her father with her eyes, he was entering a room down the hall. Jordon had come over and put his arm around her.

"He will be alright, and so will Ted. Ted is too stubborn to let a little old bullet take him down. Come over here and sit down." He sat beside her, and she was gripping his hand tightly.

Dalton arrived with coffees. The nurse's station had provided them at his request.

Jordon held the cup while talking to Emma until she took the coffee and started to sip it. He accepted another coffee Dalton held out. Dalton went back for more coffees. The nurse had four more cups poured.

"Thank you, Miss." Dalton supplied her with a big grin that lit up his black face. The nurse didn't know what to make of these strange men. One was unusually attired while others had black painted faces. Dalton realized that they must be a peculiar sight. He didn't enlighten the nurse. He just took the coffee with smiling thanks. He completed his coffee run then walked over to Emma.

Jordan said, "Emma, I want you to know that Ted kept murmuring your name even in his semi-conscious state. He kept saying he had to call you."

Emma looked at Jordan with gratitude.

"I hope he will be okay?" Her voice was weak but clear.

Jordon answered, "Emma, he is going to be fine, isn't he Dalton?"

"Of course. Ted is too tough to let a bullet bother him." His voice held more conviction than he was feeling. Ted had been in the OR too long to be a simple wound.

Malvin came back saying. "Dr. Adams thinks they know the drug that is in Jimmy's system. They are treating him for it. They put him on intravenous. He says Jimmy will be fine when his system gets clear of the drug. Thankfully he is partway there. Have you heard about Ted yet?"

"No, not yet," Dalton replied as footsteps came down the corridor.

The doctor from the OR was walking towards them. The one named Larry, Dalton recalled. They all quickly gathered around.

"Dr. Hall has removed one bullet. His arm was no problem. It was just a graze. The bullet in his back pierced his lung. We had to do more extensive work to remove the bullet and repair the lung. But we feel he will be okay."

There was a definite sigh of relief amongst them.

Detective Harding arrived on the scene, just missing the doctor's message. Emma turned to look at him with distaste. He met her look and smiled.

"Sorry to disturb you, people, right now. But I have to ask what is going on here? I hear there was a man shot, and another man is heavily drugged." His eyes never left Emma's face. He could see the dislike in her eyes, but he had to be there no matter how she felt about him. She did not respond to his smile, so he looked to her father.

"Mr. Gibson?"

"My son was kidnapped and held hostage on the Belle Star. These men freed him. Ted, you remember him, well he was shot."

The detective acknowledged knowing Ted and asked how he was.

"Ted is going to be okay," the doctor replied. "He had a bullet graze on his arm. However, the bullet removed from his back pierced his lung..." He stopped at Emma's strangled gasp. Jordan tightened his arm around her as Malvin came to her other side, gripping her arm. The two men led her away as the detective looked on with concern. He had seen she was fond of Ted at the questioning yesterday. He turned back to the others as the doctor walked away in response to a call from a nurse needing him for another patient.

"Who is the spokesman here?"

Dalton and Mannie both stepped forward. "Which one wants to tell me exactly what happened down at the docks tonight? I know there was shooting and a fire. The Port Authorities gave us the information."

Dalton related the events starting with Ted's request for help from his scuba club divers to rescue Jimmy, describing how they went about it. Mannie took over, relating Jimmy's rescue from the ship. "The Belle Star's crew discovered us before we got clear."

Dalton took over about Ted's near capture and his drop into the water, his reaching him in the depths below and bringing him up towards the surface. "Ted was shot before we could get away from the area."

"That is unfortunate about Ted after his past back injury." The detective showed his concern.

"Ted is a resilient guy. He will bounce back with time." Dalton turned towards Emma as if saying, end of the interview.

Harding went over to Emma, who was sitting between her father and a diver.

"Emma, I'm truly sorry about Ted. I'm glad they released your brother. I will be having the Port Authorities detain the ship until a thorough investigation is completed." He looked at her, silently pleading for her to understand his job was the reason he kept coming into her life.

Emma looked up, and she noted his caring look. She gave him a weak smile and said, "thank you for your concern. I hope you can prove guilt on the part of the Belle Star for Jimmy as well as Ted."

"I will do my best." Detective Harding swung away happier than when he first saw her look of distaste.

"Daddy, do you think we can go and see Ted or Jimmy?"

"Jimmy, yes. He is still in a drugged stupor, but he is going to come around slowly. I don't know about Ted I'll have to ask." Malvin went to find a nurse about Ted.

Cliff was entering the emergency as Malvin reached the nurse's station. Cliff walked over to him. "Malvin, how are Jimmy and Ted? Matilda told me all she knew, which wasn't much."

"Jimmy's had a specialist treating him, and Ted had two bullets wounds. He is going to be laid up for a while. How are things at the dock?"

"Buzzing with police and Port Authorities; that is why it took me so long to get away. The Belle Star will not be leaving on Tuesday, that's for sure. The fire, we were able to contain just to the night watchman's hut and the small shed beside it. We had so much apparatus there that there was no way that fire was going anywhere else," he said with a laugh. "The ship's crew were thoroughly entertained until the shots rang out. Then they were scurrying in every direction. Some tried to get off the ship, but the police were quick to deter them."

Malvin said, "thanks, I wish I could've been there rather than waiting it out at home. Although Emma was glad of my company."

Cliff looked over at Emma. "How is she handling things?"

"She wants to see Jimmy and Ted. But she's having difficulties which one to see first. I think that young man has made quite an impression on her. I was going to ask this sweet young lady if we could get in to see Ted."

"I will ask for you since you have such a special way of asking."

She broke into a beautiful smile as she rounded the desk to go down to recovery. She came back to Malvin, who was back with the divers. Cliff was answering their inquiries as to the dock activities.

"You can go in for five minutes. Is this girl named Emma? He has been calling for her in his delirium."

"Yes, that is my daughter." He walked over to her and told Emma she could see Ted for five minutes. She jumped up animated for the first time since entering the hospital. Malvin and Emma headed down to recovery.

They stopped just inside the door, there were three beds occupied, but Emma's eyes fastened on Ted. She glided across the room and placed her hand over Ted's. His eyelids fluttered but didn't open. Emma felt his hand turn over and embrace hers.

She leaned forward and placed a kiss on his forehead. He moved his head towards her and opened his eyes. His lips moved, but no sound came out. She leaned over him again as if to hear what he wanted to say. Their lips met as if on their own accord. The kiss lasted for only a second as he drifted back into a drugged sleep. But there was a smile on his lips.

Emma's imploring look sprang to her father with a grin as if to say, do you mind? Malvin returned her smile with a nod of acceptance.

The nurse motioned that they would have to leave. She whispered, "he is sleeping much more peacefully now." She had witnessed the kiss too and knew this man was going to be a very happy man when he recovered from this night's ordeal.

Emma and Malvin went back to the men waiting anxiously for confirmation of the doctor's words.

Malvin nodded his head in affirmation, and his happy grin said it all. The men who had been so intense for so long sat down in relief and grinned at each other.

* * *

A tired Coulter is stationed outside the Gibson's residence. He didn't know why because it was after 1:30 am. No one would be leaving now. He was unaware of the astounding activities down at the dock. He was sitting there uselessly waiting for what? He kept asking himself that over and over. His early morning wait had not been productive after taking Beth home.

He must have dozed off because the opening of the gate awakened him. He saw the lights as they went through the gates followed by a black form, appearing never-ending in the night darkness.

Maybe this was his chance at last. He was out of the car in a flash, his heart pumping. As he scaled the wall, the thought came into his head. It was still dark where could the limo be going. The night sky showed no signs of light. He knew he had slept for quite a while because he didn't feel like he awoke from an unfulfilled sleep.

Coulter was making quick progress. The dog must be inside. He was at the garage quickly. He felt around for the light switch. The light flashed on blinding his eyes. He closed his eyes and waited then gradually opened them. He quickly closed them again. Then popped them open wide what he saw the first time was apparent still. The garage held Jimmy's car. The space for Emma's car was empty. Now, what would he do as his eyes widened in horror? Where was her car? Where were the diamonds? He looked around on the floor in her car's vacant space as if the vehicle would materialize or the diamonds. Then he backed out of the garage bumping into the wall beside the door. He turned and fled out the door into the night.

Coulter knew he had to get back to the car and get to the ship to tell Captain Jorgensen. He had no idea where Emma's car was nor where the diamonds could be. He just prayed Captain Jorgensen didn't strangle him. But he had to tell Jorgensen no matter what the consequences. He had run out of ideas, his mind still concentrating on that empty space in the garage. His car sped through the night like a bullet aimed towards the dock.

As he neared the dock area, he could see lots of whirling red lights, police cars, and fire apparatus. The ship was in full light. It was the Belle Star. There were firefighters and police everywhere. His brain finally registered and sent the message to his foot to stomp on the brake. Locking wheels squealed as he looked in horror at the scene before him. He could see there had been a fire, but why were the police on the ship? They were rounding up the crew. There was some crew in handcuffs at the bottom of the ramp, and the police were talking to them. The Port Authorities were surrounding the ship with tape indicating it was off-limits for anyone but the proper authorities.

Coulter was uncertain as to what to do next. He had no one to share his latest dilemma. Did he go home and pretend none of this happened? Would Captain Jorgensen be jailed? Had his crew set the fire? Was the Captain involved? If they arrested Jorgensen, would he implicate me?

Coulter put his head down on the steering wheel and did something he hadn't done since he was ten. He cried the sobs of a dying man. Managing to pull himself together, he drove home.

The answer would come soon enough for all his questions. He went into his house a different man. A man who at one time, had everything and in one night had been reduced to a man with nothing.

* * *

Emma was sure the matter of the embezzlement needed addressing. Jimmy was recovering, and Ted was off the danger list. Emma figured it was time for her to act. The reflection on her bookkeeping was not making her happy nor the incrimination of Jimmy.

The best way she could think of was to face Alan. He was back in the office from the dock. He seemed slightly nervous and unable to settle at his desk. She had noted, he had gone out after only sitting for several minutes numerous times that morning.

"Do you know where the information on the Belle Star accounts went, Alan? They were here the other day, Jimmy said, but now they are missing. I wonder why? You did process them and put them in the journal, didn't you?" She paused to give him time to answer.

"I don't know why it isn't in there, I entered the information," Alan mumbled.

"I cannot find them. Could you find the bills of lading and re-enter the accounts, please?" Emma stood watching him without appearing too intent.

He cleared his voice, shuffled his feet, then stood and walked to the filing cabinet. Bills of lading filed by date received then by alphabet. And as there is usually only one ship in at a time that meant from the Belle Star's cargo. The drawer was partly empty.

"Emma?" Alan was looking in the file cabinet with a puzzled look on his face. "It seems they are missing for some of the days," he said sheepishly.

"How can that be, Alan? Why would anyone take bills of lading? I don't see how that can happen, do you?" Emma was ever so sweet.

Alan cleared his throat and then turned a slight shade of red. "Are you certain Jimmy didn't remove them?" he asked in an optimistic voice.

"No, I can't see why Jimmy would do such a thing. I certainly didn't." For good measure, she mentioned, "I doubt my father would have either. Now I want them found, and the accounts entered in the computer before I leave today," Emma said with authority in her voice.

Alan was worried now. He knew why the bogus accounts were missing and who had them. Coulter had been in late yesterday to use the computer. Coulter must have removed the bills of lading from the drawer when he left his office — taking them all because the numbering system would identify the missing ones as the bogus companies. The bogus bills of lading were without cargo. Alan found them attached to cargo that had a double Bill of lading.

Alan accepted assurance by Coulter that discovery couldn't happen. Now he realized it was Coulter that was off the hook. He was to be the fall guy. That had probably been the plan from the beginning. He remembered how jumpy Coulter had been yesterday. How he kept looking over his shoulder as if he half expected someone to clamp onto him.

Alan knew he was in trouble. His wife would be alone in her illness if he gave himself up. So, what could he do? Disappear? Beg for mercy from Mr. Gibson telling him about his wife. Alan was standing in front of the file cabinet with these thoughts churning in his mind.

Emma knew from his stance that he didn't see anything inside the file cabinet. "Perhaps they are misfiled," Emma said, bringing his attention back to the situation.

Alan murmured, "no, I have checked."

"Can we reproduce the information from the Belle Star's manifest that the Port Authorities are holding?" Emma asked as though that would be a possibility.

"No, I doubt the manifest would show what we need. I don't know what Port Authorities have for information," Alan said, trying to dissuade her from going near the ship's records.

Emma decided to pressure Alan some more. She picked up the phone saying. "I think I will call the Port Authorities. Mr. Mitchell has been accommodating anytime I've had to deal with him."

Alan was physically sweating now, she could see. He had turned to her when she started dialing the number. Alan came over and pressed down the button ending the call.

"Why did you do that, Alan?" Emma questioned a little nervous now.

"Emma, I don't want you to make that call. I want to speak to your father before I say anything else." Alan's voice was stronger than he thought it would be.

Emma backed off. "All right, Alan. My father should be back within the hour. I am going over to the hospital to see Jimmy and Ted."

"What exactly happened to Jimmy and Ted?" Alan was playing the innocent.

"I haven't got time now. I will tell you later." Emma went back to her office to grab her purse and jacket.

Alan sat down with his head in his hands and gave a heart-rendering sigh. He knew he was in deep trouble. But he wasn't going to be the fall guy. His only hope was that Malvin would understand about Lucy and her drugs for her illness.

He straightened up as he heard Emma's quick goodbye.

Chapter Twenty-Five

When Emma got to the hospital, she went to see Jimmy first.

"Hi, brother." Emma leaned over and kissed him.

"Hi, Emma. The doctor was in an hour ago, and he is releasing me from the hospital. I phoned Matilda to have Roger bring me some clothes and drive me home. Isn't that good news?" Jimmy said with a big smile.

"Oh yes, Jimmy, that is good news. If only I had known, I would have brought them and driven you home."

"It is okay. Roger should be here soon. I guess you are going to see Ted now."

"Yes." Emma was still shy about Ted.

"Can I go with you?"

"Sure, I would like that. I hear from Daddy he is off the critical list as he stopped in this morning to see him."

The twins walked to the other wing of the hospital.

When they got to Ted's room, Ted was sitting with the bed raised in a half-reclining position. He was on intravenous still, but the rest of the monitoring machines were removed. He had a smile on his face when he saw them standing in the doorway. Jimmy walked in first.

"Ted, it is good to see you back in the land of the living." He stuck out his hand.

Ted grasped it. It was a pleasure to make contact with this man who he had successfully saved. Jimmy appeared recovered from his bout with prolonged drugs.

Jimmy expressed, "it is good to shake the hand of the man who was instrumental in perfecting my escape. I am so sorry you got shot. Now here is someone else that wants to shake your hand." He turned to Emma and held out his hand. Jimmy drew her over to the bed and placed it in Ted's hand. Although Jimmy had said to shake hands, he did it in such a reverent way. It was as though he was giving his sister into Ted's care.

He stepped back and said, "Roger will be here soon, so I had better get back to my room." He was wasting his breath; neither had heard him. They were gazing so deeply into each other's eyes.

"Hi, Emma, I know you came to see me. The nurses told me you came in often that day and the next."

"Yes, I wanted to make sure you were okay. After all, I was the one who enlisted your aid to find Jimmy."

Ted was studying her face as if he wanted to store her into his memory. "Emma, I'm sorry I didn't call you as I promised, but I was incapacitated."

"That's all right. One of your men called me. I think his name was Jordon. He said you kept saying my name and to call me or was it, Dalton? I don't exactly remember all the details of that night. Once I heard they shot you. I knew I had to be here."

Ted squeezed her hand. "Emma, I wished I had known you were here. It would have eased my mind. I have a vague memory of you kissing me. I didn't know if it was the drugs," he said with heartfelt sincerity.

He pulled her closer. She bent over willingly and placed her lips on his. The kiss was gentle, with love. She stood back, shyly again. She had never felt this way about a man before. Her dates never went beyond a couple of casual kisses. This man affected her in her deepest being.

"Emma, when I get on my feet again, will you go on a date with me?"

"Yes, Ted, I'll go out with you."

"That's good because I intend to be with you every free moment. We will hike in that valley behind my place. I will help you scale the cliff," he said with great gusto. Was it too soon to ask her to marry him? Of course. However, he knew in his mind, this girl was to be his loved one.

"Have a seat. I want to hold your hand for a while, is that okay?"

There they sat, the outside world and its past ugliness not penetrating their minds.

* * *

Alan was sitting watching out of the window, noticing Malvin was coming. He had called Lucy after Emma had left.

Lucy was better for a month now. But she still had a long way to go before gaining all her strength back. They had a closeness people seldom have. He talked to her in a reverent tone. He was encouraging her to make his favorite dinner. The meals and housework had fallen to him. But this past week, she had surprised him, having a candlelit dinner ready on his arrival home.

He tried to keep his unhappiness out of his voice. He didn't even know if he would be going home to dinner. His heart was sad as he had said goodbye with a double meaning. If saving Lucy's quality of life, meant aiding Coulter, he would do it again. He was ready now to confess his involvement. He hated to think of Malvin's disappointment, after his kindness over the years. Malvin was a generous man, but that would end now.

"Hello, Alan, is Emma here?"

"No, she went to the hospital to see Jimmy and Ted."

"Good. Will you come to my office?"

Alan quickly sped into the conversation. "Malvin, there is something I have to confess to you." He stood up and followed Malvin to his office.

"Please have a seat," Malvin was waiting to receive Alan's explanation.

"Malvin I am deeply sorry about something. I did it for monetary gain. You have been good to me and my wife Lucy over the years. But I still did this to you. That is what I regret the most." He paused as Malvin handed him a drink. It was noticeable that Alan's hand was shaking. He took a gulp. "Malvin, I helped someone who made up bogus companies for their gain, entering these accounts with false information. I gave them access to the computer after everyone was gone. They directed funds away from the company. I hid the fact by entering their phony bills of lading, which made me a part of the embezzlement that is going on. I have a feeling, you already know. I was positive Jimmy knew, although he never said anything to me. And today Emma dropped hints. She was going to talk to the Port Authorities about the Belle Star's records. I am certain the bogus companies would have come to light." Alan paused, took another drink looking at Malvin with a genuinely repentant look, waiting for the axe to fall.

Malvin took a drink giving him time to think.

"Alan, I am glad you decided to confess. Yes, we did know you were involved. But we felt you were a minor player. The ones we want are the persons that did the actual embezzlement. I must admit I was not happy to think that after all these years, this was something you could do. The real sadness in all of this is, not the loss of the money, but the friendship destroyed and my family almost destroyed in the process."

"I feel bad about Jimmy and Ted. I wasn't part of Jimmy's kidnapping. You have to believe me. I wouldn't have done anything like that, no matter how much money they offered."

"It wasn't just Jimmy or even Ted it was Emma too. That was the biggest tragedy in this." Malvin's voice was gruff with emotion. The memory of Emma's near demise clear in his mind.

"Emma tried to end her sweet life because you made Jimmy look like the guilty one. Jimmy was innocent, but Emma thought he had betrayed us because of his forged signature. She couldn't face that fact, so she thought by taking her life, she would be protecting him. Did you know that?"

Alan looked horror-struck.

"I knew something happened to Emma, but I had no idea that she tried to take her life. Jimmy just said she wouldn't be in for a while because she was sick and under doctor's care. I would have confessed sooner had I known. I would never have let your family take the blame for me, not ever." Alan was genuinely horrified. He was glad to confess at last. Despite Coulter's threats against Lucy and his life if he didn't cooperate.

Malvin just sat there watching the emotions passing over Alan's face. He knew then that Alan must've had a good reason for doing it. Malvin waited.

"Malvin, Emma means a lot to me, and so does Jimmy. I have watched them grow up over the years. I would not have let Emma die on my account never," he said firmly. "I wish I had known sooner I would have confessed then. If you knew about me, why did you not say something?" Alan asked with a wistful voice.

"Because Alan, you weren't the one we needed. It was the others. We weren't sure you would tell us who they were. We needed to get the evidence to make an ironclad case against them. But someone is still out there manipulating things. We need to know who and we need to have the records to prove it."

Alan was ready to tell all, but first, he had to explain why he did it. It was the primary factor here for him. "Malvin, I want you to know I didn't do it for myself. I would never do that. You have been a good friend to Lucy and me as well as a good employer over the years. It was just that Lucy was getting sicker and sicker, and her medicine was getting more expensive. I love Lucy so much I had to do something. So, when Coulter approached me, I went along with it."

"Coulter?"

"Yes, Coulter Stewart. He is the one who has been manipulating the computer with my help. He comes in after you and Emma leave. Then he does things in the computer directing funds to three bogus accounts." Taking a breath, he continued. "Malvin, Lucy is getting better, so I think she can handle things if I am not there for her. I am prepared to be absent from home. I am not saying that to get your sympathy for Lucy. I want to serve my time for my crime at last."

"Alan, why didn't you tell me about Lucy? I would've helped you. You know that. Where was my thinking? I should have asked if I was a true friend. I knew that Lucy was sick." Malvin was taking on some of Alan's guilt, in his failure to recognize that Alan needed money.

"It wasn't your responsibility. It was mine, but I should have gotten past my pride and my fears for Lucy and asked. You would probably have let me pay you back when Lucy got better. That is hindsight now. I helped those men swindle you. I am just as guilty as they are, no matter the reason. I knew full well that if Lucy had known she would never have taken the medicine."

"Knowing Lucy, I think that is true. However, you are guilty, and my family was almost wiped out as a result of this situation. That is the tragedy in all of this. The only thing, if you help us with testimony and evidence, your sentence may not be as severe. I am pretty sure I can convince the authorities of that. I will look after Lucy for you when you're gone. If only I had asked how you were coping with Lucy's medicine." Malvin sighed.

They both took a much-needed drink. Then spent the rest of the time trying to form a plan to trap Coulter. Malvin thanked Alan for confessing on his initiative as he had been about to accuse him when he invited Alan to his office.

* * *

Coulter was thinking, will this ever go away. He was in deep trouble. He had to quit trying to evade the issue. What was he going to do? Could he get away and survive? Would he be better off to confess? No, he was too much of a coward for that. How soon would they find out about him? He didn't think Alan would tell because of his threats to Alan. But he didn't know about Captain Jorgensen. After all, he was very angry with Coulter because he had lost the diamonds.

He had been in to see Jimmy at the hospital, but the questions he posed innocently hadn't resulted in helpful answers. The diamonds were still missing. He had nowhere else to look. No clues. No anything.

Jimmy was doing better so that at least made Coulter feel better. He was glad that he was able to have a clear conscience on that score. After all, Jimmy was his best friend. He was not letting his mind dwell on how he had set Jimmy up regarding the embezzlement. That was something he had relegated to the back of his mind to clear his conscience.

To make matters worse, he had found out from Beth that Emma had rolled her car somehow, and it had exploded. Beth had told him this after his finding the car missing from the garage. She had also mentioned Jimmy hadn't given her all the details only that Emma was okay and under doctor's care.

He had to think, how to get out of this because Captain Jorgensen had told him if he didn't come up with the diamonds, he was going to give him back to the loan sharks and their muscle men. He knew what that meant. He was feeling sick inside. There was no good end to his dilemma. Now Diane was threatening to break off the engagement. He needed her money for their livelihood as his gambling debt had multiplied again. He shook his head in self-disgust. When would he learn gambling is a foolish man's vice? His parents had cut him off from financial aid, hoping that would curb his lousy gambling habit. But he hadn't learned, he was getting deeper and deeper into a hopeless pit. He did think about taking his life, but he was too much a coward for that.

Since the night of the fire at the docks and the seizing of the Belle Star by Port Authorities, he had been wooing Diane for the trust fund from her grandfather, trying to get her to elope with him. But she was holding out for a big wedding. He needed the trust money to get out of this mess. Then he would reform and never gamble again. He just hoped he could keep that commitment when the time came. He needed to intensify his desire for an elopement with Diane. He got up with conviction.

* * *

Dalton and Mannie were at the hospital visiting Ted. He was better, expecting a release within a day or two.

"Well, Ted, what's happening about the charges of kidnapping and the shooting?" Dalton asked.

"At the moment it has been left that the Port Authorities are investigating the Belle Star along with the police. But I have a feeling there is more to this than the Belle Star.

"What do you mean?" Mannie enquired.

Ted was not sure whether to include them in on the other incidents or not, but they risked their lives for him. So, he told them about Emma and the car episode. He continued with the embezzlement that led up to Jimmy's kidnapping and the fact that he thought Jimmy's best friend Coulter was involved somehow. Ted was debating mentioning the diamonds he had found when Dalton said.

"Ted there has to be more to this than what you're telling us. Those men on the Belle Star were shooting real bullets at us, remember? The stakes have to be much higher."

"Well, the stakes are much higher actually. I have the stake," Ted replied.

"What do you have? Is it something we should know about?" Mannie queried. "Come on, we are your friends, and they shot at Dalton too."

"Well, after I got out of the hospital, I went for a hike in the valley, doing my usual rock climbing to build up my strength again. I investigated something shiny on the other side of the river. It was a hubcap from Emma's car, and attached was a pouch that I opened. Guess what came pouring out?"

"Drugs?" asked Mannie.

"No."

"I have no idea," Dalton said puzzled.

"Would you believe a fortune in diamonds," Ted replied.

"Emma's?" Mannie asked with raised eyebrows.

"No, I thought at first, they might belong to Jimmy. But I have since changed my mind about that. Malvin isn't involved either. It is someone else that stashed them there in Emma's car for safekeeping until they needed them. I will bet you anything that the Belle Star is involved. I had an interesting conversation with a girl I used to know before we rescued Jimmy. She seemed to be concerned about her fiancée and didn't know who to talk to about it."

"Yeah. How well did you know this girl?" Dalton asked, being facetious.

"I met her and another girl in a bar one night. We kibitzed around for the evening."

"Oh yeah? One evening? Yeah, right," Mannie teased.

"Honest one night, I drove the two of them home after. I must have impressed Diane somehow as we had one date."

"Well, back to the fiancée. What is that about?" interrupted the curious Dalton.

"Well, it seems he has been gambling a lot and losing heavily. His attitude toward life has changed drastically. Now the coincidence is that the fiancée is Jimmy's best friend, Coulter. He has been asking about Emma's car."

"I smell a rat," Mannie said.

"Yeah, that's what I think too, but how to catch him is the problem." Ted looked puzzled.

"Well, first of all, we have to get you out of here. When is the doctor springing you? How strong are you getting around?" Dalton asked, getting excited about these latest details.

"Well, the doctor says I should be able to leave tomorrow just so long as I don't lift anything heavy. I can do pretty much as I please. I also have been getting out of bed and practicing walking and doing some light exercise."

"Well, why are you in bed?" Mannie whipped back to the covers. "Prove you are walking."

Ted eased off the bed and put on the housecoat Dalton had pitched at him. Ted ambled with them to the cafeteria where they ordered coffee. Mannie lit up a cigarette.

Ted took it off him and squished it out in the ashtray.

"Not with my lungs, buddy," Ted said.

"It is a bad habit, and I almost have it licked," Mannie replied with a grin.

Dalton interrupted. "We will work on the information you shared. When we get you out of here, we can meet out at your place Ted,"

"When we come, we will bring the rest of the guys, so you better have steaks for a barbecue and beer too," Mannie instructed.

"No, Ted is the injured one here. We will bring the steaks. Besides, if I know him, he will get mini-sized ones, and I want a big steak." Dalton said, looking at Mannie.

Ted gave them big grins. "Yeah, if it were up to me, you would be getting less than minis. I make a mean hamburger with the works."

"Dalton says huge steaks. If you want our cooperation huge steaks, it will be. Right, Dalton?" Mannie grinned broadly.

"Yes. Ted, we will look after the food and beer you will provide us with your company. We're so glad you didn't die that night." Dalton gave him an affectionate look.

"Come Mannie, let's get this invalid back to bed. We will make our exit. I have an idea I want to think about."

Ted's sojourn to bed was with lots of love pats as the two men were pretending, they were nurses. Ted laughed so hard his stitches were bothering him, but he didn't let on. He was just so happy to be alive and have these good friends in his life.

Even before they cleared the room, Mannie was demanding Dalton pay for drinks at their favorite watering hole. Ted knew he was jokingly getting at him because he had to stay behind. Mannie was a caring person. Knowing this, Ted yelled, "Dalton, make him pay and order a round on me and make him pay for that too." The two men's laughter could be heard halfway down the hall.

Ted laid back and thanked God for his wonderful friends and especially for Emma. The new girl in his life that had gone straight to his heart.

* * *

Emma was talking to Jimmy. "Daddy found out why Alan was involved. It was because of Lucy. Her medication was so expensive that he couldn't afford them on his salary. Daddy feels bad that he had never asked Alan how he was managing."

Jimmy replied, "Alan just had to ask. We would have helped him. Why didn't he?"

"Probably his pride and when Coulter offered easy money, he took it. How do you feel about, Coulter?"

"I am shocked and deeply hurt. He is my best friend. I knew he had a gambling problem as I went with him a couple of times. He would drop several thousand and still wouldn't give up until I would drag him out of there. Finding out he has been involved is upsetting. I wonder if he knew about my kidnapping?"

"Jimmy, he is still free. I don't know how we will get the evidence we need on him. All we have is Alan's word about what was going down."

"I know I have been racking my brains trying to think of a way to trap him. Diane is going to be shocked when this all comes out. You know she was hoping to get married this fall. The most she could get him to commit to was the hall and the church because he has been trying to get her to elope. Now I can see why. He probably needs her money for gambling debts. That is why he probably got involved in this mess."

"Did you know that she knew Ted?"

"No, I didn't," replied Jimmy.

"Well, she went to see him at his brother's place."

"Whatever for?"

"Because she was worried about Coulter. Diane was impressed with Ted the one night she and her girlfriend had met him in a bar."

"What did she say about Coulter?"

"She said he was acting funny as well as disappearing for long periods and that she was worried about him. At the time, Ted was so involved in your escape. He didn't follow through on her request to speak to Coulter."

"We are supposed to be getting together with Beth on Saturday night. I don't know whether to cancel?"

"No, don't cancel. Why don't you drop a few hints around, coming up with a supposed arrest soon on the embezzlement and look at Coulter rather pointedly and see how he reacts?"

"Yes, that might be a good idea. Actually, I wouldn't like anything to occur in front of the girls." Jimmy said with some concern.

"I'm sure he wouldn't either, so I think it will be okay," Emma said confidently.

"Are you seeing Ted tonight?"

"Yes, I am going to the hospital."

"You are getting quite chummy, aren't you?" Jimmy asked.

"Yes, only because we are good friends, and I'm thankful he saved your life," Emma said casually.

"Just friends, who are you trying to kid? I saw you the other day. Your hands were clasped tightly, defying anyone to separate you." Jimmy teased. "Be honest. Ted devours you every time he looks at you."

Emma blushed but did not deny it.

* * *

As a surprise, Ted was waiting by the elevator when Emma arrived. He wanted her to see how well he was recovering. Besides, the sooner his eyes could dwell on her, the happier he would be.

"Oh Ted, you are up and walking," Emma said as he took her hand in his.

"Yes, I am getting out of the hospital tomorrow. Tommy brought me clothes this evening. Would you like to take me home?" Ted asked beseechingly.

"Oh, yes, what time?"

"Right after you have breakfast. I will be ready even if the doctor hasn't been in to give me the final okay. How about I get dressed, and we leave right now. You did that, you remember. So maybe I should too."

Emma blushed, remembering her escape from the hospital and how mortified she had been to run into Tommy as the elevator opened. "Don't remind me I don't want to talk about that anymore. You are staying and serving your time, but I can be here tomorrow to take you home." She linked her arm through his. They walked back to his room.

They were no sooner inside the door when Ted pulled her into his arms and kissed her. "I have wanted to do that for days." He bent his head, their lips met. He deepened the kiss until they were clinging so tightly pressed together. Ted was not going to let this girl get away from him ever again. They finally pulled apart as the nurse entered.

"You're out of bed, Mr. Maxwell. That is good to see." Ted didn't want the blushing Emma to go, so he retained her hand as he walked toward the bed.

"Well, I guess I had better not take your temperature. It will be too high after that steamy kiss I just witnessed," she teased. "We don't want the doctor saying you can't go home because you have a high temperature, do we?" She headed for the door throwing the comment over her shoulder. "I will be back later much later, I think."

Emma was dying of embarrassment.

"Emma, love, she is just kidding."

"Oh, Ted, do you think so?"

Ted laughed. "Do you know what's going to happen when I get

out of here?"

"No, what?"

"All the guys are coming out to my place for barbecued steaks, and I am inviting you and Jimmy Saturday night. We are going to work on a plan to trap Coulter."

Emma told Ted about her discussion with Jimmy. The fact that he was supposed to be going out with Coulter, Diane, and Beth Saturday night.

"Well, I will phone the guys. We will make the barbecue for Friday instead," Ted mentioned.

"Okay, because I'm sure Jimmy would like to be there. He has been racking his brain to figure out what to do about Coulter."

Ted asked, "are the police having any success with the information from the Belle Star's crew?"

"Daddy says they haven't come up with anything definite or at least not that they are admitting. He says the crew is too tight-lipped. The police don't even know who fired the shots. Did you see who?"

"No, I was still too disoriented from that hit on the head that I whacked on the side of the ship. All I know was the First Officer was there along with one other crew member pulling me up so fast that I had no choice but to drop into the water. I wonder if they will even be able to charge the Belle Star for anything?"

"Detective Harding has been hounding us about the embezzlement and Jimmy, so he is leaving me alone about my situation, thank goodness."

"That's good." He had noticed how that particular detective had looked at Emma like he wanted to protect her, not question her.

"Ted, I had better go now. You should get back into bed. You don't want anything to hamper your release tomorrow, do you?"

"Okay." Ted pulled her in his arms. She pushed away from him. Quickly stood on tiptoe and kissed his lips lightly and backed out of his reach.

"Temperature, remember. You want to be released tomorrow."

"Ah, gee, I want more than that," Ted said in a pleading voice.

"Behave yourself, or I will send Roger instead tomorrow."

That did it he walked over to the bed and threw off his housecoat and climbed into bed meekly.

Emma got bold and planted another smacking kiss on his pouting lips. He tried to grab her, but she slipped away and gave him a cheeky "Goodnight."

Chapter Twenty-Six

Friday night, the gang was at Ted's place.

As Dalton unloaded the extra barbecue upon arrival, he asked, "who wants rare? Who wants well done?" Dalton and Jordon were going to be in charge of the steaks.

Jimmy and Emma's arrival abounded with friendly gestures. At Jimmy's introduction to each one, he gave heartfelt thanks for saving him. The guys passed it off as though it was all in a night's work.

Emma received kisses from all the guys. Ted accepted the ribbing good-naturedly as he knew these guys well. Emma joined in on the fun, which pleased Ted. His brother and Sally were also invited so Emma wouldn't be the only girl present.

Sally and Tommy arrived. The guys started ribbing Tommy about his nightly habits as Sally looked very pregnant. Then they kissed the little mother on the cheek with congratulations for having to put up with Tommy. They both had met all these guys on various occasions before.

Ted started yelling. "Steak, steaks, whose looking after the steaks?"

There was an immediate exodus towards the barbeques by the cooks as smoke was pouring out of them. However, the smoke was more of a warning well done for the ones preferring rare.

Dalton assured them. "The next ones will be rare." He and Jordon were removing the well done and throwing on more raw steaks. They had brought a green salad. Ted had bake potatoes in the oven. The meal was well rounded out by laughter and the usual banter.

After the meal, Emma and Sally did the dishes so the men could talk. Sally's dislike of Emma was now changing. Emma was a pleasant girl.

Emma curious, asked, "what does it feel like to be pregnant?"

Sally filled Emma in ending with, "the discomfort of waddling isn't great, but I am happy to be pregnant. Tommy is such a proud papa too. We wanted the suspense of a boy or a girl until that special day."

Emma kept glancing out the window every so often towards the men talking. What were they planning? Would it be dangerous like Jimmy's rescue? Would there be shooting? She couldn't bear it if Ted got injured again.

Sally kept up the small talk. She knew Emma was worried about what the men were planning. The small talk didn't dissuade Emma from peeking out of the window.

* * *

"Anyone got any suggestions?" asked Ted as he looked around. The group was lit by flames leaping in the air. As per usual, they got carried away with the magnitude of the bonfire.

Dalton said, "I made a few inquiries into the history of this man Coulter through a friend of mine who is an investigator. It seems he is into the loan sharks heavily. That doesn't include the bailout amount Captain Jorgensen did the first time. This man has a serious gambling habit he can't afford. Now the way I see it is if a couple of us brawny men pay him a visit letting him believe we are loan shark musclemen. We could make enough of an impression to get him to sing. What do you think?" Dalton queried.

"Well, that might work," said Ted. "But that still doesn't give us the evidence."

"Now, I just happen to have a wire and recorder that should fit the bill," said Jordan.

Mannie put in. "And just how would you happen to have come by that piece of equipment?" he inquired rather curious.

"Well, we decided to play a joke on my brother-in-law on the eve of his wedding at a stag party. We were going to play it for him as a joke at his reception. He spoilt our fun, ignoring the girl that popped out of the cake. But I still have the recorder and wire."

"Well, that should do it if we ask the right questions and use the right persuasion," said Dalton.

"Now who wants to be the muscleman, and how will we get the detective there to be in on the recording of the confession?" asked Mannie.

"Dalton, I think you look the meanest and Jordon you're a close second." Ted kidded humorously.

"Thanks, who needs an enemy when we have a friend like you, eh Jordon?" Dalton asked playfully. He had every intention of being one of the musclemen since he had heard about the guy causing injurious events for Jimmy, Ted, and Emma.

"I think I can handle it," said Jordan, "and besides, it's my recorder." He liked to be in on the action. "We will need a police presence."

Ted mentioned. "I will get the detective there. I don't think I will have any problem with that. Now, where is this going to take place?"

"I'm seeing him tomorrow night at the country club with our girlfriends. Maybe we could do something there." Jimmy offered, wanting inclusion in this.

"No, I don't think that's wise with the girls there," Mannie said.

"What about the shipping office? Jimmy, can you get him there? Maybe on Sunday?" Ted put in.

"He has been querying about Emma's car. Maybe I can say I have something he might be interested in from the car. Not that I know why he is after Emma's car, but it must be something," Jimmy offered.

Ted exchanged looks with the other guys that knew the answer and gave them a signal to keep mum.

"You know that just might work." Ted didn't want Jimmy to know about the diamonds yet. Just in case Coulter questioned him in such a way that it would make it evident that he knew about the diamonds. Ted didn't know how desperate Coulter would be whether he would show up with a gun. He was hoping not. He was a gambler, not a killer.

Dalton stated, "we will meet there at 7:50 pm at our warehouse and wait for Jimmy and Coulter to go into the shipping office then pay him a visit. We'll have to keep out of the way until Jimmy arrives at the office, hopefully at 8:00 pm. We will arrive at 8:05."

Dalton continued. "Jordan and I will play the musclemen and say we were following Coulter. We will tell Jimmy to get lost so that Coulter will be freer in his talking. The detective and Ted will be hiding in Emma's office. Detective Harding, I met at the hospital should be game for this. Well, how does that sound for a possible plan?"

"Jimmy, we hope you can pull this off, getting him there without too much difficulty," Ted inquired. Jimmy assured him it wouldn't be a problem.

"Hey, is this a good plan or what?" Dalton said jovially.

"Don't get a swelled head. It sounds workable, but we have to be careful," Mannie said.

Arnie piped up. "Dalton, I always knew you had a criminal mind."

"Not criminal, just crafty." Dalton laughed.

"Back to my concern," said Ted. "Jimmy, you have the real task, getting Coulter there. It is not going to be easy. After all, things have not exactly been going Coulter's way lately. Do you think he has a gun? Or if he does, would he use it if he thinks you're trying to trap him?" Ted had a real concern about this as he didn't want to see anyone else hurt. Jimmy was the most vulnerable in this plan. The only hope was that Coulter must have some feelings of sincere friendship for Jimmy.

Jimmy had been deep in thought, weighing Ted's concerns. He remembered Coulter and their friendship over the years. The times they went swimming and going riding and jumping horses over tree trunks and fences at a local horse farm. They separated to different universities but picked up where they left off upon returning home. They often talked about being each other's best man and ended up joking who was the best man.

Jimmy concluded that Coulter wouldn't hurt him no matter what. "Coulter will be there on time, and I will be fine. Just everyone else be in place before I get there," he said with confidence.

"Ted, how are you going to get the detective there?" Arnie asked.

"Well, I am thinking it could be a case of having to fill him in on the rest of the circumstances, including Emma's car escapade. But I'll have to get her permission first. Then I think he will want to be there out of curiosity. Neither Emma nor I have been too cooperative where Detective Harding is concerned."

"Won't he want to run things if he finds out what we're up to?" Dalton queried.

"Probably, but I am going to tell him that I want to show him something at the shipping office. Then imply I will give him the complete story once we are inside. Emma will be there with us for entry to the offices then I want her out of there. Karl and Arnie, I want you to escort her back to the warehouse, where she will be away from everything."

Mannie piped up. "Mannie will look after your precious bundle, don't worry." He didn't like being left out of things. He wished he could be with Dalton. He also knew Jordon was better suited to the role.

Ted finally went and got the girls to free them from the bondage of the kitchen. The plans were in place. Everyone knew their roles. Dalton and Mannie were serenading the group, to the catcalls from Jordan and the others.

Sally and Emma joined in the laughter. Emma was trying to hide her trepidation, knowing a special discussion happened at tonight's gathering.

Tommy whispered, making a point of reassured Sally right away that he was not involved, and that Ted would be behind the scene this time. He did not want her to worry because it was too close to her time, which was soon. Sally was happy about Tommy's comment after Ted's injures the last time. She quickly kissed her husband in relief.

Jordan said, "none of that as we all know where that leads." Looking pointedly at her well-rounded tummy.

The bantering continued. Emma sat close to Ted but kept a little apart. She knew she wouldn't like their latest plot. Aware Ted always seems to be the one getting hurt. Ted tried to close the space with a lighthearted hug, but Emma scooted out of his grasp. He knew he had some explaining to do before things would be on an even footing again. The path of love is never smooth. He thought with a sigh.

Dalton started to tell a rather lewd joke. Ted put an end to that quickly. The night had passed all too fast, and he was tiring. Besides, he wanted Emma alone to explain how he wouldn't be involved, but Jimmy was taking her home, so that would have to wait until tomorrow. Ted also knew she would probably wheedle it out of Jimmy. He was hoping, at least, for enough privacy for a proper goodnight kiss with Emma, but knowing with this motley crew of buddies, that would be unlikely.

Mannie was arranging another barbecue for next month only this time the steaks were to be on Ted. The location was Ted's still with their wives and girlfriends. The response he was getting was proving how close-knit these guys were.

Things broke up. The fire extinguished. Everyone was heading for their vehicles in the driveway. The night was over, but not the special friendships evident here.

Jimmy, Emma, Tommy, and Sally stood with Ted waving them off. Then Tommy and Sally said goodnight. Sally gave Ted a warm kiss and the comment to take care of himself. Tommy expressed his wish to have Emma and Ted come over for dinner next Saturday and Jimmy too.

Tommy and Sally drew Jimmy into a conversation about his recovery from the drugs as they walked to the cars. They were hoping to give Ted some time alone with Emma.

Emma was still in her reserved mode, but Ted soon put an end to that, wrapping his arms around her and kissing her soundly. When they parted, Emma was breathless. There was no way she could ignore this man. He had a real goal to be together. It was just these other activities that kept getting in their way. She knew he was giving her lots of hints about how he felt. The opportunity for an ideal date had not happened as yet. She knew she wanted that first, needing to sort out her feelings for this loving man.

Emma thought she loved him. But what if the irregular events were making her feel she was in love with him in gratitude. Emma needed time with him alone to discover the answer. Ted didn't mention the plan as she seemed to be withdrawing.

Then Ted gave her another fleeting kiss, and she turned down the driveway for her ride home. His eyes followed the leaving car, wishing they had the time to be together, no plots, no other people, just them.

He turned to the house. Would there ever be a time for only the two of them?

Chapter Twenty-Seven

The next day Ted got a call from Malvin, inviting him to the shipping office. Ted said he would be there. Malvin didn't enlighten him as to the reason. He arrived early in hopes of seeing Emma, but Malvin was alone. He invited him in, but he didn't look too happy.

"Alan spoke to me about his part in all this. But somehow, I can't report him to the police. Do you know what I should do about Alan?"

Ted replied, "my advice is do nothing until Coulter is caught. He was the actual one who set up the bogus companies and posted the bogus information into the computer. Alan's voluntary confession should perhaps get him some leniency." He gave Malvin an understanding look.

"I heard from Jimmy that you had a plan to catch Coulter."

"Yes, we have worked out a plan."

"Good, Coulter needs to be caught. Now then after this is all over, I wonder if I could offer you a job in the company. My purpose to spend more time on leisure things such as traveling, golf, and fishing. I think you and Jimmy, along with Emma, could run things nicely while I'm gone. Would you consider that?"

"Well, Malvin, I am not a desk person. I like being on the docks where the action is."

Malvin quickly said, "it took me a long time to be able to sit behind the desk when my father was ready for some leisure time. I adjusted by spending half the time in the office and the rest on the docks. Gradually I got used to the running of things. Discovered I liked being in control. Then I was hooked. Won't you think about it?"

"I'll think about it, but I want Coulter arrested before I consider it. We still need to clear up Belle Star's responsibility in all of this too. I am hoping Coulter will sing like a canary when caught, and no diamonds found."

"Diamonds! What diamonds?" Malvin asked with a great deal of puzzlement.

"The diamonds were hidden in Emmy's car."

"Emma's car? The car that exploded and burned?"

"Yes, someone hid them in Emma's car for safekeeping, not knowing that she was going to have an accident."

"So, there is more than the bogus companies to this?"

"Yes, that is why we are going to strong-arm Coulter into a confession."

"Where are the diamonds now?"

"I have them in safekeeping," replied Ted.

"So, the Belle Star is involved?" Malvin inquired.

"Yes, up to their necks in it. Why do you think they were shooting at us? They didn't want anyone having anything on them. They wanted to make a clean getaway with a fortune in diamonds, but Emmy's accident put the kibosh on that."

"What if Coulter doesn't confess?"

"He will confess. Dalton and Jordon will make very convincing henchmen. They will make him see the light. He will confess. I have no doubt. Jimmy will bring him to the office, but they will tell Jimmy to leave so he won't be involved."

"Where will you be? I know you will be in there somewhere."

"Yes, I will be hiding in Emmy's office with our ever-present Detective Harding. We need an official police presence to hear the confession along with the recorder. After Coulter's arrest, we will need Alan's written statement as to how he got involved with Coulter. Then we will see if Alan can get some special sentence reduction for his advance confession."

"I appreciate that, Ted. You are certainly a caring man. I am pleased to have made your acquaintance. I wish you would consider coming into my shipping company. Our ships are of a high standard. However, we also deal with other ships as well as indicated by the Belle Star."

"Okay, Malvin. I promise to think about it. I will give you my answer when this is all over."

Malvin stood up and shook his hand. "Thank you once again for saving Emma and Jimmy."

"I am just glad both situations turned out in our favor. Both were pretty hairy situations. I have the scars to prove it," Ted said with a grin.

"That is for sure. I am deeply sorry I wasn't more pleasant to you in the beginning, but I didn't know the whole situation. I would have been more thankful if I had known. I can't believe my daughter tried to kill herself. I shudder every time I think of that. Don't you?"

"Yes, I do. I still shudder at the memory. When Emma's foot caught on the window on her way out, and the car broke free from the rock, dragging us both towards the cliff edge. I would have gone with her rather than give up. I remember how hard it was to convince her that I wanted to save her because she was adamant, not to be saved. Even though she was still fighting me, it was the best feeling ever to have that girl on top of me instead of in the burning inferno below."

Malvin was very pale and sat down.

"I have never really heard what happened until now. No wonder she had nightmares. I think I will have a few of my own now that I've heard this. Ted, I am very grateful to you. Emma should be thankful you are a stubborn man that wouldn't give up."

"I am also not going to give up until I make that girl mine. I am giving you fair warning that Emma will be my wife, as soon as I can get time alone to convince her." He paused, but Malvin didn't appear to have any objections.

Malvin reached out. "Thank you for your bravery, your stubbornness in saving my daughter. And most importantly, that you succeed in convincing my daughter to be your wife." He shook Ted's hand vigorously.

Ted was grinning. "I promise if all goes well, you will be a Granddaddy within two years. How does that sound?"

"Great, but how soon can I take him fishing with me?"

Ted laughed. "Well, a little bit longer than that."

"Would you like to come home for dinner? We need to get you started on wooing my girl."

Ted gave him a wide grin, with a twinkle in his eye. "Do I get to kiss her goodnight?"

"I think I can guarantee enough privacy for at least one kiss." Malvin was grinning widely too. "Well, let's go see if Daddy's girl is waiting to see you?" Malvin chuckled as he tidied things and locked his desk.

* * *

Emma was not surprised to see Ted walk in with her father. She knew her father was seriously upset with Alan's deflection. Her father would not want to turn him in, especially with Lucy sick.

Ted was not thinking of Alan when he saw Emma. He had not seen her more beautiful or more relaxed than now. She was reclining on the sofa when they arrived in the room. She swung her legs around off the couch with a fluid motion as she got to her feet.

"Hi, Daddy." Emma came over and kissed her father and gave him an extra hug.

"Hello, Emma. Do I get a hug too?" Ted asked wistfully.

"Hello, Ted. Why not?" She came over to Ted to give him a little hug.

"Honey, I brought Ted home for dinner. The least we can do is start showing him some of our hospitality after all he has done for us." He watched Ted take advantage of Emmy's little hug to progress into a more possessive embrace. He thought he would be jealous to see another man getting some of his little girl's affection, but he wasn't. He grinned at them both, a good feeling in his heart. Thoughts of grandbabies must have done that for him.

"I think I will go tell Matilda we have a guest for dinner." Malvin left the room without a backward glance.

Ted took the opportunity to drop a kiss on Emma's upturned mouth. She returned the loving gesture then eased out of his arms. She still wasn't sure if it was just gratitude or whether she was falling in love with him. Things were happening too quickly to know for sure. She did feel thankful Ted had come into their lives.

"Are things all set for tomorrow night?"

"Yes, as best we can arrange it. We can only hope Coulter is still trustful of Jimmy in order to pull him into our web. That will be the big thing. The rest we hope will happen as we need it to."

"Did you get Detective Harding to comply?"

"Yes, he wasn't happy that we kept him in the dark for so long. But he isn't about to turn us away now that we are in the final stage." In her distraction, he had taken hold of her hand and was slowly reeling her in closer to him again.

"Did you tell him about Alan? I know Daddy is having problems reporting him."

"No, not yet, I will fill him in tomorrow night. We will need a signed confession from Alan, but I am sure he knows that. I understand your father's feelings. But Alan's part in this has to come out, to clear this all up once and for all." Ted had been inching Emma back to the sofa. He had managed to get her down beside him.

"Ted, I'm worried about Jimmy's role in this. What if Coulter brings a gun?"

"Well, we hope he doesn't. If he does, I am sure Dalton and Jordon will handle him as they both have had commando training."

Emma's worried expression relaxed a bit.

"Hi, you two, don't you look comfy?" Even though he could see Emmy's tactics of trying to separate them.

Emma jumped up and ran to her brother and gave him a big hug and a kiss.

"How come you're so loving tonight? It has been a long time since you gave me this kind of reception." Jimmy said teasingly.

Emma gave him a love tap, knowing he was referring to her evasion tactics.

"Well, Jimmy, are you ready for tomorrow night? Do you think Coulter will agree that soon after you both take the girls out tonight?" asked Ted.

"Yes, I have arranged a night out with Coulter without the girls for a change. I mentioned we probably both need it, and Coulter agreed.

He has been trying to pressure Diane into eloping. But she is holding out for a big wedding. I think he is after the elopement because of her trust fund, and the loan sharks are closing in again. That may work in our favor tomorrow night, don't you think?"

"Yes, that would make Dalton's and Jordan's appearance creditable. Please, Jimmy, don't try any heroics. You leave when Dalton and Jordon tell you and go over and wait with Emma at our warehouse. We will call you there with the results as soon as we can. I promise," he added after seeing Emmy's worried face. "I will have Detective Harding with me. I am sure he will have some back up around somewhere," Ted said with conviction.

"Can you guarantee that you won't get hurt this time?" Emma asked fervently.

"No, but I am going to be hidden away in your office, and I doubt Detective Harding will place me in the line of fire should Coulter have a gun."

"Come on, everyone, we have to change to another topic, or we won't be able to digest the delicious spread Matilda is making." Malvin had heard the concern in his daughter's voice.

"Jimmy and Emma, I want to announce that I have asked Ted to join our shipping company. Gibson and Gibson Shipping Lines are long overdue for new blood and maybe even some new expansion."

"Oh, Daddy, that's great. Isn't it, Jimmy?" Looking at her brother to see how he was taking the announcement.

Jimmy stepped over to Ted, who was now standing.

"Congratulations, I am glad you are coming on board. No pun intended," Jimmy said as he put out his hand to Ted.

Ted took his hand and shook it, but he also stated. "The announcement is premature as I have not confirmed that decision yet. I want to give it a little more thought." His eyes leaped to Emma. The look on her face was apprehension for Jimmy. Ted didn't want that kind of a reaction to his joining the company. He realized Malvin hadn't mentioned his semi-retirement to either sibling.

Jimmy wasn't accepting Ted's comment. "You will be a natural. Why not accept it? You know all about ships, cargoes, and how to deal with the ship's Captains and their crews," he said glibly.

Emma was relieved Jimmy was taking it so well, stepped forward with her congratulations. "Great Ted, I hope you do consider the position Daddy is offering." Ted looked at her in relief.

"Do I get a kiss of congratulations?" he inquired jokingly.

Emma quickly said, "you haven't accepted the position yet." Ted chuckled good-naturedly.

"Well, I will give it serious thought," he finished. "I have a few things I need to get cleared away before I make my final decision."

Matilda took that moment to announce dinner was ready. Everyone headed for the dining room.

The conversation at dinner was light and informative for Ted. Watching these three family members interact with each other. Why had Emma not confided in Jimmy or her father before her car fiasco? He could see the love flowing between them. The embezzlement by her twin, who was an intricate part of her, caused her protective instincts to take over.

* * *

The time had come, the final act was about to begin. Emma led Ted and Detective Harding into her office then Mannie appeared whisking her away for safekeeping. While awaiting Jimmy's arrival, Ted provided Detective Harding with all the details. The previous bare outline was now filled in with the missing information.

"You mean to say Emma's attempted suicide was to protect her twin?" he sounded horrified.

"Twins have a special bond. When she thought he was the guilty party, she couldn't face it. So, in her mind, she was protecting him, not realizing that an audit of the books would happen anyway. But Jimmy didn't do it as I have said. Coulter was the guilty party. That is why we are here."

"When you got Jimmy away from the Belle Star, why didn't you cooperate with the police then?" asked Harding a bit miffed.

"Because I love Emma. I didn't want her hurt again until we had a plan in place to get the evidence needed. So, you see, we had to keep quiet. But now we need your help officially to catch Coulter. I knew you would expect the missing details in return."

"I should arrest you for obstructing justice just on principle."

"You wouldn't do that when I have offered you the golden goose who laid the golden egg or diamonds in this case."

"Where exactly are these diamonds? You must have them salted away. You haven't told me where yet."

"In a safe place, I hope, or they were when I last looked," Ted replied.

"They will be turned over to us no later than noon tomorrow, or I will book you for obstruction of justice for sure. I had no idea that there was so much going on."

Before Ted could comment, they heard the key in the front door. Jimmy and hopefully Coulter had arrived.

"What do you want to show me?" Coulter asked curiosity in his voice. "Why did we have to come here? Why couldn't you bring it to my place?"

Jimmy said, "I didn't want to be carrying it around. That's why."

"Where is it?"

Before Jimmy could answer, Dalton and Jordon, pushed their way into the office, filling the small room with their massive bodies.

"Who are you, and what do you want?" asked Jimmy defensively.

"Well, you may not know, but I am sure Mr. Stewart here knows. Don't you?" Dalton said menacingly.

"Me, why would I know? I don't know you. I have never seen either of you before," replied Coulter.

Jordan said, "do you want this guy to leave, or do you want us to spell out your problems in front of him?"

Coulter looked at Jimmy, wondering what to say. He thought he knew who these men were, but he wasn't sure. He knew it was about time for Mr. Big, as he likes to be called, to pay him a threatening visit. But he had hoped they would have waited a little longer. He had almost convinced Diane to elope. Then the money would have been repaid.

"Jimmy, I think it might be a good idea if you waited outside until I finish talking to these gentlemen," said Coulter.

Jimmy looked at Coulter. "Are you sure you will be okay? I can stay if you want?"

Ted was saying under his breath, 'get out of there, Jimmy.'

"I'll be okay, go. They want to talk to me. Don't you fellas?" Trying to put on an appearance that they were all reasonable guys here.

Jimmy let himself out. Ted sighed in relief.

Dalton grabbed hold of Coulter. "Now Mr. Stewart, you have some explaining to do. Mr. Big is not happy with you."

"I'm getting the money. I will pay Mr. Big back."

"But Mr. Stewart, you are three weeks behind. You are supposed to pay every week." Dalton sounded very convincing. Jordon was shifting around Coulter like he was itching to get his hands on him. Coulter was eyeing him with some trepidation.

Dalton tightened his grip. "Look at me when I talk to you, Mr. Stewart. I want more definite answers here. Like, when is the money being repaid? Are you still embezzling money from the shipping company? I understand from Mr. Big, you once worked here and have an in with someone to let you falsify the books." Dalton lifted him off the ground. "Talk, Mr. Stewart, Coulter Stewart, isn't it?" he said menacingly.

"I was doing that, but I have eased off after the Belle Star seizure," Coulter said fearfully, now that he realized these men meant business.

"How come you stopped when it was such a successful way to get money, embezzling funds from here? How long has it been one or two years or more? Tell me, Coulter, how long was it successful?" He lifted Coulter higher.

"One year almost since I started feeding the computer with bogus information," Coulter replied in a tight voice.

"Why hasn't Mr. Big gotten his money?"

"Because the cheques stop coming."

"Did you stop the information?"

"No, it was all there when I checked on Monday after they seized the Belle Star. But I wiped it out to protect myself."

"What about the job you were doing for Captain Jorgensen? You were supposed to get big money for that?" Dalton set Coulter down, but Jordan stepped in closer as though he wanted a turn at him.

Coulter was watching Jordan again.

"Something went wrong. I couldn't deliver. Then Captain

Jorgensen was not able to leave his ship because of the Port Authorities."

"Well, Coulter, what about making delivery to me? I will pass it on to Mr. Big. He will deduct your debt from your share of the money."

"I can't, I can't find them," Coulter said frantically as Jordan was pressing against him threateningly.

"Not good enough, Mr. Stewart." Dalton gave Jordan a look to back off as though he was protecting Coulter. Jordon eased away. Coulter looked relieved.

"I hid them in the girl's car, but something happened to the car. I can't find it."

"Why did you put it in the girl's car, Coulter?"

"The diamonds were in a pouch. I was instructed to put the pouch inside Emma's rear left hubcap for safekeeping. But the car went missing, and no one would say where, when I asked them."

"You put two million in diamonds in a stranger's car?" Dalton had no idea the worth of the diamonds, but that sounded like a good round figure.

"The car belonged to Emma, Jimmy's sister. She came to work and never missed a day, so I had the assurance that the car would be available should I need access to it."

"Well, where did the car disappear to then, Coulter?"

"I don't know she just suddenly stopped coming to work about two days before the Belle Star docked. I've looked for the car, but I can't find it."

Coulter was getting worried as Jordon was standing too near him again.

"What was supposed to happen with the pouch of diamonds, Mr. Stewart?"

"I was supposed to turn them over to Captain Jorgensen, and he was supposed to pay me."

"Did you have anything to do with Jimmy's kidnapping, Mr. Stewart?" Dalton asked.

"No, I didn't know Jimmy was kidnapped until that night when Mr. Gibson called asking me to inquire around after him." Coulter was squirming around, trying to put space between Jordan and him.

"The next night, I had an appointment with Captain Jorgensen. That was when I found out Jimmy was detained on the ship. I told Captain Jorgensen I didn't want to be involved in that. But when I told him I couldn't find the diamonds, he threatened to throw me overboard along with Jimmy, when they got to sea."

"The embezzlement with the bogus companies, you must've had inside help with that who was it?" Dalton slid the question in, hoping Coulter was too scared to think properly at this point.

"Yes, Alan, the man who works here. We had an arrangement where he would let me in after hours to use the computer. He would post the fake bills of lading for the bogus companies in the book. I did that so he would be the fall guy upon the bogus companies' discovery. He needed the money for his wife's medication, so he was cooperative up to a point. It wasn't my idea. He talked me into the embezzlement to blackmail me into getting the diamonds."

"Who is HE, Mr. Stewart?"

"Captain Jorgensen of the Belle Star, he is the one that blackmailed me. So, I would deliver the diamonds to him."

"Well. Mr. Stewart, Mr. Big still wants his money. He will take the diamonds instead, so you better find them."

With that, Detective Harding and Ted walked in from Emmy's office.

Coulter looked at them in horror and looked at Dalton and Jordon. Jordon was undoing his coat to remove the wire and recorder from inside.

"Here's the whole conversion recorded on this," Jordan said to Detective Harding.

Coulter didn't know whether to run or cry.

"You aren't from Mr. Big, are you?"

"No, Coulter, we are actually friends of Ted, Emma, and Jimmy. We were helping them out to clear up the mess you created. Coulter, meet Detective Harding." He added after pointing to the detective. "Now, this gentleman wants to read you your rights. I hope you have a good lawyer. Detective, he belongs to you now." Dalton bowed from the waist as if he was awaiting applause for his convincing role as a thug.

Ted slapped him on the back. "You did really good. If you ever need another profession, may I suggest either acting or being a thug."

Jordon piped up. "I want my share of the accolades. I looked really menacing and kept crowding him to get a clear recording of his confession."

"You did well, too," Ted replied.

Detective Harding had handcuffs on Coulter and was calling for his backup to pick them up to transport them downtown.

Ted went over to Coulter.

"Some friend you are to treat your best friend like that. I'm disgusted with you. It gave me great pleasure to set up the recording of your confession. I did it for my friends, whom I value as friends, Emma, and Jimmy. By the way, I have the diamonds. That's why you couldn't find them."

Coulter looked at him in horror. "How?" he asked.

"They happened to fall out of Emmy's car. I picked them up and hid them for safekeeping."

Detective Harding thanked them all for their role in the confession. "Don't forget Ted noon tomorrow." Harding gave Ted a meaningful look. He took Coulter to the door as the police arrived to cart him away.

After Coulter was safely in the police car, the rest of them arrived. Ted looked at them with alarm. "Where were you waiting?"

"Around the side of the building," said Mannie with a smirk. "We took turns peeking in the window. We wanted to see Dalton and Jordon in action.

"Oh great," Ted said in shock. "You could have blown it if he had seen you."

"No, he was too scared of Dalton and Jordon to notice us. We were quiet," finished Mannie.

Ted had managed to get near Emma and Jimmy. "Well, did you like my speech to Coulter?" He put his arms around each of them. "It is over, and Coulter is caught red-handed. Someone had better tell Diane about this."

Jimmy offered. "I'll go. I know how to be a special friend too." With a special light in his eyes, he glanced at Ted. "It will be a solemn occasion telling Diane."

Ted looked at Emma. "How about the three of us go. She will probably need a woman around for support."

Emma said readily. "Sure, for Diane's sake, that would be a good idea."

Ted turned to Dalton and Jordon. "Thanks guys, for coming to my rescue once again. You both put on a spectacular performance. I have decided you two should get awards for your realistic role as aggressors. I sure am glad you're both on my side. Thank you."

Dalton and Jordon were taking more bows, and everyone was clapping.

Jimmy said, "thank you to all the men that helped here and particularly Ted. He made everything happen. Saving Emma, saving me, and then catching Coulter, this man is a one-man army with a few followers for assistance. Ted, we owe you so much. We will never be able to repay you. I hope you do consider the job my father offered you. I would be proud to work with you in the future."

Arnie chimed in. "New job, what new job?"

Jimmy replied, "my father has asked him to help run the shipping company Gibson and Gibson Shipping Lines. I am sure it will be Gibson and Maxwell Shipping Lines someday," he finished proudly.

"Hold it. I haven't said I would take the job yet. Do you know why not? Because there is a certain girl who needs my full attention while I court her. I intend to convince her soon to marry me until then my career aspirations are on hold."

His arm circled Emma completely. He looked into her face, which was a deep red. She was trying to hide against his chest. She knew Ted wasn't about to let go of her anytime soon.

"Well, Emma, do I have a chance? Do you still hate me?"

Emma mumbled, "no."

Dalton, Jordan and the others chimed in.

"No, to which question, Emma?"

"No, I don't hate you any longer." Emphatically she said. Ted had pried her face away from his chest.

To the cheers of the guys, Ted kissed Emma. She didn't respond at first, but Ted's deepening kiss was so loving. Emma was soon willingly kissing him back.

Ted came up for air at last and looked at Emma and said. "Daddy's girl will soon be mine."

CPSIA information can be obtained
at www.ICGtesting.com
Printed in the USA
BVHW050549140723
667188BV00003B/10

9 78199